Sailor H

By

Philip G Henley

Published by Phenweb Publishing
Text Copyright © 2024 Philip G Henley

All Rights Reserved

No part of this publication may be reproduced, distributed, or transmitted in any form or by any means, including photocopying, recording, or other electronic or mechanical methods, without the prior written permission of the publisher, except in the case of brief quotations embodied in critical reviews and certain other non-commercial uses permitted by copyright law.

Paperback ISBN - 9798335878234

The Sailing Clear Series
Sailing Clear, Sail Chains, Sails, and Sailor Knot
The Demise Series
An Agent's Demise, Rise, and Prize
The Demise Trilogy
The Observer Series
The World of Fives, and Intervention
Other Books and Short Stories
To The Survivors
The Persuasive Man
Landscape
Not Too Much
Take Four
Counter
Semblance of Storms and Re-Semblance

To Lisa…

for allowing me to spend time in my own worlds
with a frightening number of voices in my head

To reach a port we must set sail
Sail, not tie at anchor
Sail, not drift.

Franklin D. Roosevelt

CHAPTER ONE
Prologue

Despite the distance from the popular coastlines, the noise rippled along the shore. Tourists and locals alike looked up from their bars and restaurants. At first, there was a flash in the night sky and then a distinct sound. Many feared a terrorist attack until they realised the explosion was at sea. A few minutes or seconds before, there was the sound of distant fireworks. Hours later, press reports would state that a luxury yacht had caught fire and then exploded in international waters.

While rushing to the scene, other ships in the area found only bits of the wreckage of a large German-registered motor yacht. Authorities feared multiple fatalities and continued to search for survivors. According to reports, there were swift motor boats, also known as RIBs, in the area.

Eventually, film emerged from French and Spanish coastguard vessels. The spot-lit video showed bits of wood and cushions floating in a small oil-slick, on an otherwise placid sea. Reporters speculated that there appeared to be bullet holes in floating bits of wood. The immediate search yielded no survivors or bodies. Some pieces would be found over the next few days. Carefully reported, to avoid squeamishness, was the announcement of some human remains being discovered and recovered. It was too deep for divers to be sent. The cost of submersibles to search a wreck was prohibitive. The reports believed the boat, named Richtung Süden III, to be a custom-built Sunreef model. Sunreef declined to comment.

A few persistent journalists traced the yacht to its base in Port Grimaud. Harry and Josephine Rosenthal stated that they had reported the yacht stolen from its berth. The shocked couple's lawyers, a Greek based international firm, blocked all further media inquiries. Journalists tried to question the French and Spanish authorities. Spain was not far away from the site. The French police referred reporters to the French Navy and Coast Guard. The Spanish Navy and Coast Guard had nothing to add. Various sources in those nations' intelligence services declined to comment. Germany vehemently denied any involvement and asserted that the boat did not actually have German registration.

CNN International, French, and Spanish TV initially carried the reports. The registration announcement briefly piqued German TV's interest, but they quickly abandoned it. There were bigger stories to report. Multiple newspapers soon relegated the news to their inside pages. There was little for them to follow up on, and as a result, the editors showed little interest. Those same editors frequently linked boats sinking in the Mediterranean to illegal immigration or drug gangs depending on which story their owners wanted to promote or caused most clicks and sales. Gaza and Ukraine dominated the headlines or *real* news.

The mention of some possible victims' names briefly piqued interest, but the lack of bodies meant identities were elusive. The speculation prompted several British newspapers and associated websites to briefly highlight the story on inside pages. It was difficult to track down and would cost money to research. Journalists might have been keen to go, but not to pay for themselves. There was little appetite from local reporters or contributors. Even social media remained uninterested. Conspiracy theorists had bigger tales to push.

CHAPTER TWO

Major Tom

Major Tom Larring, MC, most recent military posting had been a dull stint in policy reviews in the Ministry of Defence's HQ in Whitehall London. That was before he'd been initially happy to get a task from MI6. That task had ended in near disaster. Not for the first time. The previous occasion had been an MI6 mission to Pakistan. He'd been selected to help the Secret Intelligence Service while he was recovering from injuries sustained with the SAS in Afghanistan. The Pakistan mission had more injuries but on it he'd met his now wife Effie. She was an MI6 officer and assigned to the terrorist hunt. She'd barely survived.

They'd both escaped on the last mission only with injuries to their mental well-being. Others had paid the ultimate price.

Tom was finishing an essay at the Joint Services Command and Staff College. The institution was located within the Defence Academy in Shrivenham, Wiltshire. It had been a long academic course. At least he had plenty of weekends with Effi. Tom didn't know what she was doing for MI6 in Vauxhall. She gave only vague hints about operational analysis for the Middle East Desk. She was often away, doing whatever she did for them.

Tom had not continued his own entanglements with the security services, instead accepting his posting to the staff college. His only connection after the MI6 formal debrief was to give a review to a select group of his former SAS colleagues in a Hereford meeting room. He had served with the Regiment in Afghanistan before his mission to Pakistan and the Enez operations. He'd needed the clearance and approval of MI6 before he was allowed to give a limited description. That included enhanced but redacted video footage, which blanked out the faces of the other participants. His own face was also pixelated. The description made it obvious to his audience that he was a main participant. The formal report had numbers instead of IDs. His audience knew not to ask about why and who, and instead focused on the engagement details. They had all seen the original mobile phone footage. They also asked about the Mykonos and Naples incidents. He was not allowed to discuss his previous MI6 mission to kill Bravo-One-One in Pakistan. The firefight in Enez meant he and Effi were now Russian targets for revenge.

The Joint Staff Course Commanding Officer, a two-star admiral, received a separate briefing on the potential threats. Tom, invited to a one-to-one meeting with him on the first day of the course, could not elaborate on why he was under threat. The nature of the risk was something his more junior instructors were not told about. The college dressed it up as a more general terrorist warning. All the other staff and students were aware of additional security measures for the facility. The military students were all familiar with historical threats. In the past, the IRA and the Real IRA had been the main risks, which were now supplanted by Al Qaeda and ISIS.

Despite the potential risks, Major Larring's nearly-over academic year passed without incident. If the Russians were watching and waiting, there was little sign. The Russian assets, captured or killed by MI5 and the SAS in the UK, would not be easily replaced. Tom knew the enemy agents would take their time. They all knew Putin would want revenge, even if the incidents weren't mentioned in public statements.

Tom hadn't seen FSB defector General Oleg Yegorov and his family since they parted at RAF Brize Norton. He hadn't seen Kathrine either. As he and Effi left the registry office after their wedding ceremony, he thought he had glimpsed Michelle and Hugh Turnbill. Tom had been disappointed that they weren't there in the audience, with Hugh acting as Tom's best man. Carolyn and Stephie Harper flanked them, alongside attending Italians and Greeks. Tom had not immediately recognised Michelle or Hugh standing across the street. Both were heavily disguised. It was only later that Effi confirmed that she had also seen them. She'd congratulated him on his observation, as she once told him in Manchester before their mission to Pakistan. Neither Carolyn nor Stephie said they'd seen them. They were both annoyed; they hadn't. Neither had anyone else spotted the pair, including the surveillance teams from MI5 and MI6, who were discreetly hoping to see the couple too.

As per usual, there was a simple message from them both in the email system. It wished them good fortune and said how happy they looked. It confirmed that they had not dared to approach closer or attend the small reception due to the security service presence. It finished with an even more enigmatic promise to see them soon. Carolyn and Stephie were upset not to see them. Later, Tom and Effi learned how the couple had gone to see the sisters at the sailing centre. That was before Hugh and Michelle disappeared somewhere in the world.

The occasional emails were all that they knew about Michelle and Hugh's movements. Locations were only mentioned long after the couple had moved on. Tom missed the friendship. He also missed access to the Mykonos house and yachts. One motor yacht was now in Port Grimaud. A sailing yacht was docked somewhere. Tom couldn't recall where. Another smaller dinghy had been sold alongside the Mykonos house. The building had bullet damage repaired before sale. Bullet holes fired by various nations' special forces, including an SAS team. They were trying to capture Hugh and Michelle. One of several reasons the couple had disappeared.

***

Except for the arrangements for the Turnbill's yacht docked in Port Grimaud, Antreas Katsaros, the Greek lawyer, and his wife, Sophie, knew less than Tom did. Tom and Effi were on a list of people permitted to use the vessel, but they would have to check with Harry and Josephine Rosenthal first. Neither Tom nor Effi knew who they were or why Hugh and Michelle had placed the boat in their care. Antreas, admitting to occasional contact with Hugh and Michelle, stated the communications he did have were for occasional legal matters but mostly just checks on well-being. Antreas did tell Tom that he also didn't know where they were.

Stephie mentioned that Harry and Josephine were some people Hugh knew from before he met Michelle, thus providing more intriguing details about his friend's life before he'd become embroiled like Tom with MI6.

The Harper sisters had introductory letters from Hugh to Harry. The communication was sent via email to be passed on to Harry and Josephine. The sisters almost immediately travelled to meet the older couple, desperate to discover more about Hugh's past as well as use the yacht. They provided very brief details to Harry and Josephine based on their own connections. Harry and Josephine both recognised the timeline. Stephie relayed the story to Tom that the older couple were questioned by detectives looking for Hugh. All Harry had said was that Hugh and he had been sailing friends years before. Back then, Hugh had disappeared, and the police investigation feared he had been killed. Harry and Josephine were very surprised to hear from him. They were even more surprised to be given access to a luxury yacht with all its bills paid. All Stephie and Carolyn told the older couple was that they had met Hugh while sailing around the Greek Islands.

Jules joined them all on a trip out to sea. Harry and Josephine were at least used to seeing the crew. They enjoyed their company, especially Natalie's cooking. Josephine remarked to her husband that Jules and Stephie seemed to be together before some argument separated the pair.

"Ignore them," Carolyn commented. "They're always arguing." She'd smiled but felt the absence of Lizzie. She wasn't heartbroken. Stephie then needlessly mentioned fish in the sea while they were at sea. She had been trying to lighten Carolyn's mood.

Harry and Josephine remained baffled by why Hugh had lent them the yacht. They confirmed to Stephie and Carolyn that refuelling, docking, and maintenance were all covered by a company account. All they had to go on was the letter from Hugh, plus some instructions on the boat's use and the initial briefings from Jules and Andre's father, who'd delivered the vessel. They asked the sisters about the strange compartments and safes but got few answers.

Harry had no direct contact with Hugh, although he relayed a hello via Carolyn. The sisters did tell Josephine and Harry that Hugh was married to Michelle, and they were travelling around the world.

Carolyn and Stephie planned a return visit in the summer with Tom and Effi. Whether Lizzie would still be with Carolyn then was to be agreed upon. Carolyn was non-committal.

CHAPTER THREE

The List

In Western intelligence agencies, it had long been known that the Soviet and now Russian intelligence services maintained lists of assassination targets. Some were even compiled by public Internet sites after the fact. The public lists rarely covered all the targets or attempts that the western intelligence agencies knew about or suspected. Targets were normally dissidents or defectors. It had been an unwritten rule, only rarely broken, for the active intelligence assets of any of the nations to be targeted. No service wanted their own agents to hunt or be hunted in that way. That informal agreement had changed over the last decade as Putin's estrangement from the rest of the world increased. The FSB, GRU, and SVR hunted spies inside Russia, occupied territories, and worldwide. They always had, like their forerunners, the KGB and NKVD, and would brutally deal with Russians or Soviet national spies. They would happily capture others, but they would normally use them to trade for their own captured spies. In recent years, that unwritten policy had begun to change. Recent activity and a near-war footing had made the agencies of the Russian Federation alter their approach. Whether that was at the direct behest of the president, with explicit instructions, or just attempts to please him was unclear.

The list being considered in a small ante-room in the Kremlin had been compiled after a lengthy and occasionally brutal review of several connected operations. The president had asked for speed but had to wait. His removal of senior security leaders caused further delay, as did untangling the various threads of what had happened. The first page of the report, after the plain, security-marked cover, contained a simple picture of a timeline of the events. There was then a summary of those events. The main purpose of today's discussion and review followed. It was in the opening section of the report. After the summary came a table. A complex table delivered in landscape format. They could see the president's handwritten comments on the document's numbered photocopies. There were five copies in total, three of which were in the room.

The new director of the SVR, General Akim Volkov, was still seating from his presidential meeting. "Where shall we start?" He was trying to be friendly. Volkov's name meant wolf, and his name reflected his career as a spy hunter, mostly in counter intelligence. A highly stressful role for 50-year-old. Even more stress now. He was surprised to be leading the directorate, thinking his chance had gone. He had mostly focused on China and North Korea in his career. He knew he had only been appointed because he didn't have connections to European operations or Ukraine. His uniform reflected his recent promotion and appointment and his long career.

"Internal?" The equally new director of the FSB, General Damir Egorov, replied. He was also a long-term veteran. His name meaning farmer had never been his occupation. He was not in uniform, favouring a smartly tailored suit. He'd also spent most of his time covering counterintelligence but was based in St. Petersburg and therefore not connected with recent defections, one of the subjects for today's meetings.

The two directorate heads were joined by one of the president's many security advisors. The starting question had been aimed at him. Evgeni Kovalenko was fifteen years younger than his two colleagues. If anyone dared to mention the Ukrainian origin of his name it would be a short violent discussion. He was from an ever-changing group of aggressive men who, for a period, held the president's attention. How long he would continue to have the president's favour would depend on his results. He'd already annoyed the two more experienced leads deciding that he was in charge and not either of the heads of Russia's intelligence service. "Where the president has instructed," he pointlessly replied as if anyone would dare to do anything different. Kovalenko was also the connection to the otherwise missing GRU. That organisation seemed to have permission for aggressive missions abroad.

The small group ignored the main section details of the report. They had already discussed it at a previous meeting. The purpose of today's review was to recheck the names, progress, and plans for action. Assistants and deputies were not permitted to see the report. Any actions agreed upon or initiated would be communicated separately. Previous leaders of the organisations they represented, and their various underlings, were included in the names. The names were grouped into multiple categories.

The first classification was confined to recent defectors connected with the events that had prompted the committee's formation. It did not include anyone more directly connected to Ukraine's failings or any associated Wagner operations. General Oleg Yegorov, once of the FSB and the Joint FSB/SVR Task Force, his wife Galina, and daughter Misha were listed. No timeline for action was assigned to them, although they could all read the handwritten *скоро*, translating to *soon* in large letters. There was no location listed or any indication of their current identities. Many resources were being expended in an attempt to find the missing information. A global search was not hidden by the need for security. Their photos were with every embassy and overseas agent. There was a summary paragraph describing the last known sighting and possible location, together with a probability percentage. The former general was believed to be in the USA, with an 85% rating on the country but only 10% on Virginia. His wife and daughter were thought to be in the UK. The degree of accuracy was only for the country. The last verified sighting had been at a British RAF base. That was nearly a year ago.

"Nothing new on the traitor," Volkov explained. He was abroad and therefore it was his organisation's responsibility to find the man and his family. Everyone knew it wasn't a simple as that despite the president's murmurings about incompetence.

The next category listed those who had been in Yegorov's workplace. Two other generals were already in prison, facing corruption charges. They would not leave the prison. A colonel and a major were shown as retired. Both had accurate locations as of the day before, with 100% probabilities. The small committee would decide their fate. Despite their listing in second place on the category list, they were not a high priority.

"Easy targets." Kovalenko stated. As far as the other two knew, the advisor had never done anything else but steal money, chase women and make promises to the president. His own hands might be dirty in criminal terms but he was not GUR despite his contacts. He was the son of an oligarch currently favoured by Putin, but making his own connections.

"Finance team," Egorov moved on. Two critical names were listed in the third category, that was loosely labelled as *The Finance Team*. Michelle and Hugh Turnbill were catalogued alongside multiple links to aliases. The location column was marked as unknown, with an honest 0% alongside. Not something that had gone down well with their leader. Their last sighting was given as Naples, Italy. An accompanying note stated that the occasion was in the same timeframe and near the location of General Yegorov and his family. The couple had also been at Istanbul Airport to meet the escaping traitor, and then at Enez. They had radio reports of them being tailed from Istanbul Airport. The three men glossed over some details on why the following team had not intercepted the Yegorov family in the airport. That was in the details of the main report and not the responsibility of the three in the room. The report made it clear that the finance team was obviously more than what they appeared.

The committee had watched video showing the couple and others shooting in Enez, although disguises confused the picture. Another couple were very similar-looking. The trailing team from the airport did not survive the encounter. It was probably lucky for them their fate was not extended. All the reviewed report had was the initial chase with intermittent radio and phone communications. The video of the shootings was from civilian mobile phone footage. The Turks would not provide more once the Russian IDs of the dead men were uncovered. Relations with the Turks were tricky, especially after it was clear that the Russians had fired first.

Further mention of the four Russian agents killed in Enez trying to prevent Yegorov from escaping was limited. The three reviewing men knew that if they had survived, they would have had a lot of explaining to do. Especially about CCTV obtained from Istanbul airport car parks.

The Russian deaths in Darlington and London were also missing from the table, even if attackers were noted. To make the report look better, the name Maddy King was also highlighted. There was a dead symbol next to it and an operation number. Nothing was recorded in the table about the two Russian agents who'd been killed by an SAS team attempting to rescue Maddy King.

The next category did list several people also involved in the incident at Enez. They were marked as '*Unknown Man*' and numbered 1-4, with injured or dead next to the one labelled as 1, and he was recorded as being at Istanbul airport alongside the Turnbill couple. An italicised '*MI6?*' was alongside. The identity was from Istanbul, which they knew to be fake. Man 2 had a possible identity. Facial recognition had a low probability of matching. Less than 40% of the identity of a British Army Major. Tom Larring was currently enrolled in one of the UK's military training colleges. The Turkish records had him named as Hugh Greenway, the owner of the yacht, with his wife Michelle. The coincidence of first names with the Turnbill couple had not been ignored. The similarity in appearances with the finance team was obvious. Disguises were presumed, and for some reason, the British were deliberately making the IDs as similar to the shared looks.

If it was Larring, his military record was also known based on London Gazette reports. There was his Sandhurst training, infantry regiment, tour in Afghanistan, and return to the UK before promotion to captain and an unknown, undisclosed posting. Such a listing normally indicated a Special Forces assignment. Promotion to major was listed, and the Military Cross was against his name. It had no public citation, which again indicated special forces and probably Afghanistan. He had been posted to the UK's Ministry of Defence. They had no sources that could confirm that role or any absences coinciding with Turkey. The investigators had seen film from the incident in Enez. Some of it was on the Internet. The video clearly demonstrated the man's skills and ruthlessness. The three men in the committee hadn't blanched watching the man and a woman finish the Russian team off. The president had spoken of executions fuelling his demand for revenge. Tom Larring might also have been in Naples. Another failed attempt at getting Yegorov back had been thwarted by short notice and the city's traffic.

"Dubai still difficult?" Kovalenko had heard the warning not to upset the Emirates. It was in relation to the next unidentified male. He had a false Dubai ID. Some information had been released by Turkish authorities based on the yachts encounter with Turkish customs and immigration. His picture was still being checked and bore some similarities to press reports of a failed kidnapping and murder several years before. That man was supposed to have committed suicide in a UK prison. If that was a match, his name was Doug Masters, but no one of that name and age was living in Dubai, according to sources there. Checks were on-going. An operation in Dubai would not be authorised unless they could be very sure and discrete. The unknown man could be seen shooting in Enez, near the man who might be Major Larring. If his name was Doug Masters, then there was more to discover about his previous life and why he had been pronounced dead by the British. More intriguing incidents to uncover when time allowed. His name was listed as possible, and the small committee would decide what to do once they had better information.

Three unnamed women were listed, including the one masquerading as Michelle Greenway. She had carried out one execution it appeared from the Enez video. She was also probably in Naples. One of the three unknown women was again listed as dead or injured. That was a Dubai resident and another fake ID. The next had the possibility of being a young woman called Stephanie Harper. They had that from Turkish Border Control. They were the source of other names. She was on the boat with an Italian man, who was presumed to be one of the unknowns. His name was incorrectly recorded, or it was false. Facial recognition software had failed to identify the others. The classification of the incident meant further searches were restricted. Not helped by the dissolution of the joint SVR and FSB task force.

One additional name was noted. They had a file on Justine McKenzie. She was the wife of Jamie McKenzie, who they now knew had been MI6's Moscow station head. Her husband's listing was in the next long section. They had good photos of both of them based on his life in Moscow and her regular visits. They had an address, boarding school details for their children, and a note on the currency of the last check. The probability was 95%. Putin's handwriting had a '*Yes*' next to the action. They didn't know if that meant the wife and children or just him. Given the wife was also thought to be MI6, the reviewers included the wife only.

The Enez list was followed by a brief list of glossed-over actions in Mykonos. Two female names were known there. Elizabeth Vaughan and Carolyn Harper, the sister of the woman on the yacht, were identified. Another unnamed woman, possibly Italian, an Italian man, and another man who they believed had left for Dubai. There were surveillance photos elsewhere in the report. Action lists were not noted. There was no list of the SAS and Delta Force operatives also in the area. A lawyer's name, Antreas Katsaros, was listed, but with no further context.

The original British Treasury report names were registered alongside empty action boxes. Another pending decision. Included was the former Pentro asset, Adrian Holloway, who they knew was in British custody. He had been charged with espionage. Recommended action for him was *оставьте его в покое*, or '*leave him alone*', with *согласованный* or '*Agreed*', in handwriting next to the decision. The two professional spies were pleased the president agreed. Killing agents or sources was not conducive to recruiting more.

The longest section covered various UK intelligence service personnel. Members or officers of the Secret Intelligence Service, MI6, and the Security Service, MI5. It started with Sir Rupert Paltray, noted as retired. They had an address, but the last sighting was several weeks before. Mel Kennedy was next in the table with a note about her involvement and help. She was partially responsible for returning captured Russians and some dead bodies back to the motherland. She had a long file they knew, as did Paltry. Despite her help and the seniority of Sir Rupert, both were on the list. All three thought that was a mistake, but none of them would voice it.

An unknown female operational director was the next entry. All they had managed to find out about her was that she was on a long-term leave of absence with no name. Both the SVR and FSB had sparse files on her identity. They looked back through Yegorov's record but saw no connections. They did have a side photo from Naples. There, she had been spotted greeting Yegorov, although the long-range photograph wasn't that helpful. It was presumed she was his controller. Image recognition had established other connections and vague appearances. A possible meeting in Geneva, but again, photographs were indistinct. Yegorov had not been suspected then. Surveillance in the Swiss city was not planned. He had reported no contacts other than the ones he was supposed to have. All his previous activities were rechecked. It all appeared to be legitimate. The investigators had no idea when or how the former general had been recruited.

Confusing the review of the potential controller's background, there were more notes about Afghan and other Middle Eastern operations. The photo-matching system had some low-probability connections to Dubai and Pakistan too. They had no proper identity. Surveillance outside MI6's HQ hoping to see her was high-risk, and unlikely to be successful.

Yegorov's wife's and daughter's records were also traced. The daughter's attendance at a French university was studied. They had reports from there, but there was no indication anything was amiss. Other Russian students had also been present. The sons and daughters of the Russian elite. Every interview was a minefield of potential complaints. The wife's potential drinking problem appeared to be innuendo and gossip provoked by competing generals. It was not supported by facts.

"Controller?" Kovalenko unusually wanted their opinion. The woman remained unknown.

"Possible. Perhaps just a recruiter or a lover. We" he meant the SVR, "don't have anything to suggest that." Volkov quickly added.

"We don't either." Egorov admitted.

"Next." Kovalenko couldn't help he had no organisation and he already knew the GRU had nothing.

The unnamed woman was followed by MI5's Head of Internal Security, Baz Butler. His location was noted as the same address as Mel Kennedy. Handwritten next to his entry was a quotation about two birds. The location probability was 90%. All three of the reviewers knew it was also unwise, but they had their orders. Volkov managed not to raise objections. Taking measures against foreign heads of intelligence or their senior managers was asking for similar action. It was the same reasoning as heads of state. He hadn't mentioned that to the president.

The security services list then proceeded with a lot of unnamed references to various surveillance assets and those involved with the capture of the Russian agents in the UK. Over twenty were catalogued. Only one specific name appeared. Joseph Carpenter in MI5. He was recognised by his appearance in the UK's Parliament alongside the Head of MI5. '*Small fry*' was handwritten across that section with a note excluding Carpenter from that description. His action remained to be decided.

The assembled group returned to the main lists. It took several hours and multiple arguments before they decided. No one had changed any presidential instructions. They weren't that stupid. There now remained the how and when of what activity had been decided. Some would have to wait for better information. Some would find out soon that the president was eager for revenge. The unintended consequences that would follow that revenge were unknown. All three knew that the target, the UK, would not let it pass and that their allies would support them. It was a considerable escalation of the secret war, and it was unknown what the response would be.

Following the meeting, select members of Russia's intelligence services, including the military GRU, were re-tasked. Their own organisations were given their objectives. The GRU had carried out aggressive operations before and had some assets in place. Some targets, they knew, might take years to achieve. Others would be delivered more swiftly. They all knew speed would help their own longevity in their positions.

CHAPTER FOUR

Sidorova and Morozov

Former SVR Colonel Ula Sidorova had managed to rent a small house on the outskirts of Stroyberi, south of Kirov, itself nearly 100 kilometres east of Moscow. Her former home and career seemed much further away than the physical distance. She was surprised she still had her pension. It barely covered her rent and utilities. She had managed to purchase a small car. She was trying to get a job, any job. She wanted more money to heat the house and buy food. What she had left of her savings were already dwindling. She needed work, but except for very lowly paid supermarket check-out positions, there was nothing.

Her neighbours were suspicious. Nothing unusual there, but that was not helped by the occasional obvious surveillance car parked nearby or tailing her to the shops. They made no attempt to hide. She had hoped that it would be temporary, but they were still there several times each week. She ignored them, but one of the regular watchers would leer at her, and that would send a shiver down her spine. She knew this life couldn't continue. Her anger at Yegorov's betrayal had dimmed along with her wish for revenge. She had no ability to carry out retribution. Her own problems were mounting. The action taken against her equally angered her. She had lost her career and her home and was on the verge of destitution. She had not done anything wrong, but her superiors and investigators tarred her with the brush of disgrace.

Yegorov's traitorous actions made her examine her own country and motivations in ways she had never thought possible. What could she do? In some fundamental but subconscious way, she realised that she could be imprisoned or worse. Why keep the surveillance unless they want to drive her to despair? She feared what the authorities would do next. What would she be falsely accused of in order to punish her? A discipline she did not deserve. She knew what had happened to the generals. Their arrest for corruption had been on the news. She knew what would follow in a brief announcement of trial and punishment. She had escaped that so far.

She was desperate and knew that desperation would grow. At any point the intermittent surveillance might by re-tasked to take more aggressive action. Getting out of the interrogations without a trumped up charge was a relief. It gave her brief hope but optimistic dreams did not follow into new reality. Her yearning for a positive future could be snatched away at any moment. She needed to act. To save herself from state action or just save her own mental state. She knew of stories of others who had lost the confidence of the president or his minions. They might be rumours and unreported in the state media, but Ula had once had access to western reporting. She'd controlled multiple operations against the west. Now those same countries she sought to manipulate might be her only hope of salvation, unless she could find somewhere to live.

Sidorova left her house and car and walked away in the early hours of the morning. Abandoning the not-new car might buy her some time before her absence was noted. She headed southeast. Ula had no fixed plan but wanted to get away, find a way out of the country. She knew it was not well planned. She couldn't use the Russian Internet to look. Even a library visit to look at maps in an atlas might be reported. Heading west would take her towards Ukraine. She didn't want the military checkpoints or risks there.

In her darker moments, she'd contemplated suicide. She had stopped thinking of it as cowardice. A sign of her increasing desperation. She turned those thoughts to anger and determination.

She didn't see anyone following. Perhaps she could take a train, and leave Russia, but where to go? She would try to survive, but taking her own life was rejected. She would not let them win. Not her former superiors, the politicians, or the traitors. She'd had no passport since her return from overseas duties. She had identity papers, which still showed her rank. She had some cash, including a few hundred US dollars and fifty euros. She couldn't remember where she had gotten the notes. She hoped they were current. She had over 1,000 roubles in cash. More than that in an untouched bank and savings accounts. If she tried to get more cash, it would be flagged. She remembered an exercise back in basic training. An escape and evasion test. She had done well, using her smile and fake promises to lure a civilian into giving her a lift out of the area. She'd reached the airport target and even got inside the terminal. She had been praised before being presented like a prize cow to one of the colonels. This would be no exercise.

***

Sergei Morozov had taken to drink, but he could not afford it. He was shocked by his own service's actions, despite his innocence of any involvement with the traitor Yegorov. His Facebook connection to Adrian Holloway, his former asset, exposed him to suspicion. Other officers forcefully took over his operations. His desk was swept clean. Days of interrogation, asking questions he couldn't answer because he didn't know anything, led to his official retirement. He didn't hide. When asked if his superiors might have known more, he could only concur. He agreed with everything they said. Sergei knew he was tainting them with additional suspicions. He was saving himself from a worse fate. Although there was no actual physical assault, the threat persisted. Exit processing took his uniforms back before he had to clear his home. He had to vacate the apartment he rented in a government building. He had nowhere to go, and no friends would accept him. He had no friends. No family either. He was on the streets; jobless, and homeless. He didn't know what to do.

Sergei tried to stay in a hotel for a few days, but this depleted his already meagre savings. Despite his best efforts, the bureaucracy of state security held up his references, preventing him from securing a room or apartment to rent. He suspected the loss of his references was deliberate. He left the hotel before his money ran out, becoming homeless and living on the streets. He was unable to afford to rent a place in Moscow. The lack of references and a home address, meant Morozov was also unable to obtain a job. He was aware that he might be forcefully conscripted and sent to Ukraine to die. His fate would be similar to thousands of others. He actually considered volunteering. He suspected his references would be suddenly adequate. Perhaps his rank would be restored. At the very least, he would receive nourishment, if he wasn't so cowardly. He was well aware of what was going on in the special military operation thanks to his access to western media. His knew his country was a pariah within the European countries where he had once spread disinformation.

Instead, Sergei made an effort to acquire funds by pleading and asking for them. It was not long before he found himself back in a cell, albeit a police cell. The Moscow police did not like the homeless or beggars. Not a single person came to his aid. He returned to the streets after spending a few nights in detention. A judge issued a warning fined him, further depleting his savings, and threatened prison for a repeat offence.

Sergei knew he would not last long in prison. He would not last long anywhere, and why would he want to? He stole a bottle of vodka and managed to evade a chasing security guard. He went to Gorky Park, tottering from the alcohol's effects. He walked onto the Crimean Bridge. He felt the push and the rush through the air. The impact and then the cold of the water produced a brief sobering effect, before he lost the ability to fight to the surface. Water in his lungs. He'd clung on to the bottle.

CHAPTER FIVE

Revenge

Sir Rupert Paltry had been on a long cruise with his wife. Something she had wanted to do for years, but his roles in government and in particular as the head of MI6 had not allowed it. Not least because some countries might take the opportunity to have a discussion with him. Now, after long flights, they were back home. The dogs would be picked up from the kennels tomorrow, thus allowing them time to settle back in and unpack. The trip had been a four-week section of an around-the-world cruise. It had passed pleasantly enough once Sir Rupert relaxed. That was easier on sea days than port days. His wife had suggested writing a memoir to keep him busy. It would be better than gardening, he thought. If he were allowed to write it, he would need government permission.

The cleaner had been there that day, his wife noted. She complained that the gardener had not mowed the lawn correctly. It was not the first time. They were both tired from the journey back from Sydney and took themselves off to bed with their main cases unpacked.

He awoke with the security alarm buzzing. He was momentarily disoriented from sleep and location, despite being in his own bed for the first time in weeks. His reactions were not as quick as he would have wanted, and his wife's were slower. Her hip replacement last year had reduced her mobility. They had practiced the emergency procedure only the week before their trip. His wife, as usual, dismissed the need. He reassured her that it was a remote possibility of Russian revenge. He had been a security target all his senior career. He'd received the briefings, some training, and additional security measures. She knew that, too. He also had field experience and training. Some of that never left you, no matter how many decades had passed since he had walked East Berlin Streets or waited in Hungarian cafés for a contact.

In the director's role, he'd always had permanent security assigned. The teams were removed on retirement, despite Mel Kennedy's wishes. Resources would not be allocated. Finance and the new brooms in place didn't comprehend the real risks. Sir Rupert had not complained because he knew it would be pointless. Nameless civil servants sat in dusty rooms in central Whitehall. They had no comprehension of what enemies could and did do.

The alarm's warning was what he dreaded. He swiftly dismissed the possibility of burglars. They would have had over four weeks to act without the risk of the couple being present. It would be bad planning and timing to try a robbery now. It was something else.

He managed to get moving towards the safe room behind the master bedroom. His wife was also disoriented, which slowed progress. The master bedroom door was thrust open. The shots were nothing more than soft expressions of air, breaking the silence. Initially they went into the empty bed before the shooters re-aimed. His wife's immediate scream of pain destroyed that near silence. He felt her jerk with more impacts even as he tried to pull her through the opening. He could already feel his own injuries. He managed to get through the door and somehow get his wife in too. He had to push the door against the on-rushing attackers. He gave the hardest kick he could manage, and the door shut. He knew instinctively that his wife was gone. He crawled to the power switch for the room. He barely had the strength to reach. He flicked the switch. It immediately sent a further alert to the police and security services, along with the main alarm's trigger.

How long would they take, and would he still be alive when they got here? He forced himself to look at his wife's face. Her eyes were staring blankly and no longer in pain. He wanted to close them for her. He didn't have the strength to move. He should have told her how much she had meant to him all these years. Apologise to her for all the late nights and unexplained absences. The dalliances too: a field agent's life is often a lonely place. She had probably known, but she knew he would come home to her. Those adulterous liaisons were years in the past, despite women like Kathrine regularly crossing his path.

Sir Rupert had not been around much to help with the children. What would they think or do? Inherit, he casually thought. He waited now. If the attackers had explosives, then the safe room would not hold. If they had the code, they could open the door. Only his wife knew it. The code was inside a sealed envelope inside the operations centre within MI6 HQ. He had changed it on departure. He knew it would take time to get it. Authorisations would be needed. He considered, as he drifted, trying to ignore the pain and the pooling blood, what other activities the attackers had planned. He guessed they were Russian, but he and MI6 had plenty of other enemies. He lost consciousness.

***

The Sabre team consisted of five surveillance personnel from MI5. They had been assigned to watch two men purporting to be Ukrainian refugees. Their initial identities had been checked by UK immigration. The fact that two men of that age were claiming refugee status and were not injured or on the front lines, led to suspicions from the immigration officer at the airport. Concealed buttons had been pressed. Those suspicions led to further checks and then assignments. The investigators decided to watch rather than arrest. The two men's proximity while staying in a hotel near several potential VIP targets also raised concern. A trip to a lock-up garage was watched. Their departure from the hotel in the early hours of the morning raised more concerns. The team scrambled to cover while alerting control rooms and rapid response teams. The suspect's car stopped near a red-flagged VIP house. The team watched but could not stop the men from gaining entry. They could see they were armed, but they had no orders to interdict. Those instructions changed, but only after the men were inside the house. Sabre checked their weapons, and two members went to the back. A further two covered the front door, while one stayed near the target's car. The house alarms briefly sounded disturbing the night-time silence.

Unlike the initial entrance to the house and the shooting in the bedroom, the shooting at the front door was very loud. The rear team had gained entry through the same broken door as the attackers. The two targets had decided to exit via the front door. With weapons raised and warnings shouted, the front members of Sabre had no choice after the attackers started shooting. The attackers were caught in the front and rear crossfire from the Sabre operatives. The rear and front teams both fired. The Sabre team was still searching the bodies when other vehicles began to arrive.

After they received the code from MI6, police and paramedics were able to gain entrance to the safe room. They began emergency first aid on the one barely alive occupant; the other was obviously dead.

***

Justine and Jamie McKenzie had spent a quiet evening together. The children were at boarding school. Justine had given Jamie a full account of the trip from Moscow via the gunfight at Enez to her disembarkation from the yacht and return to England. It was more detailed than her more formal debrief with her former service.

Justine's account included the firefight on the dock at Enez. He was horrified to know that one of the blurred figures running to the yacht was his wife. She didn't want to watch that nor the end of the film. That showed the bodies of Lila Cotton and Liam Green being taken on board. She didn't want to talk about that part either. The fact that Jamie had been involved in organising the defector's and his family's escape from Moscow just added to the strange story.

Jamie, in turn, had little more to say except the tension of his departure from Moscow. He was amazed that she had been involved in the fight and received a minor injury that had resulted in a small white scar on her leg. He was happy to have his wife back in one piece. He got to meet Effi in the office, where she helped identify photos of the Russians who had died in Enez. He'd seen what she had done in Enez and there were rumours of other operations. Justine wanted to invite her and Tom Larring to dinner. Jamie wasn't sure that was a good idea.

Jamie was pleased with his promotion to desk head, although he was not as keen on the new director, Elliot Parnell. He was surprised that Kathrine wasn't around at the office. William

Thatcher told him it was temporary. Jamie didn't know. He didn't particularly like William's new assistant or aide, Sam. Sam made a few snide comments about Kathrine while implying that it was his own abilities that had driven the successes. He made one of them in front of Effi she shook her head but said nothing, which Jamie noticed.

Jamie avoided a glass of wine before he joined his wife in bed for an early night. A promise of more than that, led him away from a TV documentary.

***

Lina Smirnov was not her real name. She'd had many names before this one. She was 35 and in her sixth European country of residence in the last five years, killing in four of these. In one, she had been pulled out before she could complete her mission. Studying the photographs and planning, she knew that two targets were more difficult, even if they were co-located. She knew their names and the address. She'd been advised of possible security and that they would be surveillance-aware. She was told they were unlikely to be armed. The house they lived in cost a small fortune, she knew. She had floor plan layouts from an estate agent's listings. London prices shocked her.

She knew her success was due to a lack of suspicion as well as her skills. She was physically small, barely 1.6 m. She knew she had no attractiveness. A square face with a short neck made her look overweight, dumpy, and older than she was. She could further disguise herself as an even older woman. Her stocky build hid her physical strength. She had been trained for years and received abuse and support in almost equal measure. Taken from a young offender's institute to the SVR centre. She had been detained after attacking and almost killing two boys and a girl who had been teasing her. Not a fight, but a carefully planned, pre-meditated assault. Her capture taught her that her pre-planning had not been good enough.

She was associated with the SVR but not officially in it. She held no formal rank, nor had she graduated from the more formal basic training. Instead, she was diverted to other courses. Her recruiter sensed a different skill set. He handed her over to an SVR controller as a new raw asset. She had learned two foreign languages, English and French, and had a smattering of Spanish. She learned multiple techniques of physical assault, along with communications and codes.

She liked living in Europe. She liked her work. She liked the time she had between missions to explore museums and galleries or to visit famous buildings and viewpoints. All while enjoying the fact that her fellow tourists had no idea there was a trained killer among them. She imagined killing them all. She craved solitude on the visits, but she had to put up with other humans wanting to see what she wanted to see. She loved watching 'Killing Eve' and imagining herself as the assassin Villanelle. She did not think she was a psychopath. She also did not share the character's fashion sense or good looks. It made her laugh. It was rare that she laughed or even smiled. She had no lovers. Her sexual experience was confined to the abuse during training. She liked to plan killings of the rich, famous, or just good-looking.

Lina's new targets must be rich to own a house in this area. Their most recent photos were blurred; older photos showed them as reasonably attractive. Enough to trigger that response in her. A response she knew she needed to control.

A forced entry into their house would be complex and likely to trigger hidden alarms. She could lie in wait, but according to the briefing, they rarely came home at the same time. There was always a chance that one late arrival would notice something amiss. Except for a date to act, Lina had no instructions on how. There was a warning that if she delayed beyond that date, the targets may have additional security. That made her realise other attacks must be planned, around the world or in the UK. It was not something she could ask about. She decided on an evening approach just after dark. Now, she had to wait for them to arrive.

It was getting late almost 22:00 local time when the woman finally walked down the road and entered the house. The man had been home for two hours. Lina had been lying in an opposite garden before that. That house was empty, with a large rental sign displayed. Not directly opposite the target but close enough to have a view of the front. It was not overlooked by the neighbours. The assassin was cold and stiff from lying still, despite her designed outfit. Lina was not wearing gloves, and she had to squeeze her hands to get circulation going. She knew she could have waited longer, but nevertheless, she was pleased to be moving.

Giving the woman a few minutes to complete any arrival routine, she approached the front door. Lina noticed the video camera embedded in the doorbell. Further complications. She rang the bell. The porch light came on. She ducked away from its glare and away from the video camera. Lina heard the comments of the occupants before the door opened.

***

Baz, 2B, Butler had managed to get home early for once, but his partner, Mel Kennedy, was still at work in Vauxhall Cross. He was thinking about making dinner but knew they would end up with a delivery after Mel got home. Eating late was normal. Working late was normal. He was subsumed in thinking about internal Thames House issues when Mel's text finally told him she was on her way and to get Thai if he hadn't cooked. She knew he hadn't. He ordered the delivery and opened a bottle of wine. Hopefully, they might get away from work earlier tomorrow and get some relaxation time. That was, of course, provided that nothing critical happened, dragging one or both of them back into the office.

He heard the front door and greeted Mel with a kiss and a glass of wine.

"Thanks, I needed that."

"Tough day?"

"As always, that idiot Parnell wants more cuts just so he can look good to the Chancellor." She was being a little indiscreet, but they had discussed the new head at MI6 and his actions. Mel had disagreed and strongly argued with the new DG, allying herself with William Thatcher, the formal Head of Operations. Unfortunately, the new broom had set out his stall early. Mel didn't want to be replaced. She suspected Parnell was planning William's removal. The Treasury report, which almost caused a disaster the previous year, led to more scrutiny of all spending. "How long for dinner?"

2B checked his phone and said, "It should be here. I

ordered it to arrive as soon as you got home."

"You'll have to knock a star off."

"Hopefully, it will still taste okay and not be cold like that Chinese from…"

"Not ordering from them again." Mel went and hung up her coat. She sipped more wine, trying to clear her mind of work as she had done walking from the station.

The doorbell rang.

"At last, I'll get it," Baz Butler said, going to the front door.

***

Lina outside the front door didn't hear a reply. There was no chain. It was the man pulling the door open.

Lina shot him through the right eye. The soft splat of the weapon was masked by traffic noise from the main road. He fell backward. She fired a second shot through his forehead. The woman came out of what the floor plan had told her was the kitchen. It was at the end of a short corridor. Lina fired again. The woman spun with the impact, followed by the sound of a wine glass smashing onto white tiles. The woman was trying to kick the kitchen door closed. Lina ran forward and had to push against the weakening woman. She fired around the door frame. She wasn't sure if she hit, but the pushback stopped. She pushed again, and the door squeezed back. The woman was trying to crawl away. She fired into the woman's back, then into the rear of her head. She didn't move again. Lina turned her over. There were no exit wounds, despite the short range. The woman was dead.

Lina reloaded with her spare magazine. She grabbed the target's handbag and rifled through it for her purse, phone, and ID. All were present and correct. She switched off the phone and disconnected the battery. She went back to the male and the still-open front door. It had started to rain. She pushed the door, using her elbow, to almost close it. Lina found the man's wallet and his phone. His ID was in a different pocket, red from his blood. She placed the captured items into her utility trouser pockets. She risked going outside and forced the video doorbell off its mount. There was a small memory card inside. There may well be a cloud Internet backup, as Lina knew. There was nothing she could do about that. She took the memory card. She used her coat sleeve to wipe the places she had touched. She shut the front door using her sleeve. She didn't like gloves.

As she turned, a delivery driver was coming up the pathway. He looked surprised to see her. She didn't hesitate. Her seventh and eighth bullets, the first and second rounds from her second magazine, went directly into the Asian man's forehead. The food spilled from a hot carrier he had been partially opening. A moped was idling on the road. She ignored it as she hurried away. The phones would be posted to a pre-arranged mail box as soon as she was clear. She hurried towards the nearest tube station.

***

Joe Carpenter received a call at 03:00. It was a full alert based on the Sabre Team's report. Not that much was on the phone. He called Jermaine. He didn't wake his wife, but she stirred anyway and silently went towards the bathroom. It saved her life. The man was just coming into the bedroom. Joe wasn't in bed. The light was still off. The door was pushed open, and the man fired into the bed. Joe was dressing in darkness, behind the bedroom door. He slammed the door on the man's arm. The gun dropped. Joe couldn't see it. He slammed the door again, and the man grunted before pushing into the room. Joe knew the attacker was younger, bigger, and stronger than he was. The bedroom light flooded on, blinding both of them. He heard the sound of the gun. His attacker went down. A stomach shot, Joe realised. His wife was holding the gun. He went and searched the unconscious form. He found no other weapons, but the man did have a small phone. He went and grabbed his own phone, dialling the emergency code. He took the gun from his wife. He indicated she should stand aside. She looked very determined. The assailant wasn't going anywhere, judging from the amount of blood leaking onto the carpet.

Joe moved out onto the bedroom's landing. His children's bedroom doors were closed as usual. If there was another attacker in the house, he would be exposed, but he had to check on his children. He lay down and crawled to the first door. He was petrified of what he might find, but all he saw was his son's sleeping shape with a dangling leg, half out of bed. He moved further along. His wife was following him, commando crawling, something he had never expected to see. He gave a silent prayer for his wife's forbearance and intelligence. Before that evening, he already knew, he was lucky to have her. She was keeping quiet, no questions or screams. Not yet. Their daughter's bedroom was the same. She was older, but she was sleeping too. Joe indicated by waving the gun for his wife to go in. She shook her head at first, and he whispered, "Please." He shut the door and retraced his crawl to his son's bedroom. He sat with his back to the door. The gun pointed down the stairs until the cavalry arrived.

Jermaine Harris, armed and scared of what he might find, was five minutes behind them.

***

Tom Larring was shaken awake in his room in the Officers' Mess at Shrivenham. He'd been awake until late, finishing a paper. His room was on the upper floor and identical to multiple others in the building. There were two armed RAF airmen standing in the door, and the duty officer, a Royal Navy Lieutenant from his uniform, was apologising for waking him. Tom was furious with himself that he was so tired that he had not heard their approach.

The lieutenant explained what had happened within the fence of the base. Some of the extra security ordered at the base included dog patrols. They were performed inside the wire and not obvious to external views. One of the patrols had intercepted two men attempting to enter the base. They had not been captured but had been chased off. A brief police chase ensued, ending when the patrol car was shot at. Luckily, no injuries had been sustained. The attackers' car had been abandoned in Swindon, where the two assailants disappeared from view. A full search was underway, with counter-terrorism officers added.

They waited while he hurriedly dressed. He wanted to be armed, but that was not offered. A further call came in to the lieutenant with instructions. They would have to wait for a helicopter. He tried to call Effi, but got an engaged tone. His phone started ringing immediately.

"Major Larring?"

"Yes."

"Vauxhall here. Sir, you should have been told that a helicopter is on its way. It will bring you to HQ. Please wait with your escorts until it is ready for you."

"What's happening?"

"I've just been told to advise you of the trip." Tom knew it was pointless to ask the control operator.

"Okay, how long?"

"Five minutes, Vauxhall out." The line was disconnected. Tom called Effi again, but the line was still engaged. Now he was getting more concerned. Tom could hear the helicopter approaching. The lieutenant and the two airmen escorted him out. Their activity woke some of his fellow officers, as did the noise of the helicopter so late at night. There were two more armed airmen waiting at the top of the stairs. Waiting outside the building were a Land Rover and an RAF Police car. Tom went in the back of the Land Rover. With three of his guards for the short drive to the helicopter.

The civilian-looking Dauphin 2 was waiting with its two crew in the cockpit and four black-clad special forces troops waiting for him on the helipad. Tom knew the aircraft was from 658 Squadron. The Special Forces assigned unit. He gave his thanks to the RN Lieutenant and his team and hurried aboard. The four-person team joined him without comment. He nodded his face in recognition at one of the men. Tom thought it wasn't a coincidence that it was a man he'd last seen in Naples.

The helicopter's pilots completed a gut-wrenching tactical departure, and they headed east. There was another stop.

***

Effi was waiting, escorted by a four-person armed police team. Her night had been disturbed by an early alarm going off. She had thought it was a false alarm until the call from Vauxhall. She then had to wait ten minutes for the police armed response to arrive. They found nothing to report nearby, but no one was taking any chances. Effi was bundled into the back of a police car and driven a couple of minutes to a school playing field.

She stepped on board, leaving her police escort. Relief on

her face at seeing Tom. She came and sat next to him, grabbing his hand after strapping in. The helicopter quickly departed from what Tom could see was a school playing field. It was half a mile from their new home. The helicopter noise was too loud to talk, and they had not been given headsets.

***

Sam, her former aide, was reluctantly waiting for Kathrine to come out of her apartment in Battersea. She had been called. Their purely working relationship had deteriorated since Naples and the rest of the aftermath. Now she was called in, and he had been sent to get her. Two armed members of Mel's security team accompanied him. William Thatcher had called him and Kathrine. After checking, they were both still alive. That had been enough warning.

"Sam," she greeted him.

"Kathrine," equally cold, was his reply. Kathrine noted the additional security as she climbed into the car. There was a police car escort waiting too.

Kathrine didn't ask what was going on. On waking, she had been concerned that MI6 was going to take sterner options with her. She dismissed it when William had been polite and told her she was to come in. He didn't offer any further explanation, not that he could. She no longer had a secure phone.

***

Stephie and Carolyn Harper were woken up in their apartment by their own security team. Lizzie was with Carolyn but refused to leave with them. Police cars were around their apartment once more. They were calling Antreas and leaving emails in draft folders, with barely time to grab laptops. Phones were not permitted. They were carried away in a stream of cars.

***

The last deaths of that evening were only discovered when the armed response team dispatched from MI6, assisted by the Special Branch, and supported by local police, entered the house. The bodies of Justine and Jamie McKenzie were found where they had been shot. They did not appear to have been woken by the intruder or intruders. Jamie's phone was on silent. They would need the autopsies to discover the time of death.

**

Armed police were also dispatched to homes in Darlington. Paul Stubbs and Uliana Doubek were not happy to be greeted by armed officers once more, despite attempted reassurances. Uliana was contemplating an offer to move back to London to join another branch of government. It would be part of her fast-track scheme, although an unusual placement. After the attacks in Darlington, which neither she nor Paul were allowed to talk about, she wasn't sure if she wanted a role in the Secret Intelligence Service. Having armed police sitting in her lounge in the early hours of the morning didn't help that decision.

CHAPTER SIX

William Thatcher

The Operations Director for MI6, William Thatcher, paced as he waited. He'd spent the night in his office, a not unusual occurrence, on another unconnected operation. It had gone smoothly according to the reports. Another target removed by a drone, coordinated with the CIA. He'd been hoping to get a few hours of sleep on the rollout bed in his office when the alerts started. A brief knock on his door from Sam and a request to go to the operations room he had left only a few hours before. His first thought had been that something had gone wrong with the strike, but Sam quickly told him it wasn't that. He didn't have the details and looked just as frazzled as William. He'd quickly authorised activity while relaying information to his MI5 counterpart. He knew sleep would now be a long way off. Sam had attached himself to William's staff since Kathrine's suspension. As soon as he was briefed, William had sent Sam to get Kathrine. It kept him out of the way so that William could think for himself. There was a lot to contemplate and more horrors to discover.

The new director was on his way in with a suitable armed guard. William knew the man would be defensive. He had removed protection and downplayed risks in multiple minuted meetings. William had already held a brief informal discussion with the Foreign Office Permanent Secretary. He'd relayed the lack of protection provided, the consequences becoming apparent, and all under the direction of the new director. Thatcher knew he was playing politics, and that could backfire, but the man would have to take responsibility. Thankfully, the Perm Sec agreed with William. That man was, in turn, waking the Prime Minister and Foreign Secretaries. More disturbed sleep and likely angry fearful reactions.

A COBRA meeting was highly likely. The Home Secretary was also aware and had authorised a counter-terror alert increase. A public response, achieving nothing, William thought. Bolted horses came to mind.

***

The first to arrive at Vauxhall Cross, the headquarters of MI6, the Secret Intelligence Service, was Kathrine. She was escorted by Sam.

"How bad?" She asked with a brief handshake as her greeting.

"Getting worse by the hour." He pointed her toward the freshly delivered coffee. They were in the same meeting room, where part of the debrief about Enez had occurred. They all waited in silence, only broken by occasional runners bringing bad messages to William.

The new director finally arrived. Elliot Parnell had no background or previous roles in MI6. He was a new broom personally appointed by the Prime Minister after Sir Rupert Paltry's forced retirement. A long-time career civil servant, he had spent a couple of years in the Foreign Office, but was not connected to MI6, or even the Diplomatic Corps. Most recently, he had been in the Home Office as the Second Permanent Secretary. He was flustered when he took a seat.

William Thatcher didn't spare him any details.

"Sir Rupert is in the operating theatre, his wife is dead. Two unknown assailants that Five was trailing are dead on his doorstep. They'll have more on them."

"Five's fault?" Parnell tried but stopped, seeing his Operations Director and effective deputy's expression. Parnell had been planning to replace Thatcher. Now his own future would be seriously in doubt. He didn't know who the Kathrine in the room was, but he had heard rumours. He didn't want to open old files. He did know Sam, Thatcher's aide, but not his background. "Where's Mel?" He tried instead.

"Mel Kennedy and her partner, Baz Butler, didn't make it." Kathrine couldn't believe that either. Parnell swallowed, but kept quiet. William continued, "Shot at home; it looks like a delivery driver got in the way too. Multiple attacks on home addresses." He mused, another strand to investigate he knew. "We also have a potentially thwarted attack on an Army officer at his base. His new wife may have avoided an attack; it's unclear. They are on their way here."

"Why?" Parnell asked.

"They are our assets." Kathrine answered.

"And who are you?" The Director tried to impose some authority.

"Their former controller." She gave the Director a very hard stare.

"Kathrine," William warned. "I'll continue, if I may?" Kathrine nodded. "Katherine is someone you are going to need." The Director again said nothing. He realised he wasn't in control of this meeting. The people in the room were very angry, and he was part of the cause. This Kathrine looked like she wanted to kill him. He had done nothing. It was just a resource issue, but he knew his refusal to provide protection, would now be regurgitated. He realised that doing nothing was the problem.

"For context, Sir, Kathrine was an ad hoc director until her recent suspension, which I'm now lifting." The Director didn't object; he didn't know what she was suspended for. "She was also responsible for the special finance team, the in-house analysts, and coordinated the efforts to bring to the UK our biggest defector for a decade."

"Fingers in all the pies," The Director mumbled. The finance team, he knew that MI6 controlled certain additional funds. There had been a big hoo-hah about it last year. Not that he had direct knowledge. This Kathrine was in charge, but she'd been suspended. Perhaps there was something he did need to know about. He'd have Mel… He had no one. The main finance director knew nothing. He was also relatively new. Only a few months more than his own appointment. They didn't like each other but were trying to have a working relationship.

Thatcher decided to ignore the comment, "Five also have

attacks reported on some of their staff. Another casualty on the attacker side." The group in the room considered that news.

***

Another knock on the door, and Major Tom Larring and Effi, his wife, arrived. Kathrine hugged their safe arrival. Introductions followed.

"Having you all here allows for a single briefing, and at least we know who's safe. Before you ask, the sisters are on their way to a safe house. They have sent messages to the couple, wherever they are." Thatcher thus made it clear that Parnell didn't know.

"Couple?" The Director was now wishing he had read some files. Everyone else appeared to know who was being referred to. He'd been warned at his appointment to concentrate on the future, not past operations. Now, he was regretting not getting some historical briefings, especially about operations in Moscow and Turkey. It was bad timing and too late. "I'm presuming; I don't need to know?" Thatcher merely nodded. Parnell hated being woken at night. He also hated high-speed escorted drives from home to the office. He had left operations to Thatcher, not that this was an MI6 operation, except in security terms. Not for the first time, he was regretting accepting the appointment.

"2B and Mel didn't make it," Sam told a disbelieving Tom and Effi.

"2B?" The Director didn't know who that was.

"Baz Butler, as I said. He's Mel's partner and also her counterpart in Five."

"My God!" The Director was slowly understanding how bad this was. Both internal security heads had been killed. Why were they in a relationship? Surely, that wasn't permitted? The two newcomers were husband and wife, he'd been told. Then, there were the two sisters and another couple.

Another interruption, with another message passing to Thatcher. Kathrine noted the dynamics in the room. "Five's Ops has also reported an attempt on Joe Carpenter and his wife. Joe is currently head of UK surveillance, among other roles. The assailant is in the hospital. I've invited them here, but I suspect more safe houses will be in use. Worse news, I'm afraid..."

"Worse?" The Director asked the question that none of them wanted answered.

William Thatcher shook his head; he could scarcely believe it either. "Jamie and Justine McKenzie." There were gasps from all present. The Director knew Jamie from his arrival. He'd had a one-to-one with each desk head. Meetings, which were full of jargon and references to the three codeword names for operations. It had taken him weeks to get used to the terminology.

Kathrine was in operational director mode: "All Russian targets, Sam and I too, I'm guessing."

"I was in here," Sam added, "and maybe they didn't know where you lived?"

"Maybe," Kathrine admitted. She knew CCTV would have to be checked. She wouldn't go back there until she was sure it was safe, which might mean never.

"They had me at the Staff College," Tom reported. "Two men chased off, apparently. Shots fired in Swindon from the getaway."

"We found nothing at the house, but the alarm went off just before the call from ops." Effi responded and had already confirmed this to Tom on the short walk from the helicopter drop-off.

"Has to be Russian," Tom started but stopped on a look from Kathrine.

"Agreed, Russians," William Thatcher concluded. "Sir," it wasn't said with any respect, "they want you at Number 10 at 07:30."

The Director of MI6 looked around the assembled meeting. He knew he was way out of his depth. His Operations Director was effectively dismissing him from the meeting. He could sort that out another time. He checked his watch. He had just over an hour.

"I'll have a brief for you before you go." William Thatcher pre-empted any order.

"Thank you, William. I must go and prepare for the Prime Minister. I'll talk to Thames House too." He left the room.

***

More coffee was delivered.

"I didn't tell him that Five and Perm Secs will be there. Kathrine suspected the Director may not be in post much longer. His removal would be carefully announced and publicised. The politicians needed to avoid the regurgitation of news articles at the time of his appointment. The PM and Cabinet Secretary had allegedly proceeded against the Foreign Office Permanent Secretary's advice.

"How can we help, William?" Kathrine asked.

"We need to plan a response and, for the last time, get hold of the damn finance team. Kathrine, your lead. Tom and Effi, with Sam, get them back in contact as soon as possible. If the Russians have them..." He left the risks unsaid. Thatcher knew there was a dead man's switch on the accounts. Dead or captured, it would be equally devastating. "Just get hold of them; make sure they are safe then…"

"We'll sort it, William." Kathrine looked at her small team. She didn't know how, but she knew she had to help. It was also her way back into the fold. She could see Sam wasn't happy, but as long as William was, Sam's opinion wouldn't matter. She missed Sam's organisational skills, but he had manoeuvred to avoid any blame for Turkey and the finance team. His own performance in the limited field exposure had been poor. She remembered him cowering in Naples as they extracted General Yegorov and his family. Kathrine had depended on him for too long, and he had jumped ship as soon as he could. He didn't even seem to be upset with the loss of agents on the missions, notably Liam Green. He'd been shot dead in Enez. Liam was an excellent agent, much missed, and another killed by the Russians alongside Lila Cotton. The four attacking Russians had paid with their own lives.

Sam, instead, seemed to spend the last couple of years arranging his own future. She couldn't prove he had assisted others in MI6, but she wasn't sure. Mel wouldn't help, and now she couldn't. She would have to keep a close eye on Sam. At least she had Major Tom Larring and Effi née Miani to help. Perhaps the Harper sisters too. She would need all their help to get Hugh and Michelle Turnbill into the fold. That was if they were alive or not captured by the Russians.

There was still the complication of the Americans and the NSA. If they got involved, Hugh and Michelle would not cooperate. She needed a list of who could help and who couldn't. She guessed that Tom and Effi, as well as the sisters, still had at least some email contact.

"Tom and Effi, do you still use the email system with Hugh and Michelle?"

"The Director doesn't have their names," Thatcher reminded them.

"Guessed that," Tom was intimidated by the man, whom he'd only met as part of the debriefing over Enez. Although he was pleased to see Kathrine alive and well, and Sam, for that matter, his trust in MI6 had been nearly destroyed by the Turkey operation. Effi may still work for them; in some capacity, she didn't tell him, but her own trust was also limited. "Yes, we get occasional emails."

"We don't know where they are. They don't tell us that." Effi added.

"Were they at your wedding?" Sam asked. The surveillance team hadn't seen them, but he guessed they had been there.

"In the vicinity, we saw them."

"They still trust you?"

"To some extent." Effi hesitantly answered. "I'm still in the service, so I come under that suspicion. Sorry, Sir."

"That's okay; we can't cover that all again."

"Tom with Hugh; maybe more so."

"A bit, yes, and they both trust you, Effi. Especially after Enez."

"Perhaps," Effi conceded. She noticed Kathrine's lack of comment. Effi suspected that she was already busy plotting. "They do trust Carolyn and Stephie, and Antreas, of course."

"Antreas?" Thatcher asked.

"Antreas Katsaros, the sisters' Greek lawyer," Tom answered.

"Thanks."

"He's also Hugh's and Michelle's in some aspects." Effi continued. "Don't forget Carolyn's partner Lizzie, but Michelle and she don't get on."

"I need to call Antreas; check if he's…" Tom decided.

"Do that," Kathrine agreed. It was also an instruction, and Tom took it as that.

***

Before he could call, there was a knock on the door. Jermaine Harris, the former Special Branch and now MI5 Surveillance Supervisor, was shown in. Introductions followed. Effi gave him a hug. They had worked together before.

Jermaine looked at her hard and offered, "Thank God!" As a comment. He paused before continuing, "Joe Carpenter sends his apologies. He and his family are in a safe house, and our director told him to stay put while they deal with the police. Luckily, only shock. Pure luck, he told me. Their attacker, his wife, shot him; he's not so lucky, critical."

"His wife?"

"Yes, there was a *scuffle*, as Joe called it. She got the attacker's gun, and anyway, they and their children are okay and safe, we hope. I hear others are not."

"No."

Thatcher gave a quick summary, explaining, with others input, the connections on targets, if not giving all the names.

"I can't believe 2B and Mel…" Jermaine sighed at the end. "Poor delivery driver. Collateral?" He hated using the description.

Thatcher continued, "It looks like it. We'll eventually get a timeline, but they may have been the first, several teams coordinated by the look of it. We are all guessing at the moment. Mel and 2B's phones went dead late last night. Sir Rupert was in the early hours and triggered the other alerts. One of your teams was following?"

"So I'm told. I was on call, at home with Sally, my partner, not on the desk. I went and saw Joe. There was nothing at my home. The only details I have are that they were suspected Russians masquerading as Ukrainian refugees. They got flagged, followed, and started acting suspiciously. Of course, we're now running other potentials. There's going to be a lot of false alerts."

"Hopefully get the two who came after me." Tom added.

They reviewed the list of potential targets and checked statuses for the next twenty minutes.

"Jermaine, thanks for coming over; we need to ensure others are alerted and are safe." William Thatcher needed to get on with the short brief for his director.

"Let me guess, Hugh and Michelle Turnbill, and the Harper sisters?"

Kathrine nodded, and Thatcher looked on, questioning how MI5 knew the names. "Jermaine knows more of the history, William," Kathrine explained. "He was in the very first investigation with Special Branch." William nodded. His understanding was also limited. He had not read all the files either.

"Sally was too. That was a crazy mess, and now this." Jermaine often struggled to sum up how he ended up in this position, working for MI5. Hugh Turnbill's name and connections had been a too regular part of that career. He'd never even met the man, although he knew several in the room had.

"What about your teams?" Effi asked. She had been with Jermaine in Darlington. She had quickly explained that connection to Tom when Jermaine came in.

"All alerted, and they are all okay so far, I hope." They all knew that other teams could be hunting targets. "The Russians, if it was them, we have a high probability, on our side of the river…"

"Ours too," Kathrine added.

"We will have some information from the captive if he survives. We'll have some photos, but not necessarily identities or locations. It could have been worse." He knew it could have been. He was a possible target. After the alert, he'd warned Sally Nugent, his partner, who was currently on maternity leave from the National Crime Agency. She needed to be warned; he needed to protect his own young family, just like Joe. "I need to head back."

William Thatcher shook his hand as he departed with an escort from outside the room.

***

By lunchtime, the Russian Ambassador had visited the Foreign Office for a very frosty discussion. He had denied everything. More likely, he had no knowledge. The worst moment was when he was asked if he wanted the bodies back, like last time. The Foreign Secretary was suitably angry. Diplomats had to keep people's cool; nevertheless, the Ambassador left in a fury, ignoring the shouted reporters' questions. He was angry with Moscow too, and he knew he would have to calm down before he called home. They had not told him. He knew his predecessor had faced the same issues when the Salisbury attack took place. He was Putin's man. He wouldn't criticise.

By the following evening's news, police, with the help of the intelligence services and the MoD, had issued blurred CCTV. The pictures showed a small, dumpy woman wanted in connection with an attack on two members of the Civil Service and the death of a local delivery driver. The delivery driver's absence had triggered a police response when he failed to return or answer his phone. A local police car was already arriving when an armed security team from MI5 arrived. Luckily, no one did anything stupid or reacted. The MI5 team found the other bodies, one inside the front door and one in the kitchen.

Next, pictures of two men were shown, supplied by the MoD and police. CCTV from the Defence College, then from Swindon's rail station. The press also knew that there were armed guards at two hospitals. One for the critical Sir Rupert Paltry, who was known as the former Head of MI6, and one for an unnamed attacker. Sir Rupert's wife's death had not been announced, although several members of the press had seen the funeral director's vans arrive and depart with multiple bodies.

CHAPTER SEVEN

Hugh and Michelle

Hugh and Michelle were, for the first time in months, afloat. They were trying out a new yacht. That's what the salesman thought, but they were only likely to rent it for a few days. It was smaller than the yacht that had once been their home and was now docked in Port Grimaud, near St. Tropez. Hugh had written a letter to Harry and Josephine Rosenthal and implemented the support company to pay for the costs. They also knew that Carolyn and Stephie had visited and sailed with the older couple. Lizzie had not gone.

Michelle knew Hugh was glad to be back on the water. They had spent months touring Southeast Asia. Land travel for the most part. Rail, bus, and occasional taxis. Border crossings in quiet locations mixed in with other younger backpacking tourists. In between, they still managed the operational finances for MI5 and MI6. Hugh's mostly automated system was still moving funds around the world and arranging supporting logistics. They visited tourist spots and did volunteer work. Their hosts never knew that the couple helping to build walls, put up fences, and plant trees were billionaires. Their money had been obtained from Britain's security services. They still managed it, although these days Hugh's software applications did nearly all the hard work.

They had started sailing around Greek islands until their presence became untenable due to NSA tracking and Russian attempts to get them. MI5 and MI6 were not trusted either. They both knew that the security services wanted the money back under direct control. Despite the antagonism, Hugh and Michelle had more actively supported some missions. Notably for Tom and Effi

Larring, although they weren't married then and had different names when they first interacted.

Hugh and Michelle had reluctantly left Greece, their house on Mykonos, and most upsettingly, the modified Sunreef yacht. A couple of trips to the UK covered some individual meetings and watching Tom and Effi's wedding from afar. They had then headed first for Borneo. There they worked on rain forest reclamation, seeing and helping orang-utans in the wild. Michelle was equally taken by the Sun Bears. After Borneo and a spectacular cave, they headed further south to Komodo Island to see the endangered dragons, but neither liked the trip. Too many officials might ask too many questions. Train trips followed in Vietnam, Cambodia, and Laos. Cambodia included a visit to the Killing Fields. Another demonstration, like in some Vietnam locations, of man's hostility to fellow men.

***

Their stays in each country were made for discretion, not luxury, with identities changing for each new country. Entry visas would have no corresponding exit unless they really couldn't avoid it. They hadn't led extravagant lifestyles before if the house on Mykonos and the yachts were discounted. The house was sold with bullets holes carefully filled in. The yachts were loaned to others or docked in ports that were now inaccessible for them.

They were in Singapore for a few days, mainly as a stopover on the way to Australia or New Zealand, if they went. Hugh was monitoring spending in both countries to see if an operation was being staged against them. There was nothing other than he had been requested to set up bank accounts for a mother and daughter, which he had been asked to do for Wellington. A third bank account for a man was dormant but waiting. There had also been deposits for a house and a car. He'd been asked to facilitate a transfer from a Swiss account to New Zealand. Hugh and Michele could guess who the accounts were for. They'd met the family in Istanbul, and they fired shots to protect them in Enez. They'd last seen them in Naples, handing them over to Kathrine and Sam with Tom and Effi watching.

The boat they were renting in Singapore was for sale for $4 million. It was a 2022 Italian Blue-game model, which was nice but not as nice or as customised as their older Sunreef yacht berthed in France. They had the hired vessel for two days, with a night out. $20,000 a day, and some convincing on the ability to look after the yacht. The credit card guarantee blew another company ID. They had quickly discovered that Singapore wasn't ideal for finding isolated coves like the Greek islands were. For less busy scenery, they needed to head away from the port. They also knew yachting and sailing would attract watchers if they were still looking. They'd been assured that neither the USA's agencies nor GCHQ were hunting and tracking. They'd been warned that probably the Russians would be looking, especially after their involvement in the defection of an FSB general. Hugh's regular checks and changes of servers provided some reassurance. He had multiple Honeypot fake servers running too. He'd started that in Istanbul and expanded. The pots were designed to expose lookers. After the tracing, probably from the NSA, he hadn't seen any attempts. The honeypots remained full. It didn't rule out photo or other surveillance, and Michelle kept a keen eye wherever they went.

Staying mostly hidden also kept them out of the way of Mel Kennedy and Baz Butler, whom Michelle knew wanted them in a secret interrogation facility. The UK wasn't safe, and going there, even heavily disguised to visit friends, was a significant risk. They hadn't seen Carolyn, Stephie, Tom, or Effi for months, except on hasty video calls with bad connections covered with Virtual Private Network, VPN, and Internet connections. There were email draft messages, but it wasn't the same. Hugh and Michelle missed their friends, even Lizzie, Carolyn's partner, whom Michelle did not trust. Antreas in Mykonos had more regular, normal messaging.

They decided not to use the boat's satellite data connection. Hugh didn't want any traces. During their night away, they had sailed to Bintan and Batam, enjoying a chance to snorkel. They didn't bring diving gear with them or hire any equipment, despite the temptation of the coral. All their stops seemed to be crowded with overly friendly other vessels, hailing and trying to strike up conversations. They were not unfriendly, but they both yearned for the private coves on small Greek islands where they could be alone and rarely clothed. The expensive yacht attracted its own attention and they had to respond several times that they were just hiring it. There were a couple of drinks invitations on board other vessels.

They politely declined.

***

It was only when they returned to Singapore, and the tablet Hugh nearly always carried pinged email alerts, that they heard about the attacks in England. It took several hours and an immediate departure from Singapore by rail to Kula Lumpur before they risked a longer response than '*We are ok*' in the draft email to the sisters, plus another message to Tom and Effi. No one even checked their fake passports in the crowds. There was a plan for a high-speed rail link, but that was delayed, and who knew when it might open.

By the time they were ensconced in a business hotel near the Petronas Towers, they had read most of the messages. Michelle had gone out for new IDs. Alone, Hugh had read all the remaining mail draft communications, including some from Kathrine and Sam. Michelle was back in under two hours. She had not managed to get a gun. She didn't say how or where she'd been. New passports and other IDs would take another day. It was not a contact she had used before, and Michelle knew that would be a risk. They sat in their locked hotel room, eating supermarket sandwiches, not daring even to use room service until they could assess the threats.

"We're okay." Michelle tried. She wanted to be armed but they weren't.

Hugh was risking using his systems. He had a regular routine to be as irregular as possible on the systems. There were no fixed times for connections. Multiple changing data connections from different geographic locations. The laptop and tablet were both in use, extracted from backpack luggage. The laptop was his preferred system, but he relied on the tablets for regular use. Now Michele was watching him whizz through systems and screens of information.

"There is nothing on operational spending anywhere near us. There's the usual Six stuff, regular in and around as there was in Singapore."

"Clear then?" Michelle asked.

"For us and no tracing that I can see." Low risk wasn't zero risk.

"Russians will be here or nearby. They'll have our photos. Airports will be a risk. That person in Singapore."

"If that was surveillance?" Hugh noticed his wife shrug; she thought so, and he trusted her instincts. "Why would they be looking for us here?"

"They'll be looking for us everywhere. Singapore, Dubai, anywhere with transport links. That's why we need to be concerned. Poor Justine and her husband."

"I can't believe that. Not even Mel, and 2B. I know they weren't that friendly to us but…"

"They were doing their jobs. We knew they wanted us back in London, but it wasn't personal; in that sense."

"I know. 2B made me laugh when we met. Mel reminded me of you."

"They were both good operators. I knew the Russians might retaliate, but I never expected this. There will be others we won't hear about. Around the world, any agent or source is at risk."

"They'll have protection or retaliation. The Americans won't let them…"

"If they are involved and if they want to be our ally." Michelle thought about it. "They will. When push comes to shove they'll support. They'll be debriefing Oleg. Those things mean a lot. One or two attacks maybe, not what's been done. It implies they'd do more. More failed attempts we haven't heard about. There was all that stuff in England. Plenty of failures."

"The HMRC girl, Maddy wasn't a failure. Lila, Liam."

"I know, but the Russians paid a price not just in direct losses but operations. I would have thought some senior people there would think again."

"Oleg didn't think so. He was appalled even before this."

"But he's not there anymore and we don't know how much influence he did have. I can't comment on Russian mentality, I'm well out of date. I wasn't on their operations when I was in, before you changed my world." She stroked his cheek and gave her husband a loving look.

"Changed mine too. We've had a good run."

"It's not over yet. Not by a long way. Don't think like that."

"I try not to." He decided to change the subject to more immediate issues. "Tom was downplaying the potential attack on him."

Michelle was relieved. She needed her husband focused and thinking. "Good spot in the language in the mail." Michelle was still training and teaching him despite the years together. Hugh had never undergone any formal intelligence officer training. Michelle had done plenty. Effi helped on her visits back when they could visit and had the yacht. Tom had corrected both of their shooting skills. That was before Enez and the need to put firearms practise into use.

"Thanks, and there were other attacks on Five. Between Effi and Tom's messages, I think we have most of the story. Kathrine and Sam, as usual, say nothing, but want us to contact them."

"No change there. I can't believe Sir Rupert either. I don't know the Five folks, but Effi knew them." Michelle checked the mail messages again. "She and Tom are hinting that they are back with Kathrine and Sam. The last we heard from them, was that Kathrine was on extended leave, which is the code for injured or suspended."

"Effi may have mentioned that; I can't remember."

"Did she? Anyway, at least they are on the inside, and they also want us to make contact. They'll have orders to follow. We need to decide. Kathrine will have asked them, if not others. I don't know William Thatcher or the new head. There's nothing more to go on to help us decide. They'll have a big push from above. Politicians and civil servants."

"Don't care about them, but perhaps the services are really concerned?" Hugh wasn't sure.

"True, they are bound to be. They always have been, despite our efforts keeping the system going." Michelle couldn't assess properly. She was tired and stressed. They were cut off on the far side of the world trying to guess on motivations of their associates and the risks from traditional enemies.

"Do we tell them we are here and ask for protection?"

"If we do, they'll have us."

"What options do we have, except continuing to hide?"

"I don't know. We can't stay in a hotel room forever. I'm pretty sick of them." The room wasn't that big or attractive. There was no bath, just a walk-in shower and a small TV. Nothing was on CNN, and the BBC wasn't provided.

"I miss the house and yacht."

"Me too."

"At least there's a big bed."

"One-track mind." They had each other. They had money and IDs, but they did not have safety. They had never been secure since they had taken the money. Something had to change; they knew that, even if the familiarity of each other was welcome.

CHAPTER EIGHT

DCI Sam Fox

It was not the first time that Detective Chief Inspector Sam Fox of the Special Branch had visited Thames House. He was accompanied by Detective Inspector Adrian Deans and Detective Sergeant Jeff Proctor. Their assignment to him was welcome, if a bit surprising. He had requested, and they had immediately been released to his team. It was easier with Adrian Deans, as he had already been involved in one of the investigations. Jeff Proctor had been unhappily assigned to anti-fraud and welcomed the reunion with Sam Fox. Together, they had spent several hours liaising with investigating police forces about the various incidents now under their remit.

Escorting them in was the former Detective Constable, Jermaine Harris. He was now a senior supervisor in MI5. In the Security Service, he had progressed up the ranks faster than the more traditional Metropolitan Police career path would have allowed. Promotion with fewer exams, less bureaucracy, and, if press speculation was right, less institutional racism than the Metropolitan Police.

"Hi boss," Jermaine greeted an incredulous DCI Fox and the others in the visitors' reception area. It was a warm greeting from the team after their initial surprise that Jermaine Harris, the most junior member of their old team, was meeting them. Only Sally Nugent, Jermaine's partner, was missing from the original group of investigators into Hugh Turnbill's disappearance. Sally was on maternity leave. There had been rare social meetings over the years since the team had been disbanded. Jermaine was always deflecting questions about what he was up to. That old team had investigated Hugh Turnbill and a lot of missing money. They had been hampered by the security services. The initial request to find him had come from the Treasury and a now-dead senior civil servant. It had been mixed up with organised crime and a high-level corrupt officer. They had not found Turnbill or the money, yet the operation had been viewed as a success thanks to other findings.

Jermaine's success was helped by the fact that he had been involved in several successful MI5 operations. Several involved Turnbill, albeit on the periphery. Waiting in the meeting room was Joe Carpenter. It was several days after the attacks. Joe had reluctantly left the safe house where his stoic wife and oblivious children remained. The late-night move to a safe house was just exciting for them. They didn't see the nearly dead Russian, and he and his wife had not mentioned him in the children's hearing. His sleepy son and annoyed daughter had been impressed with armed police and fast cars. The children were also impressed by the lack of school, game consoles, and willing participants from their watchers, even if they knew their parents were upset by something.

***

There had been multiple security service briefings before this meeting with Special Branch. There was a politically forced agreement for an MI5-led joint task force. It was reluctantly agreed upon between the respective directors and the civil service permanent secretaries for the Foreign Office and Home Office. It was to be assisted by the Met Police and, unsurprisingly, assigned to Special Branch. William Thatcher had wanted to lead, but he was already effectively the acting director of MI6. The current actual director, Elliot Parnell, had been re-tasked by the Prime Minister to lead an unneeded, but suddenly very urgent, review of GCHQ. It neatly kept him out of the way and avoided difficult questions for the PM. Two of the victims, Mel Kennedy and Baz Butler, would have been expected to be involved if they had survived. Despite Joe's direct involvement in one attack, there wasn't anyone else in Five who had enough background or seniority.

Waiting in the room for the Special Branch Team with Joe Carpenter were Kathrine, Sam, Major Tom Larring, Effi Larring, and Cindy Laughton. Cindy had been pulled from leading counter-terrorism surveillance teams. She had taken part in the operation against Russian agents that had probably triggered the mess. The introductions were brief, although the backgrounds and some previous operations would be mentioned to give context. They settled down with mugs and screens, as well as a presentation screen. It could easily be mistaken for any company sales meeting.

The first part took until lunchtime. It left the police officers incredulous and concerned. Even Joe and Jermaine did not have all the background on what MI6 had been doing, in Turkey and elsewhere. It also made them look at the others present, knowing that all of them were potential targets. Several had already had lucky escapes. There was a buffet lunch provided in a separate room to keep them focused, along with a stream of coffee and tea deliveries. Toilet breaks from the visitors had to be escorted. Two armed guards rotated outside the room. Before they reconvened after lunch, Sam Fox and his team spent 30 minutes getting a further update from the police, not that there was much to add.

"Our turn now?" Sam Fox asked. The other Sam had not given a surname like Kathrine, which Sam Fox was intrigued by. She was elegant and exotic, but several looks showed the harshness underneath. Nevertheless, she smiled at him, and Sam realised he was being manipulated to some extent. He had to smile himself when he realised before he double-thought himself. She knew that he knew that she was doing it. His brain needed to focus. Luckily, she had a string of messages to deal with over lunch too. Kathrine and Miss Miani, or Mrs. Larring, had several whispered conversations. Mr. or Major Tom Larring looked like he wanted to get out of the building and start shooting. As the incidents from previous years were partially explained, he looked agitated.

"Please." Joe agreed to Sam Fox's request.

"Immediate threats appear to be covered. I'm sure those in this room are okay, unless the attackers have additional unknown resources." He looked around. The Army major was armed, as was his wife. They weren't hiding it. Jermaine wasn't, but his MI5 boss was. He couldn't tell if this Kathrine or her aide Sam were. The Special Branch Team was not. Cindy was likewise equipped, the holster obvious under her arm but over her blouse. It made Sam Fox uncomfortable. The vast majority of his police career had not included firearms.

Joe Carpenter added, "Yes, we've had Adrian Holloway moved into an isolation cell in Belmarsh." HMP Belmarsh was one of the UK's highest-security prisons. Holloway had been a Russian agent exposed by leaking a Treasury report to the Russians. He was on remand, awaiting trial for espionage.

Sam Fox continued, "Good, there's a protection team on. " He had to check his notes: "Uliana Doubek and Paul Stubbs."

"They were the Treasury team who wrote the report. The Russians were following them and might have attacked." Jermaine confirmed.

"One Russian was killed, and one exchanged in their part of the operation." Cindy added elements from her own supervision of the operation. It was a bad way to start her promotion in many ways.

"Miss Doubek will soon be starting here with suitable protection like ourselves. I don't mean she'll be armed, Sam." Kathrine explained the surprised looks from Special Branch. "Her former boss will still need to be protected. As you know, he was also part of the threatened group last year."

Sam Fox didn't know what to think. He knew most of what had happened the previous year, but not until that morning had he been given all the links. He decided to concentrate on what he did know. "We'll start with Sir Rupert; you'll have his medical status and already have the Five Team's reports."

"Yes, we sent them," Cindy answered. "The Sabre team is back on other duties. You can talk to them, but it will need to be planned to avoid other operations."

"We really need them in the field, Sam," Joe stated, "but if you want them, I'll see what I can do."

"I understand." Sam Fox would have liked direct access, but he knew that would be difficult. He preferred his witnesses unwarned. Not that there was anything for the team to hide. Body-mounted CCTV showed the whole fight. It took less than 30 seconds to kill the two attackers. MI5 had allowed the police to see the faces of the surveillance team. Weapons had been provided to match the forensics. "What put the team onto the attackers?"

"We got a flag from Border Force Immigration," Jermaine reported. "They couldn't prevent the attack that killed Sir Rupert's wife. He remains critical. We've run the attackers DNA and fingerprints."

"As have we," Adrian Deans replied. "Not on our main lists."

"GRU," Jermaine pre-empted Cindy's response. There were nods around the room.

"False names and IDs; we're trying photo matching," Cindy explained.

"I see, and any help on locations or co-conspirators?" Sam Fox asked.

"We passed on the lock-up location where they probably got the weapons. Drop point."

"Yes, no clear ownership that we can establish. It looks like cash sub-lets. That section was flagged by counter-drug for *county line* use, but not anything to us. We have forensic reports waiting, but we're not hopeful. No other meetings or contacts?" Sam Fox wanted to know if the security services were going to cooperate, unlike the investigation into Turnbill.

"You have the full report from Sabre and the initial alert from immigration. We do have one undamaged mobile phone. Burner, with one text message in English to another UK mobile number. It's timed just before their front door shooting, so after their attack. One word, 'Excalibur' in English. No response. It was purchased in France, we think. The other phone was very badly damaged." Jermaine was being polite. He wanted to help his old boss and teammates, but he knew he couldn't be as open with them as he once had been. He worked for new masters now. There were three bullets' worth of plastic and metal disintegration. Bullets that progressed into the target. He didn't pass on the details about the credit cards that had been passed to MI6. They had requested any details on bank accounts or credit cards with a cover story about financial applications. Train tickets to Nottingham were also found. They didn't want anyone else outside the limited group in MI5 and MI6 to know. No police, not even the small Special Branch team, were allowed to know.

"We are using GCHQ to trace the other phone. So far, they have had other texts sent to that number, but not the content of the messages." Joe Carpenter neatly concentrated on the phone.

"Location of the receiving phone?" Deans asked, guessing the answer.

"From GCHQ, it's in the vicinity of the Russian Embassy. Not a full triangulation." The other Sam responded.

"Implication yes, but the tracking is intermittent," Kathrine added.

"It was them," Tom was sure.

"We don't know that for certain, but there is a high probability. We'd need an outgoing call to pin-point the location, and we don't have that." Joe could see that the Army man was itching for a fight. The loss of friends and colleagues could do that. He also knew that the man sitting in the conference room had killed multiple times, most recently in Enez, Turkey. His wife had also killed there. Kathrine's brief explanations that morning also implied other deaths on other non-disclosed missions. They took a brief break.

***

"Shall I continue?" Sam Fox asked.

"Sorry, Sam, please do," Joe Carpenter permitted.

"Jamie and Justine McKenzie, both shot in their bed. Double taps, sorry." He now knew the other attendees knew most of the victims. "All we have to go on is some blurred CCTV from across the street. It looks like another two-man, correction two-person team. We're trying to trace movements before and after, but that street has three exits, and they all go to other combinations. There is no immediate evidence of a car. There are multiple alleys linking streets, and then there are taxi and bus stops. They may also have had a driver. We're trawling through street footage, but we don't have them coming in or leaving. The search is already taking hours and lots of resources. Where was their security given the threat?" Sam Fox asked.

"Good question, but not one for here and now." Joe Carpenter was also furious with MI6's official director's decision, even if his own agency was complicit in not providing security. He hadn't requested any, as he didn't think he was a target. A mistake of his own doing. He remembered the alerts after the surveillance operations and associated killings. He now knew that Turkey, Cyprus, escaping defectors, and Naples also raised threat levels.

"From what you said this morning, Mrs. McKenzie was also a target?"

"Yes, she was at Enez and left Russia with the defector." Effi remembered the journey on the yacht out of Turkish waters. "She also knows Michelle Turnbill. She was an analyst in Vauxhall, pre-kids."

"Her husband did the messaging in Moscow to the defector." Kathrine was horrified at the loss and wanted her revenge too. She would rather the connection to Michelle not spread wider, but her requests to contain information were overruled.

"The defector, he and his family are safe?" Proctor asked.

"Yes," Sam replied. "Additional security is on them. I am not saying where they are, of course, but they are not in the UK."

DCI Fox grumpily added, "One less threat to worry about."

"Mel and 2B?" Kathrine asked. She had been fairly taciturn after having to, very reluctantly, talk about her operations in the morning. In particular, she had been told to tell about a finance team, an operation on the Turkish Coast, and the escape of a defector. She was trying to use her charm on the DCI but realised he was aware of her attempts. She looked at Tom Larring. She had charmed him into the hunt for Bravo-One-One but he had lost trust in her. She needed to work her old magic.

"Have you seen the video?" Sam Fox asked. He got some nods from the room. He noticed Tom Larring leaning in close to a screen. Effi, his wife, was just as close.

"Grainy on the CCTV near the house. She waited and was in the house less than 2 minutes. Six bullets inside all hit. Specialist ammunition, according to our forensics, comes from a presumed 9 mm Glock like the others. She took their IDs and service phones, and as you can see at minute 35 on the edited CCTV, she pulled the memory card from the doorbell CCTV; it wasn't cloud-backed up. We had more luck on her exit. Straight to St. Pancras and Eurostar across the channel. The French are looking, but she could be anywhere. She was out of Gare du Nord before any alerts. We did get good photos, though." The small woman appeared on the screen. "Lina Smirnov was the name she used. Ukrainian passport. False, but it didn't get much of a check on the way out. If she came in on that passport, we don't have it. We're trawling."

"So are we. We do have connections via photo matching for her operating elsewhere, and that timeline is linked to other killings." Jermaine added. He was also taking a keen look. He had a very good memory for faces. The alleged, his former police mind added, 'alleged', assassin, was now in that memory bank alongside other pictures.

"Moving on, Joe, your attacker." Sam Fox continued.

"Still alive?" Jermaine asked.

"Yes, just. His prognosis is not good. He lost a lot of blood. Probably brain dead."

"Good. The Missus did brilliantly," Joe added.

"She did; she saved you." Jermaine waited a suitable pause and said, "Thankfully." He got a smile from his boss. He may be in charge and determined to catch the attackers, but he was still in shock.

"Yes, well," Sam Fox continued, but the lighter-hearted comment was a relief from some of the tension in the room. "There is no ID on him. Similar burner phone with one pre-programmed but unused number, the same as the text that went. Purchased in Ostend. Have a possible match on the Dover ferry. If that ties in, he was on a Turkish passport." The Turkish potential connection prompted some looks away from screens.

"You two," Adrian Deans said, looking at the Army Major. He got a stern stare back. He would not like to be on the wrong side of Tom Larring. His wife was equally as stern. "They backed off when the dog patrol spooked them." Tom knew that. "Rental from Heathrow, although there is no record of them flying in. They dumped it in Swindon and probably got on a fast London train. They don't show up in Paddington, but they're not anywhere else either. Train CCTV is being scanned. The name on the rental was Harvey Goldman."

"False?"

"Yes. The credit card for the car was in the same name. There was only one man on the airport CCTV, so he picked up his accomplice elsewhere. We have CCTV from motorways on the way to their target."

"Me." Tom didn't seem concerned, although the glance from his wife was not so confident.

"One of our forensic photo people thinks they were disguised in the car hire too." DS Proctor contributed. It was one of the few things he had helped with since re-joining Sam Fox's team.

"No hits on our systems, so far," Jermaine added.

"As you can tell, Tom and Effi are very keen to meet up with them." Kathrine tried to make a joke of it. Sam Fox and the other police knew that such a meeting would probably end in illegal acts in multiple ways.

"We've got some CCTV from your home, Mrs. Larring," Proctor stated politely. It still took Effi a couple of seconds to realise he meant her.

"Effi please."

"It's not very clear, Effi, but it looks like a single person who could just be a regular burglar. Amazing coincidence, if it was. Your alarm sensors and security floodlights spooked him." Tom and Effi watched a shape in their rear garden briefly lit. There was no sound, but Effi knew the alarm had also sounded. Neither of them could take credit for the security system that may have saved Effi's life. The system had been installed by the previous owner.

"All of them are probably back in Russia," Joe speculated.

"More likely in Ukraine; they failed," the non-policeman

Sam added.

Sam Fox continued, "We have police protection for the Harper sisters. They have private security too, from what you've told us. I've gleaned from other police forces that it's not the first time they have been threatened.

"Best we don't cover that any more than we already have." Kathrine didn't want their kidnapping retold. The fact that Stephie had helmed the yacht to Enez put her in Russian sights. The connections between Hugh, Michelle, and her sister had been exposed by Adrian Holloway, the NSA, and the Russians.

"What about Carolyn's partner, Lizzie?" Effi asked. Tom and she had spoken to the sisters, but Carolyn wouldn't discuss the state of her relationship with Lizzie. Tom had a very brief, unsatisfactory call with that woman. She didn't want to talk about it either. Tom and Effie speculated that the relationship between Lizzie and Carolyn, which had already been difficult after kidnappings and Mykonos, was now doomed.

"She doesn't want direct protection, but we have cover on her anyway," Sam Fox replied.

"Good. Effi and I will try to speak with her again."

"Which leaves us with Hugh and Michelle Turnbill."

"We don't know where they are." Kathrine thought that Tom was a little too quick to say that, and Effi wouldn't look at her. "We have sent messages, and they have replied." William Thatcher had already confirmed to Kathrine and Sam that routine operational spending messages were still being actioned as normal. The Special Branch officers didn't need to know about that. There had been no response to messages in draft folders that Sam and Kathrine had access to. Tom added, "Carolyn and Stephie have also had messages, as has Antreas."

"The Greek lawyer?"

"Yes, Antreas Katsaros is in Mykonos, although his firm has offices in London too. He may know more, but he won't say." Kathrine doubted if he did, and the not-saying was more likely Tom and Effi. She wanted Mel or 2B's take on the conversation, but that was never going to happen. She'd mourned her colleagues in private. They had their disagreements, most notably about what to do with Hugh and Michelle Turnbill, but Kathrine was just as shocked as anyone that they were dead. The poor innocent delivery driver too. The callousness and ruthlessness of the attacks shocked Kathrine, although she was not unused to violence in pursuit of her own targets.

Now, Effi was working in MI6 on analysis and nominally in charge of the old team Kathrine had once controlled and once more officially controlled. Effi also split her time between the now deceased Russia Desk, Jamie McKenzie, and the Middle East, focusing on Dubai, where she once worked. She helped with IDs and names in Dubai.

The formal meeting concluded with the departure of the police officers. They would reconvene in two days for an update. By then, Joe Carpenter's attacker was dead, but Sir Rupert continued to cling to life.

CHAPTER NINE

CHAIN 3865 Tarot CC 00643

"Surprised to see you, been awhile."

"Recovering, heart."

"Okay now?"

"Triple bypass but hopefully sorted."

"Why add to the stress?"

"The attacks."

"Those. Russians are going nuts, last year was…"

"All connected."

"Shit!"

"Yeah, need a full brief."

"Full?"

"From the very top. I'll send links and access codes. A national response plan is being drawn up."

"Serious then?"

"Yes. This time they over-stepped, made senior people very nervous about their own vulnerability."

"Not surprising given who they hit."

"Full list is not public."

"You mean it's worse?"

"Yep, and several thwarted attacks too."

"Jesus! Okay, when you say *all*, you mean?"

"I'll edit most of Tarot out, and obviously we'll change the numbers. First chain."

"The one we forgot."

"Un-forget."

"Tarot and penetration into the task force?"

"Not that."

"Defector?"

"Yep, but without details. No mention of Navy operations on yachts. They never happened."

"Okay."

"More on the defector and his family?"

"Just the timeline. He's over here, safe, but you didn't get that from me. No need to mention current location. Just Turkey, Mykonos and the previous sailing activity."

"New yacht traces?"

"Nope, stay well away as we agreed on shut down. I'm told it's not in use."

"The systems?"

"Also keep clear, this is just a dull review background briefing. Summary timeline, bullet points. Justification for executive decisions."

"Okay."

CHAPTER TEN

Analysts

Greg Birch, Troy Williams-Roberts, and Ali Watson were a team of analysts employed by MI6 to watch over the finance and accounts system. They were supervised by Effi Miani, who was still using her maiden name at work. She was supposedly away from operational duties. Although she had dabbled with surveillance and occasional other tasks for Kathrine prior to her suspension.

As part of the team's induction, Effi had helped to coordinate their briefing which included an appearance by Hugh Turnbill in an external conference room. Michelle would not allow her husband to be cornered inside MI6's HQ. Effi had also been present before that meeting with Michelle when she did enter the building for the first time since she had run off. Those circumstances were still highly classified. Michell had helped the team inside Vauxhall Cross, the iconic green and cream home of MI6.

The original analysts had been combined with a fourth member. He was no longer in MI6, and they knew, due to press reports, that he was no longer alive. Suicide, the coroner had ruled. Mo Gadhi had been a traitor, passing on their secrets to a terrorist organisation. The three other analysts had all been investigated and eventually cleared. Their original tasks back then, had been to find the couple and alternatives for the finance system run by Hugh and Michelle Turnbill. They had failed in those objectives hindered by the traitor in their midst.

The team and its operations had a new MI6 codename. Operation *Slump-Grown-Salvation* was not a great name, but at least it was obscure. The team's main task was to collect reports from

Hugh Turnbill, process any internal actions, and try and use a new application Turnbill had written. All aspects had become more difficult since the previous year's operation. Effi clearly knew more about it but didn't spread the news. She had arranged for the team to be given other tasks while *issues* were resolved. Kathrine, Effi, and even Mel Kennedy had told them not to be concerned.

Now, the team was aware that Mel Kennedy was dead. She had been named on TV. Security in and out of Vauxhall Cross had increased with the terror warnings. The new assigned work for the team was under other code names, and it had increased, but it felt like piecework compared to the financial issues.

Most recently, William Thatcher himself delivered account numbers for credit cards. They tried to use the application to start tracing, but it delivered multiple error messages. When working correctly, they knew the application could trace financial connections. They used it on their own MI6 and MI5 accounts to trace activity. It was not easy to use, but now it just stopped. The security protocols on bank accounts and credit cards at home and abroad change regularly. They had received updates from Hugh Turnbill in the past, but not recently.

Effi was in their office. They were explaining again why they couldn't use the application.

"These aren't our accounts, you understand?" Effi was limited by what she could tell them. She had her own news to pass on. A new member of the team would be reluctantly joining. It would be safer for her inside MI6 than in Darlington.

"Hugh told us, in that one briefing,' Greg officially led the team, "that he wanted to expand use to potential enemy accounts, but none of the accounts are working anymore." Their shared experience made them close-knit. That was when Ali and Troy were not arguing about something. He didn't ask, and they didn't tell, but he knew when they weren't always together.

"We've had success before on Visa and Mastercard accounts." Ali Watson added.

"So what do you need?" Effi understood their frustration. She knew they were a bit scared of her. Canteen rumours about operations in Turkey. They also knew her phone number had changed again and that she and her Army husband had moved house at short notice.

"A new version of the app, if we can get one? We need new updates as well. It's all been cut off since…" Troy tried

"I know when," Effi snapped. "Sorry, tense times. No, I'm not going to tell you, and no rumour mongering in the canteen."

"Effi, we're not saying anything," Ali said. Effi gave them a hard look. "But not speaking about it attracts attention. We can't just say nothing."

"I know, I know." Effi understood the problem. She had lots of looks around offices and comments behind her back. Unexplained absences did that, and Middle East Desk could gossip, even if they didn't know below desk head what had happened in Turkey. She had a security escort to and from the safe house she was living in. Tom had to commute to and from the Defence College with an ever-changing vehicle allocation, different often longer routes, and an assigned security team. He was not happy, even if he was happier being armed. Another situation that caused comments among his military colleagues. Still, he only had another couple of weeks to go before graduation. Their social life, which she had enjoyed on the base, was now prohibited. She'd been looking forward to the Mess Ball.

Effi focused on her news. "We'll have a new member of the team joining, hopefully tomorrow. She has a computing background and used to be in Treasury. Her name is Uliana Doubek. Greg, please do the usual onboarding after HR and security have finished."

"Okay," he said, as surprised as the others.

"She knows about some aspects of the finance team and the process. She'll be able to look at computer programmes and trace accounts. She's had a tough time. Connected to what has been going on, but please don't probe."

"Can you ask the finance team for a new version of the app?" Ali asked. A new member of the team would be welcome, especially one who had better computing skills than they did.

"Sort of," Effi admitted. "It's not easy; they are at risk too."

"Not us! Not this time." Greg wanted it made clear.

"No, the source of those cards."

"Russians," Troy added

"Speculation." Effi didn't deny it. She wanted to brief the team wider. She had Kathrine back in the offices with Sam, whom she didn't trust. William Thatcher was okay. Likewise, the MI5 team. Jermaine Harris, whom she knew from surveillance in Darlington, with Cindy Loughton. There was also Joe Carpenter, Jermaine's boss who she had met during debriefs on Darlington.

Other than Tom, who could Effi trust? She was not supposed to talk about MI6 operations with him, and she didn't, except in the vaguest way. He'd been stretched academically by his course, and his own determination to do well. She knew he was much happier fighting, than in a classroom. She wanted to talk to Michelle, preferably on the yacht away from ears. Michelle would understand. Now, Effi had a Russian target on her back. She was nervous. The deaths of colleagues made her nervous. The analyst team wouldn't understand but might be able to help.

***

Effi's thoughts were interrupted as Kathrine came in unannounced. She hadn't told the team that Kathrine was back. They all looked suitably surprised. Thankfully, there was no Sam.

"Hello, and we can close mouths, and some questions won't get answered."

"Kathrine, hello," Greg managed. Ali and Troy added greetings.

"Has Effi updated you?" Kathrine asked after pleasantries on well-being had been provided.

"A bit. I've told them about Uliana, but…"

"It's okay Greg, Ali, Troy, sorry, Effi, I only just got clearance from William. Sam's with him still. First off, this is UK TS, not Five Eyes; any GCHQ requests via Effi, please." She meant United Kingdom Eyes Only, Top Secret classification. The analysts all sat up. "No direct to Cheltenham. The operational code will remain *Slump-Grown-Salvation*, but with Codeword *Plaintiff* for output, if and when we get some. It's also strictly compartmentalised. You may only discuss among yourselves, Uliana, when she gets here, Effi, of course, Sam, and Acting Director William Thatcher." Another rumour confirmed Greg realised. "Five liaisons as necessary, but only via Effi. She has direct contacts with the head of the joint security service investigation, who is in Five. They in turn will deal with all police liaisons via Special Branch, whom Effi and I have both met with. Others may be added as and when. IT has been briefed on the updates needed. They are not cleared for this. Understand?" They all did, and having it spelled out reminded them of previous operations. "We, I mean Effi and I, can tell this part of the operation more, and you can pass that on to Uliana. Shall we start with the cards? Effi?"

Effi nodded at Kathrine. The woman was back in her normal confident manner, which meant she was plotting and scheming. "The cards were taken from two dead Russians." That got the team's immediate attention. "They were killed after they attacked Sir Rupert Paltry and killed his wife before an MI5 team got them."

"Jesus," Greg shook his head. Some of it had been on the news.

"Mel Kennedy and her equivalent at MI5, Baz Butler, were killed the same night alongside a civilian, a delivery driver." Kathrine added to the shock in the room. It had also been on the news, but not all the identities or the brevity of the report from Kathrine hammering the news. Deaths were rumoured, but now they were being briefed. The three analysts looked around at each other and the two women. "Effi will be too modest to admit it, but she and her husband were also targeted. A further Russian died from injuries after attacking another senior MI5 man. A further Six senior officer, along with his wife, who also used to be here, were also killed. That has not been disclosed and must not be. We, I mean, Effi and I, knew them too. That one has not been on the news."

The McKenzie deaths were being covered up as carbon monoxide poisoning to avoid any more headlines. Their children, released from boarding school, were being cared for by Justine's parents, who, thankfully, knew enough not to press for a different investigation.

"What the…" Troy was shaking his head. They all looked shocked. Kathrine gave them a few moments. They again looked at each other, shaking their heads in disbelief.

"But you were okay?" Ali eventually asked Effi.

"Never got near me thanks to my home, former home's alarm." She thought about luck and had a short flashback to bullets flying in Enez and Pakistan. "They tried to get to Tom on the base. That was the two in Swindon on TV."

"Hence all the extra security," Greg pondered.

"Yes, and Kathrine was also probably targeted; several others are still at risk. Some you know about. Uliana may also have been targeted. She'll be safer here."

"Hugh and Michelle Turnbill?"

"Yes, but also…"

"Not the sisters, not again," Greg added. He had been involved in identifying them, and then they had been kidnapped. Greg had guilt all over his face. Although his own actions had helped uncover the traitor Mo Gadhi, it was not before other stupid actions had been taken.

"Old ground, not needing to be covered again." Kathrine wanted that back in a closed file. She also knew it was another reason trust was not forthcoming from Hugh and Michelle. She didn't know for sure, but she suspected that Effi and Tom also knew all about it. It was in the past and should not have happened, but it had. Now she needed Hugh and Michelle back in contact. That meant she needed Effi and Tom to persuade the sisters to ask Hugh and Michelle. She also needed Effi and Tom to directly reach out to Hugh and Michelle. Her own draft emails had elicited no response. "As you've probably guessed, all our colleagues were targets of the Russians. That was due to another mission. One Effi and her husband were directly involved in it."

"Oh!" Greg could only manage the exclamation. More rumours were being confirmed.

"It was a defection they helped escort out."

Effi, with a nod from Kathrine, continued, "It didn't go well; I mean, part of it didn't. It's on the Internet if you want to look." That got a surprised look.

"The gunfight in Turkey?" Troy asked. He was an avid follower of some social media sites. He thought the film was faked by some CGI recorded from a video game.

"Yes." Effi didn't like admitting it. "Look, that's not important. We need to get Hugh and Michelle back in contact. They were also in Enez, as was one of the sisters. Close your mouth, Greg. Tom and I are trying, as are Carolyn and Stephie, the Harper sisters. They are also in a safe house. For now."

"No more detail, Effi." Kathrine stopped her from making any further disclosures. "No discussing in the canteen. If you must watch the Internet, do it privately. Obviously, you," she said, looking at Troy and Ali, "might watch together. You do need to update your security records if you are going to live together." Ali and Troy both looked embarrassed. "Not for now," she said, preventing them from replying. "The cards from the Russians, what's the issue?"

Greg decided to respond as team leader. "We just told Effi that the application that Hugh gave us, no longer works for any accounts. We've been trying to follow his code to see why, but we have limited skills in that area. This Uliana might be able to help. We do need a programmer, and he or she would need to understand all the bits and pieces that Hugh uses. He hasn't sent an update since…"

"I know when," Kathrine was blunt and didn't apologise. Her sense of urgency was palpable. "Okay, so we'll try and get an update. In the meantime, I've given you access to the joint files that we are working on with MI5. Tracing Russian assassins. Special Branch also has some access and will feed into the police investigations. Get the IDs, photos, and so on up on some of your boards and get me connections. You'll also have access to some aspects of the photo matching system. This is a highly privileged, very high-profile operation. We want to know the routes up into the GRU, FSB and the SVR. Even above to Putin's gangsters."

"That high?" Greg asked. He was already impressed with being involved and what he had been told. He had seen the faces around the building. Steely determination to do something, expressed in mumbled words about Russia and Ukraine.

"We think so; the defector was very high up. Five wrapped up a network of Russians last year. There were more deaths at the time. That's also part of Uliana's connection, so please don't ask her directly. She'll tell you if she wants. Those attacks were passed off as drugs and counterterrorism. Please don't go digging there unless links pop up with your new targets. Check with Effi; she knows about all that." She got nods from the team, and Effi got more looks. "I don't want to hammer it home unnecessarily, but no leaks. You know what happened with the threat Gadhi created. We can't waste resources chasing internal leaks."

"We understand, Kathrine." Greg was getting annoyed but understood the warnings. They had all been suspected, and some smoke always lingered.

"Don't talk about it at home, bugs." Ali and Troy looked shocked. "Internal security will sweep when they get a chance. We don't have Mel to help prioritise. That team has their own shocks to deal with. Also, review your home's physical security. Alarms, CCTV, and so on. Internal security has some guidance. They'd normally assist, but…" That made them look up. "Anyway, there's no reason the Russians should know you or target you, but they are not playing nicely. Threat levels are up everywhere. Effi, we need to visit some sisters."

Kathrine swept out as fast as she had swept in. Effi nodded to the team and followed. She hoped they would not watch the Internet, but she knew they would. They would also soon know she was one of the blurred participants. They would probably see her executing one of the Russians. Even if he was dying already, Tom said he thought it was Hugh's shot, but she had finished the man off. Just as her husband had done the others. How Tom tracked who had shot which target was beyond her comprehension. The Turkish authorities had not shared forensics, as far as she was aware.

CHAPTER ELEVEN
Ula Sidorova

Ula Sidorova had spent several days travelling south. The weather was better, but train and road connections were not as common. She'd managed to reach Orenburg and wanted to cross into Kazakhstan. People were suspicious of her. She did not look like the majority of the locals. She was trying to get a lift to Aktobe. A truck looked to be the best bet. Ula had no passport, and her funds were dwindling. She'd refrained from using dollars or euros on the trip. Train fares and walking kept costs low, even with doubling back and taking diverted routes. Brief stays in dilapidated hotels who would log her journey in thankfully paper records. Eventually, she would be traced.

She found an open café and ate a meal of stew and dumplings, washed down with awful coffee. There had been a couple of men giving her long looks in the café, but they had departed. She knew the main road south was near, but she had no map to get a sense of how far she needed to go. She asked the waitress for directions to the nearest library. At least she was pleasant, and she directed her to the Scientific Library OSU on Prospekt Pobedy. She passed her bank's ATM on route. After the library, she thought. The reception staff were helpful, especially after she showed them her papers. They had some maps and some Russian Internet terminals for public and student use. She knew her presence would be logged and even reported so far from Moscow. But she needed time to research, even if it exposed her location. She checked the maps and saw the route. She changed maps, creating a false trail. She chose Zharsuat and researched the crossing and transport links from there. Not that there was much information adding Uralsk to her searches. She needed to leave.

Ula was on the street at the ATM. She was surprised her accounts were still accessible. There was a daily withdrawal limit from her savings and checking accounts. She used the maximum. Glancing back at the library, she noticed the fast car arrive and two men go in the front entrance the same one she had left barely five minutes before. They would have the ATM soon. She needed to move. Not that she had done anything illegal yet. She could return home. She had no job and no requirement to let anyone know where she was. Leaving the country without a passport was another issue.

She walked quickly away. Thirty minutes later, she was at a filling station, looking at vehicles. She saw several with Kazakhstan plates. That was what she needed, now to entice a driver. She found a rest room and did some makeup. She had a few clothes in her bag to make her look more attractive. She had carried clothes for comfort, not to seduce. She checked the mirror, remembering other checks and looking in other mirrors. Men were easy, she told herself. They were all the same in the end.

***

It took her less than five minutes before a small fifty-year-old who called himself Adylet agreed to give her a lift to a road junction near the town of Kornilovka. They set off. His truck was carrying paper and cardboard into Kazakhstan, he told her. It was a poorly paid return for the fruit and vegetables he had taken north. He told her about his family even while checking her blouse and legs. She had no skirt, but he was mostly looking at her chest and the tops of her bra. She left a little on display that he could see through the open buttons.

Behind the driver's seat was a small bunk bed, which Ula knew the driver would like to get her into. She let him think she would. His Russian was heavily accented, but she smiled. She slowly introduced the possibility of continuing with him into Kazakhstan before she apologised for the difficulty given that she had lost her passport. She traced her neck as she told him. Her fingers idly extended to the curve of her pale breast as she enticed. They passed the junction she had originally asked for. The next stop was the Russian customs post just before the border. She was lying in the bunk. By that point, her blouse was undone with her bra on full display, promising access to the contents. Ula wanted him to think she was promising more than that degree of intimacy when they were through the border. Russian Customs officers barely checked the paperwork or the truck. The driver was on their list as a regular traveller. The guards did take a cursory look in the back at the rolls of paper and flat cardboard sheets, but Ula, shaking behind the screen of the cabin, did not get disturbed.

"Next bit harder," Adylet told her, enjoying the innuendo of thrusting his groin at her. She fake-smiled sweetly and cupped her still-bra-clad breast. Encouraging him to hurry.

The truck edged onward. Ula closed the curtain. She felt the truck turn right and then slowly creep forward. She couldn't risk a glance out.

"Adylet," she heard the driver's name, but that was all she could understand in the Kazakh language. Forms were exchanged. Ula could just see a $50 bill clipped to the noticeboard. Her driver was either protecting her or doing something else. Another short check in the back, and then the truck moved once more; she was out of Russia.

"This is near Martuk; stay in the truck," he stated as he pulled the curtain back, having stopped briefly. It was almost dark outside.

"Why?"

For once, he was not leering at her breasts. "We stop unload some stuff. You stay here; stay lying down but curtain open; otherwise, they search. Very dangerous men, if you come out. Understand?"

"Yes," she said, confused. She had thought they were clear, and all she would have to do would be to dissuade a sexual assault or let him have something. She watched him reach beneath the console. He pulled out a handgun. She couldn't tell the type. It looked old. The driver tucked it into his trousers' belt under his stained shirt.

"Many like you are running from Putin, young men, children of bosses. I help for money, but I also bring other stuff for others before they leave. You nice bonus." He took the opportunity to grope her breast. "We have fun later; now we careful. You quiet."

Thankfully, he stopped the examination of her chest. He left the curtain open and drove on for a few minutes. She could see no road signs from her position lying down, but the road surface changed. She noticed some power lines passing across the view, lit by full-beam headlights. A few seconds later, Adylet braked and pulled in. She could smell diesel. She could partly see a low-rise building. No lights were on.

"Quiet and stay," he said as he climbed down from the cab. The cab had no light on when the door opened.

***

All Ula could hear were unintelligible voices. She tried to see in the absent driver's rear-view door mirror what was happening. The voices were louder. Some Russian words she thought, although she could not make out words. She heard the clang of the rear doors opening. Then there was rustling and boxes moving, she guessed.

"You, open it?"

"I check no drugs, sniffers at crossing."

"Where's the rest?" That was all she heard in Russian, no accent. The conversation got louder but was back in Kazakh, or another language.

She clearly made out two gunshots, then three more. The sounds were different. She didn't know how many weapons there were. There was a bullet hole in the cab, half a metre above her prone position. She waited. The cab door slowly opened.

"Help me," Adylet gasped. She moved, automatically closing her blouse as she climbed from the bunk. He had sunk down near the step of the vehicle's door. She looked around. She could see the unmoving feet of someone near the back of the vehicle. "They dead," he said something in Kazakh and then swore in Russian. She looked at him. His hand covered a wound in his stomach. The darkness was only broken by a dim hanging lamp casting shadows onto the wheels and reflecting off the metalwork. Despite the darkness, she could see that there was blood coming up through his fingers. There was a lot of it, almost black in the night. He went to move, but then passed out.

She watched him die. She had not touched him to help, instinctively knowing there was nothing she could do. His gun was still in his hand. She managed to extract it from his dead grasp. She extended her arms as she had been taught, having already checked for ammunition. It was an old revolver. She'd never fired one before. There were two rounds left. She tried to remember how many had been fired. She realised she didn't know how many the gun had been loaded with. The hammer was still cocked. A deep breath. She tried to steady her racing heartbeat.

***

Ula very carefully manoeuvred towards the back of the truck, pointing the revolver at the unmoving body. The first man was dead. He was lying face down with a large part of his skull missing. Ula wanted to vomit after seeing the brain splatter and gaping hole.

She risked a glance into the back of the truck. It was lit inside, the light spilling out onto the ground, giving her the view of the head-shot man that she could do without. Looking inside, another man was face-up, his body sprawling across a large box. His eyes were open. His chest was covered in blood. His eyes did not blink or move. Ula climbed up inside the container. She moved closer again, pointing the revolver at the centre of the unmoving target. A gun, an automatic, was lying on the floor. There was no need to be concerned, as she finally checked for a pulse. Nothing. Three dead men, two guns, at least a truck, and a container of paper. She noticed a smart mobile phone near the dead body, lying on another box.

She went back out to the doorway, using the height of the container to scan around the outside. She noticed the rear of a car parked to the side of the building. She searched the men's bodies. Adylet's trouser pockets yielded still-wrapped bricks of $100 bills, two of fifty bills each. She took the money. The rest of his pockets had a wallet with a mix of currencies. An opened packet of condoms was placed back in his pocket. She took the cash.

She riffled through the back of the vehicle. It didn't take

long to find the suitcase and a leather briefcase. An open but empty hidden cupboard at the rear. There was space for a human as well as the bags, she noted. The case wasn't open and wasn't locked. It was full of cash. Dollars, euros, and roubles were in bricks. Far too much to count now.

***

Forty minutes later, Ula was driving a five-series BMW with three-quarters of a tank of fuel. The SatNav was programmed with a route to Aktobe Airport. Not that she could fly without ID. She'd spent five minutes wiping her fingerprints from the cab of the truck. DNA would be impossible to remove if anyone looked. She had carefully pulled the bodies of the driver and the head-shot man, back behind the truck. She left the other man in the truck where he was. She didn't take time to hide them further or want to get blood on her clothes. She had closed the door as best she could to the rear container.

She had three guns, spare ammunition for two of them, a suitcase full of cash, a locked briefcase, and two expensive mobile phones with working SIMs and data. She considered throwing them away, but she could use the Internet. There was even a packaged sandwich on the front seat. The phones had both been unlocked with fingerprints from their dead owners. Ula quickly reset the protection to a 0000 PIN code. The BMW had bags for the men, but neither carried identities she recognised. The chest-shot man's ID was covered in blood. She didn't want to go near the head-shot man, but she somehow managed to check his pockets, managing not to throw up. He had the keys to the car.

An hour and a half later, she was in a Dastan hotel room. She had found it on the Internet but couldn't book it. The BMW was valet parked, and a porter helped her with her suitcases and bags to reception, where she paid for a room with stolen cash. She signed the register as the wife of one of the dead men, neatly covering her real ID papers and rank. No passport was requested or offered. Extra cash, a $50 bill from the pile that had been in Adylet's pocket helped the transaction. The porter happily accepted a $5 tip also from Adylet's wallet.

She showered, ate the nearly stale sandwich, and, naked, slipped into her bed. She was exhausted from the tension and the long day. She noticed missed calls on the phones that were set to silent. She would need new SIMs or phones. She struggled to believe what had happened. She didn't even fully check the suit case, except to see where the fistful of dollars Adylet had taken had disappeared into his pocket. She recognised the name of the film but couldn't recall what it was about. The wrappings were the same. She didn't try to open the briefcase.

CHAPTER TWELVE
Russian Hunt

The three men tasked with enacting Putin's revenge met once more. The discussion started well. Much better than the presidential audience. They first reviewed successful operations against Mel Kennedy, Baz Butler, Jamie, and Justine McKenzie. Each name was neatly crossed off the list. Sir Rupert Paltry's entry was listed as partial. His current condition was not believed to be conducive to recovery, but he was not dead, even if his wife was. A brief note was added to the table.

The successes had partly assuaged the fury of their president's response. All three had gone to face the ire of their leader. Luckily, he was distracted by the lack of progress in Ukraine. The FSB's representative also had to account for several internal issues regarding saboteurs operating inside Russia's borders. Progress in some border areas was not enough.

Military commanders waited in the reception areas. Each of them was waiting for their own turn to discuss their failings. Their endless pleas for more troops and working equipment fell on apparently deaf ears. There was no point in blaming others. It was a distinct difference from the carefully choreographed TV pictures of Putin meeting with his security advisors and generals.

The Russian hunt for targets continued. Yegorov and his family remained the number-one priority. Their locations were still marked as unknown. There were no changes in probabilities. They had indications that the former general was in the USA, but they didn't know where. The family could be anywhere. It was likely they would be hidden in a British colony; they knew that from previous exits. The head of the SVR, General Volkov, was in charge of that search, but he had nearly buckled under the president's unsympathetic gaze. He felt safer away from the Kremlin.

The head of the FSB, Egorov, another general, also had a difficult time recounting how one of the joint team members, former Colonel Ula Sidorova, was now missing. Little compensation was forthcoming from the brief announcement of the death of one former major, Sergei Morozov. The FSB had tracked Sidorova to a library in Orenburg, and the woman had used her bank card to withdraw some cash nearby. They had missed her by a few minutes; the failure was not seen as bad luck. Her accounts had not been frozen, despite a request from the FSB to the banking authorities. Someone else would be explaining that failure. Due to a suspected smuggling ring, the intelligence service was active in that area. Using external assets, the route was also used as a cover for an operational messages. Something the FSB had only recently learned. The smuggling ring was officially under investigation, suspected of taking running conscripts, the rich, and money out and bringing black market goods into the country. It was also a method of sending secure information to contacts who couldn't directly fly in and out of Russia.

The investigations back in Moscow had again questioned several members of the former task force. The interrogators discovered that Sidorova would have had no knowledge of or access to the ring. The map searches she had carried out indicated she had headed south or, more likely, west for the border. She had not been seen, despite alerts. They suspected that she had either retraced her steps or found another exit path. The surveillance officer assigned to watch Sidorova's apartment was now in Ukraine. Another failure that was not reported up the chain.

Egorov did not mention a potential coincidental incident inside Kazakhstan. That was, unless someone else heard about it and mentioned it. The anti-smuggling operation was a good reason why FSB agents were in the area. The SVR agents in a foreign country were not briefed. The loss of one of those agents across the border need not be mentioned. He had little information except for a gunfight reported by the local authorities with three dead. He didn't want to report any more failures, especially with a missing Colonel at large. Not that he had any information to prove she had been involved.

They all wanted her. Her departure put her own previous record in considerable doubt, rather than just her association with Yegorov. Her interrogations had been satisfactory but were now also being reviewed. The Head of FSB knew that people were claiming connections that didn't exist, just to deflect attention from themselves. Allegedly, Yegorov and Sidorova were long-term lovers, based on a throwaway comment from the soon-to-be executed General Tarasov. He'd said Sidorova had been ordered to try and compromise the general. General Kuzmin, awaiting his own calendar appointment with a brick wall, denied issuing any order. Instead, he claimed Tarasov was just trying to undermine his rival for promotion. This only highlighted his own failure to spot that Yegorov was a traitor. The final decision on whether and when they met their bullets was still to be made. Putin had asked for a hold, just in case more information came to light.

***

When the new Director of the FSB, General Egorov, had some private time, which was rare, he idly speculated if this was what it was like during the Stalin purges. He knew he could just as easily be in the same place as Kuzmin and Tarasov.

He managed to tilt the review towards other targets and the failings of his SVR counterpart, the GRU, and their overseas agents. Little time was spent covering the losses of the attackers. Two were dead at the house of Sir Rupert Paltry. Following the attack at the house of Joe Carpenter, one more person died from his wounds in hospital. All were carrying cell phones with a single pre-programmed number. That number terminated on a handset allocated to an SVR agent. They were non-diplomatically accredited but based inside the Russian Embassy in London. A few successful calls had been sent when the handset was outside the embassy. The ambassador did not know the asset, but the British had told the diplomat that the calls were connected. They apparently did not have the asset. The ambassador huffily denied any Russian involvement.

Back in the Embassy, he wanted to be angry at the incompetence but couched his words carefully. Using his own diplomatic skills with Putin and his Foreign Secretary. It was a small problem, according to the president. The three of them briefly discussed the British response. Putin wanted the British to know he was taking revenge, just like Salisbury.

One successful agent was listed on Interpol. She had gone to ground in France. She was making her way somewhere safe before making any contact. At least she was successful, and not for the first time. Unfortunately, her picture was with every European and international police force and had been broadcast on British television. She would have to retire if they could get her back to Moscow. The head of the SVR also knew there was a further question about whether she would willingly return. Her controller stated she enjoyed her western life.

A further failed two were also on their way back. They were also on Interpol's list. A long route through France and onwards across Europe, then to Turkey, before flying back to Moscow. That was if they made it and were not arrested. The French in particular were cooperating with the British, according to agents there. There was concern in the GRU that the two failures might decide not to return. Their futures would not be bright, and they probably featured a posting to a trench in Ukraine.

***

The three men continued their review of progress.

"The military base had extra protection," Volkov explained on behalf of the SVR.

"Poor target location choice. His home would have been better."

"Yes, but he wasn't there."

"His wife was." Effi Miani/Larring's name was next to Tom, her husband. Army/MI6 was against both their names with the handwritten question mark.

"A planning mistake," the security adviser, Kovalenko, was enjoying the discomfort of the two heads.

"GRU agents, not our own." A quick blame deflection.

"Yes, GRU," blame now apportioned to the military agency not present but connected to Kovalenko. He instructed them.

They all agreed the couple would stay on the target list, joining Joe Carpenter. He had a Putin note against him. An additional line in the table had been added for the security team, thought to be MI5, who had killed the two agents after their attack on Paltry. Not that anyone had names.

The Harper sisters now had an unknown location against them. The team on Paltry was supposed to have gone to them after their first target. New agents would need to be assigned. Agents were thin on the ground in the UK, despite Ukraine's refugee infiltration. All would be checked by the British, given that was how two of the dead men had entered the UK. Men would be noticed, but female agents who would undertake the necessities were also rare. The woman who had killed the security heads was a notable exception, but her future use was doubtful with her photo everywhere.

"These two," the security adviser pointed at Hugh and Michelle Turnbill's names. "Singapore, you said?" He was looking at Volkov.

"An associate, not an agent, and it is a low probability. He was unable to follow, but there was a yacht connection."

"We have the report from France as well," Egorov contributed. Happier ground for him. Despite the supposed separation of actions, sometimes the Russian FSB, like MI5 and MI6, also operated overseas. He struggled with the pronunciation of Port Grimaud. "We have some assets in place. A different mission watching one of our leaders business acquaintances." He confessed to the other parties and got a nod from Volkov. "They will watch the boat." He used they, implying a team.

In reality, he had a single woman working for occasional money. She was tasked with watching mega-yachts. It was not a difficult task for a young, attractive woman on the French beaches and harbours. It was an expensive place, hence her willingness to exchange information for money. Her background as a Russian from the Donbas area allowed her to masquerade as a Ukrainian refugee. He checked his handwritten notes: "Harry Rosenthal and his wife Josephine appear to be using the boat. It looks like the one used in Enez, but it has a different name. High probability it is the same boat but not certain. It has a German registration now, via a nest of companies. A maintenance trip to Naples was witnessed there, and some occasional crew came from the city too. More links for my colleagues to trace." He tried to smile at Volkov. Their interception failure of Yegorov's defection was another reason why the head was the new head.

"New targets?" The security adviser asked. They were not on the list. Naples sparked all their interest, even with the reminder of their predecessor's failure.

"Collateral," the FSB replied, condemning and dismissing in one word. There were no complaints. He then added, "However, one Italian crew member has a potential photo match with Enez." One piece of positive news to relay in this meeting. Good work from his team. Not that he would receive any praise.

"Identity?"

"Our asset heard him being called Jules. The other crew is a married couple, possibly the brother of Jules. No other names; the assets couldn't get that close. They were surveillance-aware. The assets had to withdraw."

"Most interesting," said Evgeni Kovalenko. He was happy. He'd have something positive to report to his boss, the president. "Are the assets useful in other ways?"

"Not an active team, just some information and limited surveillance capability. They have other targets to watch. Bigger yacht targets. I would rather not share identities unless directly ordered."

Kovalenko was deciding if he wanted to know or let the SVR know. "Not for now; you have more?" He suspected who the targets being watched were. From the location, he could make guesses.

"Yes, another link with the brother. One, or both of them, are also linked to that incident on Corfu, a Greek island. The one that the joint team linked to possible terrorism. Again, the yacht is possibly the same one."

"Possibly?" Volkov asked.

"Superstructure is slightly different." Egorov was also

disappointed that the news was not definitive. "It's a low probability on both photos. They might be the crew, and possibly the prime target finance couple were there. In Corfu, I mean, not France." Facial scanning of more photos sourced from social media followed. The couple appeared in the background of several, with varying degrees of probability. The SVR had also tried to get the Greek police files on the two arrested people at the scene. Another one had been captured in bizarre circumstances. Reportedly, he had been found tied to a lamppost on a different island. Normal Greek files were easy to get, but the counter-terrorism ones were not. The three captured men were now believed to be with the Americans via obscure rendition routes. The Greeks knew they were not nationals. Given their capture, they were not very competent, either. Why they were involved with the Turnbill couple in Corfu was unknown.

"Has the crew been added to the list?" Kovalenko wanted to report action, not information.

"Yes." They took a short break.

***

"Dubai?"

The SVR had made progress. "Surveillance assets have confirmed the possible Doug Masters target. He is working in Dubai under the name Kevin Little. He is allegedly a consultant on security affairs, also working with a younger black man. They share an apartment. Not homosexuals." He added it for clarification and to avoid someone suggesting different approaches. "An operation is underway."

"Timing?"

"Another week, they are…"

"No details; we just want results."

"Very well," Volkov didn't like that Kovalenko continued to think he was in charge. The man was a current Putin favourite, but that could change.

"To resources, given recent losses."

"Limited, and some exposed. We have a possible additional

supply from some allies." Volkov announced.

"Syria? The President called their President." Kovalenko conveyed the information as if he were a party to the discussion and agreement.

"Yes, thank you for that," he could be grateful, "but they come with a warning. They are not ideologically aligned."

"Who is?" A mistake from Egorov that he regretted as soon as he said it. He quickly covered. "They will work for money, though?"

"Yes, money, but they are mostly jihadists looking for funding."

"I meant that they are our enemies' enemies, but can they be trusted?"

"They have done tasks before." Volkov was enjoying Egorov's mistake.

"I know, but this needs delicacy, not terrorist outrages."

"The instructions from the president are clear, regardless of collateral." Kovalenko would tell the president about the comment. The president always wanted to know who was performing well or not. Who was plotting more than normal? Kovalenko knew his own climb to power meant providing such information. His own background was business connections, as it was euphemistically called. He ran internal security for one of the unofficial organisations that handled finance in Russia.

"Very well," Egorov knew he had made a mistake, but he didn't trust Islamic activists. "How will they be informed, briefed, and assigned?"

"Documents are on the way via a secure route and an asset overseas. A long route, but it stays secure." Volkov didn't want to say more, not when that route also exposed the missing colonel's involvement.

"Where will we use them? The UK will be difficult."

"Dubai, better cover there. Ethnically, they won't stand out." The slightly racist comment was not mentioned by the others.

"Yes, they would fit in." Egorov was trying to recover his position. It was better that they were operating there rather than in Europe. He had his own experiences in Chechnya and elsewhere. He knew his comments would raise questions about him, but he also didn't want terrorist bombs on his conscience. He was unconvinced that the attack on British interests was necessary. It was not how spies normally worked. They had lost good people in the attacks and the British responses.

They had gone too far, in his unvoiced view. Networks had been uncovered. Agents were captured, and some were killed. Long-term interests were harmed purely for short-term, petty revenge. He suspected more would follow. The British would also act again, dragging their American friends in too. Russia already had a real war in Ukraine, that was killing thousands of young men. It didn't need a war among spies too. He wisely kept his thoughts to himself. He was in enough trouble already.

CHAPTER THIRTEEN
Sanzhar Kaliev

The smuggling enterprise that Sanzhar Kaliev had built was the result of thirty years of tough, mostly criminal, work. At the beginning, he focused his attention on routes that ran from east to west, transporting a wide range of drugs into Russia and then further into Europe. The trade was something that he had learnt from his father, who had grown the firm during the Soviet era.

At that time, the majority of the goods that were being transported came from the south. Cheap goods diverted from routes to Western Europe fetched black market prices when transported to Moscow and other Soviet cities. The fall of the Soviet Union created chaos and opportunities. It also saw the rise of competitors, one of whom ended Sanzhar's father's life.

The types of items and the destinations were altered as a result of a number of different crackdowns and changes to the political and territorial landscapes. The finances of his father had been bolstered by the acquisition of guns from Afghanistan for a limited period of time. They were delivered to Iran as well as locations throughout the region. The Taliban received armaments through Kyrgyzstan and Tajikistan after the attacks of September 11, 2001 and the invasion led by the United States.

Heroin was smuggled out of Afghanistan in a covert manner and mixed in with other authorised commodities. This trade had been significantly disrupted as a result of the Taliban's reappearance.

Sanzhar had to adapt and did. An entirely new sector of the economy emerged as a result of the increasing constraints placed on Russia. Young men who were attempting to avoid being conscripted were offered a one-way journey that cost them $5,000. While they were concealed for the departure from the border with Russia, they were nevertheless entitled to enter Kazakhstan on their Russian passports, if they possessed one. They might be able to purchase a new Kazakh one for a higher price. There was also the possibility of obtaining a passport from Turkey, Pakistan, or even Europe; a gold standard for a considerable additional fee. The passports stolen from western tourists and adopted for a new arrival. They would not get through biometric screening at an airport but simple border crossings were easy. If the new holder was caught it would be long after Sanzhar had his money.

As a result of the Russian sanctions there were additional requirements that the small organisations could assist with. Money, documents, jewels, artworks and other items needed to leave Russia, unofficially. Sanctions blocked many transfers. Individuals in the business world who had been confronted by the leadership in Moscow also wanted goods to leave to join them in exile. It was virtually a daily occurrence for one of Sanzhar's trucks to pass through one of the border stations that separated the two countries. Official legal trade in fruit and other farm products was successful, but it was nothing in comparison to the remainder of the hidden items. Ordinary drivers transported ordinary commodities mixed in with the flow. Not every truck smuggled. Not every border guard or customs officer allowed unchecked passage. Nevertheless, it was successful and that success meant larger more powerful people wanted to use the facilities.

***

Almost twenty years had passed since Adylet Tsoy had first established a connection with Sanzhar Kaliev's family. He was dependable and, for the most part, did not steal money or things that were being smuggled. The thefts were normally a few hundred dollars taken from travellers allegedly as extra bribes for guards, but that went into Adylet's pockets. Kaliev knew and didn't care as long as goods weren't taken or people detained.

Adylet's vehicle would normally be met by two of Sanzhar's men at a gas station close to Martuk, just across the border. On this planned trip they were supposed to retrieve a suitcase full of cash that belonged to a former Putin associate who was now in exile.

The client was going to be waiting at the airport with his private jet. When it came to the customer, the suitcase of paperwork was of greater significance. Despite the fact that Sanzhar was unaware of the contents he knew it was valuable. The businessman had spent a sum of $50,000 merely to retrieve the bag. An additional $10,000 would be required to get the accompanying suitcase transported without being opened. They were large payments.

Both his men and the truck driver were unaware of the contents of the briefcase as well as the true value of the item. They were going to be distracted by the suitcase, but Sanzhar was confident that his threats would keep the money safe. In spite of this, he was able to monitor the BMW by using a small device that was connected to the interior of the wheel hub on the right rear wheel. This allowed him to consume a meal while he watched the tracker make its way to Martuk as it had been intended. After then, he noticed that it was driving back to the city. He was content. The transfer to the customer would soon take place at the airport. He continued his meal. It was not until the man called and enquired about the location of his belongings that he became aware that the vehicle was not now in transit. On the contrary, it was in the vicinity of the Dastan hotel. Why were the idiots going there?

Sanzhar went to the automobile and checked it out. No one was there. A parking sticker for a valet service was displayed in the window. He went to the hotel, not somewhere he would normally visit. Even after trying to handover over a $50 note, the receptionist wouldn't assist. She did not provide the room number of the woman who had checked in; all she did was acknowledge that she had done so. Being in close proximity to the night porter made it impossible for him to threaten her. He was going to have to wait, but he couldn't just sit about in the lobby of the hotel. He couldn't afford to have the local police attend. He did pay for some assistance in the forces but his contacts were limited and he couldn't be certain any men dispatched would recognise him. For the most part, he carried out his tasks discreetly and without attracting the attention of the authorities on either side of the borders. He paid small fry to look the other way, not bosses who would want bigger cuts.

When he stepped back from the disappointing engagement

at the reception desk, he saw a man waiting to check in. He was standing back and glancing at a booklet on his way to the front desk. He appeared to be Iranian. They greeted each other with a polite good evening and nodded to each other as Kaliev continued his departure. As he moved out of the room, Kaliev tried to call his missing men. It was not the first time they had missed a response.

He considered what little information he had obtained. Who was the woman driving his car that was valet parked and had now checked in. He did not employ any females in his organisation. Even if he was involved in smuggling some, he was not implicated in sex trafficking. Some of his acquaintances owned whore houses, but he continued to engage in ordinary smuggling.

He reached out to two additional contacts. Favours that he would be required to repay and pay for at this time. It was imperative that he discover the identity of this woman and, more significantly, retrieve the briefcase and suitcase if his missing men had placed them in the vehicle. He requested that the new men keep an eye on the BMW as well as the hotel. In the event that someone attempted to steal the BMW, they were to stop them. He had no idea what the woman looked like or how old. The fact that he had not dealt with the foolish girl behind the counter in a more effective manner irritated him.

It was necessary for him to call the customer. He had already declined two calls. They were late delivering. The man would be angry. In the event that he was unable to retrieve the briefcase, he would be even more dissatisfied. Since the luggage contained nothing more than money, it would be necessary to issue a refund. Kaliev was not aware of the amount that was intended to be included within it. Other connections were held by the customer. The reputation of Kaliev was formed on the basis of his safe delivery. It was necessary for him to live up to it.

***

Sanzhar decided to take a look at the pick-up site. See if there was anything there to indicate why his BMW was in valet parking and his men had disappeared. Perhaps the truck driver, Adylet Tsoy, could be found and shed some light. He could call him, but was wary of doing so. Contact was normally only made to pre-agree pick-ups and drop-offs.

He drove to the fuel station near Martuk. It was obvious something was very wrong. Very wrong. He could see flashing police lights. An ambulance was present but the paramedics were just standing around. He had to drive slowly past the site. He could see a truck and what looked like bodies covered in sheets. Harsh halogen lights lit the scene. There were multiple uniformed and civilian-clothed men standing around. A junior police officer waved him to go past. He could ask his limited contacts in the police force, but that would take time and money. Via an alternate road, he returned to the city. He considered returning to the hotel. That would attract attention. The police may go there anyway, if they had a lead on the woman. There was no CCTV at the filling station but some vehicles had dashboard cameras.

He had one lead. The unnamed woman was in a hotel. He wanted to find her, find the suitcase, but mostly find the briefcase before the Russian client decided on his own response. That reminded him that he needed to contact him. He returned to his home, not looking forward to that call and what might result.

***

Sitting in his small office at his home, he placed a call to one of his limited police contacts. The associate only had restricted information. He would provide more for extra money. It was not a good start. Sanzhar had managed to get a man to sit in reception. Not a very good one, but he would have another there in the morning. Kaliev deployed another man to the car, just in case it was used. He suspected it wouldn't be.

There were other deliveries to coordinate. If Sanzhar diverted all his resources to looking for the Russian's goods, his whole business would grind to a halt. He made some other calls ensuring his operation was unaffected by this issue. A large truck had dropped off fruit supplies across the border. It was due to collect five running conscripts or AWOL soldiers. He didn't care which. One girlfriend was with them. A $40,000 package on the return leg of a $10,000 profit fruit delivery. Bribes at the border would be a few hundred dollars. That was better news to lift his spirits. He called the client.

"What happened?" The man had already complained about missing his calls.

"I don't know yet. The police were at the scene."

"You have contacts?"

"Some, not good ones."

"I pay you for access and delivery."

"I know. I have a lead. I am chasing it." Kaliev tried to sound in control.

"Your men have stolen…"

"No, Sir. They are dead. My contact did tell me that."

"And my goods." No sympathy expressed for the loss.

"The police may have them, or this other person who was in the car. My contact will try and ask."

"Who are they?"

"I am finding out. Please give me time to find your goods."

"Some time. I need that briefcase. Noon tomorrow!"

CHAPTER FOURTEEN
Gavin King

Gavin King was a fifteen-year CIA veteran. Most of it had been spent as an illegal undercover agent operating in the Middle East and the various 'Stans south of Russia. It was a hotbed of information about smuggling, which provided routes in and out of Russia if the right bribes were paid. He also had links in and out of Iran and further smuggling routes, evading sanctions for that nation. All activity the CIA monitored and even used for their own purposes. Information from inside Russia, especially who was escaping, was valued, as was Iranian regime activity.

Gavin had spent more and more time monitoring the mostly organised crime networks of Sanzhar Kaliev. This was due to his involvement in helping Russians escape their mother country, for whatever reason. Many of these were conscripts, but there was always other activity.

He too had a tracker on a BMW Five Series car, and when planting it, he noticed another tracker. It was a western-model tracker under the right wheel hub, meaning a left wheel hub for his own tracker. He didn't think it was the FSB or SVR doing the tracking. He guessed it was probably Kaliev checking on his own people.

Gavin knew one of them was probably FSB or SVR. He had a couple of bad photos of the man. So far, Langley had been unable to confirm or deny his ID. He didn't have time to chase that lead down.

His priority was an exiled Russian businessman waiting at Aktobe's airport. He had left Russia several weeks before appearing in Aktobe and then flying out. Other assets were tracking him and his private jet, but he was the only resource on the ground.

The jet had recently been in Syria, thus proving that the man wasn't running from Putin but was more likely working for him or one of the intelligence agencies. Using the cover of a disgraced oligarch to escape attention. A forlorn hope Gavin thought. The man had contacts in Syria, other parts of the Middle East and the Far East where he often stayed. His file claimed various salacious exploits in Thailand. Of more interest were potential links to Iran and arms deals to Russia. Any links there were of interest with or without the supply of weapons to end up in the war on Ukraine.

When the BMW was heading back to Aktobe, he too thought that the vehicle would go to the airport. It was not the first time this route had been made. It was how Sanzhar Kaliev had been spotted in the first place. His target was waiting by another small private jet, but he did not board. He watched him through binoculars make a very agitated phone call before leaving in a large SUV; the jet stayed unused.

Gavin could see that the car he tracked was parked near the Dastan Hotel. He, too, wondered why. He managed to get near the car in time to see Kaliev open it and check the interior and trunk. The man then marched towards reception. The location was used by a nearby hotel for valet parking. Gavin King also rushed to reception, where he was in time to see Kaliev questioning the female receptionist behind the desk. He did not look happy with the response.

He nodded at his target and offered, "Good evening, friend," in what little Kazakh he spoke. He didn't want to use his fluent Russian. He got a polite smile before the man's expression changed, and he left.

***

Gavin King made a snap decision to check in. He was using his cover identity as an exiled Iranian businessman. He had an Iranian passport, which he used to grab a room. He was carrying an often-used small overnight bag. It did have some toiletries and a change of clothes. It also had a 9-mm automatic in a hidden base, just in case.

As he finished the check-in process, he asked the receptionist in English if his friend who had left had checked in.

"No, Sir, he was just asking about another guest, a woman."

"Oh, I thought he was going to stay?"

"He is a friend? Sir?"

"More an acquaintance," Gavin corrected.

"I see. No, he is not a guest."

"Thank you," he said, handing over a $10 tip and taking his room key.

"Do you know the woman?" The receptionist suddenly asked. "Your friend," she didn't believe his description, "was also asking?"

"I'm afraid not; thank you again." Gavin didn't want to push. That would attract more attention. He had established some bits of information. He could not hang around in reception. He still had the tracker on the car if someone decided to take it. He could follow. The battery on the device was good for another few days.

In his own room, he took the opportunity to update his masters via a game application on his adapted mobile phone. He got a message to continue as he expected before he also grabbed some sleep. Unknown to him, Uliana was asleep in her own room, a floor below.

***

He woke to a game app message and was sent a linked photograph. A woman's photograph. According to the message, she was thought to be running from Russia. NSA or CIA monitoring had picked up on alerts to various Russian border posts. They came from FSB HQ in Moscow. Gavin suspected a trap, because it was too much of a coincidence. Then again, it could just be what it appeared to be. He wondered if she had been aware of the smuggling route and used it to get out of Russia. That's if the woman in the hotel was the same woman. He would have to wait. He also had to consider how he could use the woman, or any information he could get from her. Perhaps she wanted to defect?

Why run first? Too many questions with too few supporting facts.

He headed down for breakfast. He was given a single table. The restaurant was half full. He'd been sitting for only a few minutes when a single woman came in. He tried not to show any surprise and quickly looked away from her. She was being shown to a table in the other half of the room. What was Ula Sidorova, former Colonel of the SVR, doing in Aktobe?

He casually watched her. She was watching the room and briefly scanning him in return. He didn't avoid her gaze. He knew he was taking a risk by showing interest. She looked stressed and tired. Perhaps she thought his interest was due to her looks. He could see she had once been beautiful. In better circumstances, perhaps she still was. He ordered another cup of coffee and waited. He wanted to see if she would make the first move. She was speaking Russian to the serving staff who delivered her tea. She wasn't hiding her origin in that sense. He hadn't asked reception if Ula Sidorova was staying. She would be stupid to use her real name. Stupid or desperate.

Gavin finished his breakfast and stood to leave. Did he gamble that she would want help? How could he get her to respond? It was risky, and he might lose the opportunity that had arrived in the room. He was not concerned for his own safety, but he was for hers. He hadn't seen any FSB or SVR actors, but he might have missed one. Kaliev wasn't around, but he could have stationed a man in reception or in the restaurant, although no one had attracted his attention. No other guest had come in for breakfast since Sidorova.

She was finishing her meal. He needed to act, not dither.

He walked up to her table. He saw her tense. Was that a gun she was carrying?

In Russian, he told her, "Ula, if you need help, my room is 320." She looked shocked at the quiet mention of her name.

"That is not my name." Was her poor reply.

"Others are looking for you, not just your former employers."

"What are you talking about? Please leave me alone. I don't

know you."

He took a bigger risk; in quiet English, he added, "I have friends who can help. If you want it. The hotel and your car are being watched. Please come." He turned and walked away. He may have blown it with such a bold approach.

He walked into reception. A scruffy man was sitting in the lobby, making out he was reading a newspaper. It wasn't Kaliev. Gavin didn't think it was a Russian operative either. The man was not skilled. He would have taken the opportunity to take a photo of him, but he needed to protect what he hoped would be a new asset or assist in getting an SVR Colonel into the USA.

He created a small diversion by heading to the entrance and demanding from someone on a faked phone call why his car wasn't waiting. The man waiting in the reception area watched him and therefore missed Sidorova exiting the restaurant and heading to the lifts. She looked at him, and he looked hard at the man watching him. Sidorova quickly hurried into a lift.

Gavin finished his fake call and returned to the lifts. Reception, who had heard the call, asked if they could get him a car if he was having problems. He politely declined. The man who was waiting returned to his newspaper. Sidorova's lift had gone to the second floor, he noted. He was tempted to follow, but instead he went to the fourth, then walked down the stairs to his room.

He quickly packed and was brushing his teeth when his door was knocked. He checked through the peep hole. Sidorova.

CHAPTER FIFTEEN
Oleg Yegorov

The one-time general officer of the FSB, Oleg Yegorov, was well aware his former compatriots would be hunting him. He had been briefly told that attacks had taken place in the UK, although his current hosts, the CIA, did not give any details. US TV news had little coverage. He was also reassured about his own family and then allowed to call them. They were fine. Time zone differences meant they were four hours behind on the clock, but it was already the next day. They were breakfasting in their current safe house in Wellington, New Zealand. The intention was that they would all be there next month when the debrief was due to finish. Wellington was unlikely to be their final home, but Galina, his wife, and Misha, his daughter, had been there for two months. Oleg was yet to travel there.

Almost eight months in the UK had followed their arrival at the RAF base. That was after a brief, nervous vehicle ride in Naples and an RAF flight. The trip to the UK followed the dangerous trip out of Turkey, a firefight in Enez, and then hiding on a luxury yacht.

With the British intelligence services, he was slowly and meticulously debriefed. His daughter attended a nearby university to finish her degree under a false name. His wife helped with charities and translations for the local Ukrainians who spoke Russian but not English. They all had additional English lessons, with an emphasis on removing accents. They always had security with them, disguised as friends and colleagues, whenever they left the safe house. Misha's at the university had been a woman who appeared to be of similar age. They also had briefings on new future identities that were being created.

He suspected that Hugh and Michelle might be involved. During their time onboard the yacht, Hugh showed him his own bank account in Switzerland. He had been amazed to watch the man manipulate the funds. It was no wonder his own former service and it appeared others, wanted control of the man.

Kathrine had visited him only once after he was in the safe house. They had not been able to discuss much. His debrief in the UK was conducted by a small group of MI5 and MI6 officers. An occasional American listened in. After a short break, when they were taken to a holiday home in Cornwall for some fresh air and limited freedom, Galina and Misha reluctantly left via a circuitous route for New Zealand. He headed for Utah.

His debrief in the USA started with his entire FSB career before and mostly after his recruitment by Kathrine. They were thorough, constantly returning to his previous statements and teasing out every last detail he could recall. They wanted names, and he spent hours in front of screens showing blurred and sometimes very good photographs of FSB, GRU, SVR, unknown, and other leaders. There was a lot of focus on senior officers, especially those thought to be near Putin's inner circle.

His own questions about the group that had assisted his defection were answered briefly but with no detail. He knew two had given their own lives to help his escape. Liam, his greeter, and Lila, who had died before he could know her. His only memory of the woman, her dead body lying on the rear of a luxury yacht. He mourned them, as he mourned other former colleagues. Even the four who had tried to kill him and his family on a dockside in Enez, Turkey.

He knew his former colleagues had tried to get him again in Naples, although the car journey and RAF flight had not been prevented. Tom and Effi sat with him on the plane for some of the journey. Effi was talking to and reassuring Galina and Misha as Tom practiced his Russian with Kathrine, who smiled at him. Sam, Kathrine's assistant, was not so friendly. He hadn't failed to notice Tom talking to the security team. He also recalled Tom and Effi as friendly as they appeared, finishing off some of his attackers with close head shots. The other soldier, Doug, had been upset by the loss of Lila.

***

He had provided a full account of his escape and the incident as it was described in Enez. He had to repeat all of that for the Americans. They were fascinated by the operation and wanted details on the participants. His MI6 and MI5 handlers had warned him not to talk about it, but the Americans used the names and photos. They knew who the participants were, including the enigmatic Hugh and Michelle Turnbill. He couldn't provide details of what the couple did, as he didn't know, except that it was complex and included financial logistics. He skipped over his own bank account. After all, they had arranged all the travel, and with Tom and Effi, he and his family's arrival and departure from Naples.

Next to be discussed were the Harper sisters, similar in age to his own daughter. One, Carolyn, with her friend Lizzie, who was upset by everything it seemed. They were believed to be a couple but showed little affection on the yacht. He had heard arguing. Stephie had her Italian boyfriend, Jules, who flirted with Misha. The other Italians who joined them were Andre and his wife, Natalie. It was a strange collection of couples and personal relationships.

He and his family had been treated well and protected. His trip out of the UK had been as secretive as his arrival. A car drove to what appeared to be a US military base, where he was driven into a hanger and boarded a plane in that hanger. The only familiar face was Sam, who only nodded as his UK security minders handed him over to a US team. They flew with one stop to Utah. He had not gotten off in what he presumed was Washington, DC.

***

In a safe house, on the outskirts of Salt Lake City, he started again with recollections and some new photographs. It was only a brief news report that alerted him to the fact that several people had been killed in the UK. Additional security was provided, which he barely noticed. He was shown three new photographs and was able to give names. He recognised the new heads of the FSB and SVR, Damir Egorov and Akim Volkov, respectively, although he personally knew neither of them. He had no name for the third man, but thought he had seen him in briefings.

He was shown a photograph of a small, dumpy woman he did not recognise. Other men's pictures followed, but he did not know them either. His regular discussions then returned. More details on his time in Iraq. The Americans still expressed astonishment that he had worked for so long for the British. They wanted to know not only about that but also what he knew about US citizens and Saddam's regime. Not a lot he could tell them, as he didn't know apart from the Embassy social events he had attended. A long series of new photos then appeared. These were scientists involved in WMD programmes in Iraq and were now thought to be either dead or working for other regimes. There were a lot of questions about Iran that he couldn't answer because he didn't know.

"Your contact in Moscow." The woman called herself Aileen. CIA, he presumed, and she did most of his US debriefing. She was in her early fifties, short and grey, although well dressed. She switched effortlessly between Russian and English, and her bright green eyes watched every response. She had apologised for one session when he was polygraphed. Other than that, their discourse was probing but pleasant. She didn't rush, except when the post-attack photos were shown.

"I didn't have one."

"I meant for your escape."

"I didn't know his name. We only met at the pick-up in Gorky. A jogger but with a team covering him. Very slick drop-off, considering they were being watched."

"Were you?"

"Not that I saw. No, I don't think so. Neither I, nor my family, would have gotten away if they suspected me."

"Had you seen him before?"

"No. I did see him again at the airport. His wife, Justine, was with us on the yacht, and she was on my flight before she was accidentally mixed up in the trip."

"Accidentally?"

"Yes."

"We think the British arranged for her to be on the same flight as you."

"Maybe, but I didn't know her. She didn't know me. We only started talking as we left the plane."

"And this was only Justine?"

"Yes. He was at the airport in Moscow when I left." He tried not to show any frustration. This was at least the third time they had covered the escape.

"I'm sorry to say he and his wife were victims of the attack. He was the British head in Russia."

"Dead?"

"Yes, I'm sorry."

Oleg couldn't believe it. He was shocked, although he knew that if the Russian team in Enez had been successful, he, his family, and their escorts would all have been killed or captured. "She was kind," he sighed, "a small bullet injury in Turkey to her leg. She was in the car on our trip from Istanbul. She knew Michelle; I think she said she was in MI6 before." Oleg was upset.

"Your comrades are taking revenge. Yes, she was an analyst at MI6 before she had children. The British have told us a little. Her husband was newly appointed as Head of Russia Desk." It was more information than she would normally divulge, but she had been asked to see his reaction. One hypothesis was that Yegorov was a plant designed to expose various British assets that could then be attacked. Aileen didn't believe that, but people had been attacked. His reaction was one of genuine shock, as she could see.

"They are not my comrades anymore. We don't do that. I mean, take revenge like that. Not in FSB or SVR. GRU, well, they have their own work. There were attacks before I left. Stupid attacks or incidents, surveillance sent when we already had information."

"In Darlington?"

"And London. I don't know much about it. I was leaving,

and those operations were not in the task force."

"An unwritten rule on attacks?"

"Yes, but… I mean, I have not heard of such actions before. Yes, for defectors." He stopped, as if realising he was now one of those that would be. "Me now, I suppose, but we don't attack other countries', agents. We want to know who they are, not kill them.

"Others on your trip were targeted. Your friend Kathrine, *Salamander*, you called her, has sent a report."

More shock on his face. "Are they safe?"

"So far." He didn't comment. "There are alerts worldwide. You've seen your extra security?"

"I thought something had changed. My family?" He knew they would be threatened to.

"Yes, your family has extra precautions. We don't think their location or yours here is known. We do know that your being in the USA is known. I can't go into how we know that."

"Thank you for telling me. This must be a change of policy. Putin must have ordered it; only he could. We don't usually attack other agents; capture, yes, trick of course, but…"

"We know. It's causing considerable concern among all our agencies and allies. I'm afraid we'll have a lot more photos for you. Your British friends are planning their own response."

"I don't know anything about that."

"Kathrine is leading part of it."

"I told you, she recruited me, but I don't know what else she did or does."

"She kept you very quiet." Aileen's smile was complimentary. "We had no idea about you, even if we occasionally had output."

"I wouldn't know. Our messaging was intermittent, just the occasional letter."

"By email?"

"Yes, in recent years. London does not wish me to discuss the method." Aileen knew she couldn't push that bit. It may be intriguing, but it also probably meant that the techniques were still in use elsewhere with other assets. She focused on the main purpose of the debrief. "The trigger for your leaving was the Treasury report?" Aileen skilfully changed tack. This was her technique. Oblique references, and then a sideways question to get another nugget.

"Final trigger. The investigation I was part of…"

"With Colonel Sidorova and Major…"

"Morozov. Yes." He recalled the discussions. "They appeared to be suspicious of me. I think Sidorova was ordered to be more friendly. It was too late; I had already triggered my exit."

They took a short break.

**

"This was all Pentro?" Aileen recommenced.

"Part of Pentro. We've already covered this." Occasionally, Oleg grew bored with the process.

"Sorry, Oleg Ivanovich, we have to check." She was all smiles.

"I know. The Treasury report highlighting the UK finance process came from Adrian Holloway, Persano, in Pentro. I was told he was arrested?" He was asking, but he didn't get a response. "He was not my asset. It was not my part of the operation. Morozov ran that asset and Pentro. They were all in the other half of the task force. Morozov reported to Sidorova, who reported to General Tarasov, SVR, who in turn reported to General Kuzmin, FSB, my boss also." They had covered this and his own tasks, spreading disinformation.

"Kuzmin and Tarasov have been found guilty of corruption."

"Dead?"

"Not yet."

"The president is not happy."

"No. Major Morozov is dead."

"Oh," Oleg remembered the meek officer. He wasn't shocked. He knew the response would be harsh.

"Suicide, according to the news report. A fall off a bridge while drunk."

It was nice to be exchanging information rather than endlessly answering the debriefing questions. He raised his eyebrows at the news of Morozov, expressing his disbelief in that verdict. He recalled other bridge jumpers. Instead, he asked, "Sidorova?"

"More interesting, she's disappeared. Discrete alerts out for her on the borders, like yourself."

"Defecting?"

"Running, we think, we are keeping an eye out."

"I don't know her; she was a cold fish until she, English expression," he tried to think of the words, "batted her eyes; that's it."

"And she batted her eyes at you?"

"She had started to."

"These three?" She showed the photos again.

"Yes."

"They are in charge now of FSB, SVR, and with a direct line via him to Putin."

"I don't know him. I said I've seen him, but I don't know his name. There have been others like him. They don't last long. They have connections through money and friends of the president. Some have been at meetings. We didn't trust them but they have the president's support. Not just his others in the part and political leadership. I said I had seen this man, but not met him."

"Okay, that's fine. Let's move on. What do you know about

Syria?"

"We support another madman; I mean, they support him. More stupidity, like Iraq. Anything to twist your tale." She tilted her head at the comment. Yegorov rarely raised his own loyalty, but occasionally a possessive crept into his language. Aileen knew there was nothing in it, but she also knew some in the CIA would take it as a reason to distrust the information. Oleg continued, "He does fight ISIS and other Islamic groups."

More photos were shown. Mostly bearded men in varying Arabic dress. He thought he recognised a couple of faces. "Targets for our own operations," he explained. "Supporting Chechen rebels."

"They seem to be realigned."

"Really?"

"The British were successful against three assets defending their people, and several others, like the small woman I showed you, are now known."

"Like the GRU men who attacked in Salisbury."

"Yes, but this is more blatant. We now think the three leaders are getting extra assets from Syria."

"That's crazy. Do they want a war?"

"An intelligence war, maybe. Hence all the concern. Not for us. Let's take a break, and then I want you to go over your old operations into the EU."

"Okay." He had no choice, but his former compatriots actions scared him.

CHAPTER SIXTEEN
Harper Sisters

Carolyn and Stephie Harper were thoroughly bored in the safe house that the police had moved them to. They had even stopped joking, and Stephie was no longer flirting with the private security team who were in the house. The police were mostly outside. They were on a new estate outside Lincoln. No work for Carolyn; extended sick leave; not that she was enjoying the graduate scheme she had reluctantly started. Stephie was effectively finished with her own degree and had been thinking about a law conversion. She was fighting off disappointment at missing out on England's and, therefore, GB's sailing team selection. She had a nasty suspicion that someone had interfered with a quiet word that she should not be selected. The assessors all thought she needed more time. It was a disappointment delivered in a management process, ruined when someone younger and less experienced than her was selected.

She had been contemplating who to complain to when the alert came in. The private security team had immediately acted, moving them south to a Birmingham hotel before, with the police, they reluctantly moved to a safe house. They had calls with Tom and Effi and a very brief check that they were okay, from Hugh and Michelle, wherever they were. Their response meant the warning had been received from the sisters, Tom and Effi. Effi had said Hugh and Michelle had been given more information. She wouldn't discuss it over the phone or on email, not that they could use Hugh's system to talk to each other.

TV box sets were almost exhausted, and books were being read. They had their ebook readers and could still get content. Fresh air was confined to individual escorted trips into fields near the house. There was private security on either side of them and a policeman hovering nearby, trying to hide the fact that he was armed and just as bored. Dog walkers were smiled at politely, but no discussion other than a hello was permitted. The sisters both knew that they risked attracting attention, as if two women in a house with mostly extra men hovering around didn't. There was one woman on the protection team who reminded both the sisters of Lila Cotton. The outside, sometimes uniformed police, did have a woman present, but they didn't come in the house. The house was at the end of a road, and as far as they could tell, the other immediate neighbouring houses were not occupied. Carolyn had suffered a flashback to another house where they had been kidnapped. They weren't tied up here. An unfriendly Lincolnshire Police Detective Inspector told them they would be placed in protective custody if they tried to leave. Stephie almost laughed at him. He had no idea what had happened to them before.

***

The front door opening unannounced was not unusual when the teams switched shifts. They were both sitting in the lounge when Effi walked in, followed by Kathrine. Hugs with Effi and over-polite handshakes with Kathrine followed. Cups of tea were suggested, and Carolyn and Stephie noticed two more non-private security and non-policemen settled in the kitchen. One immediately put the kettle on.

They sat on sofas, with the TV off and ebooks closed. Tea was presented in mugs. The two guards went and hovered in other rooms and windows. They had four targets in the house, not just two. Every car and pedestrian were being scrutinised. Kathrine didn't appear to be armed, but Effi made no secret of her weapon.

"You guys okay?" Effi started. Kathrine and she had talked on the way up, sometimes heatedly. Kathrine could have played the superior officer card, but she knew it wouldn't work with Effi. Not since Turkey. In the intervening period, Effi had been switching between running the analyst team and supporting the Middle East Desk. She had allies and supporters in Vauxhall Cross as well as support in Thames House. Tom Larring was really Army, despite his MI6 dalliance. He would be expecting to re-join his old regiment or, more likely, be back with the SAS.

Kathrine could influence them and their careers, but only if she was fully back in the fold. Without Sir Rupert, she needed William Thatcher to support her. He would, up to a point. Annoying Tom and Effi would not get her that. Kathrine may dislike Vauxhall politics, but she could not ignore it. She may be respected for the operational missions in the Middle East and then the extraction of a senior defector, but she had plenty who didn't like her attitude. She needed Effi and Tom onside, as well as the sisters.

"Bored," Carolyn answered, her head swivelling between the two other women.

"How's Tom?"

"On base, fuming."

"I bet." Stephie remembered him in Enez and Effi, for that matter. She didn't have a clear view, but she knew what they had done.

"Carolyn, Stephie," Kathrine started, "we need your help. We also need to find a way to keep you safer after this is resolved." The sisters knew they would be targets as long as Putin was in charge in Russia. Tom had made that clear in his call to them. Kathrine corrected herself. "We're all targets as long as that madman is in charge or his henchmen. All we can do is minimise the risks. That means a low profile as well as additional security."

"We know, we don't have a high profile; we don't even do Facebook." Carolyn exclaimed.

"Sailing?" Kathrine asked.

"We know. I didn't make the team," Stephie told Effi. Effi already knew but tried to look sympathetic.

"You knew?" Carolyn asked.

"Did you?" Carolyn and Stephie were both very quick.

"We couldn't let you be exposed, more exposed." Kathrine answered. She could see the anger. "Before you get cross or try to run off, this is serious. Not just for you but for all of us. Not just MI6, but MI5 too. There were attempts on them as well. Mel and Baz were killed, as were Justine and her husband, Jamie. You knew these people."

"We knew Liam and Lila too." Carolyn was almost shouting.

"I know, I know," Kathrine said, feeling the meeting was out of control. She went and made a call to give them all a quick break.

***

When Kathrine returned, Effi was at her most persuasive. "Carolyn, Stephie, we could argue about the past for hours. I have already." A guarded look at Kathrine. "It doesn't matter. We need Hugh and Michelle." She paused and got the nods she wanted. Kathrine admired Effi's skills. "They won't come in unless we, that's you two, Tom, and I can persuade them. It needs a team effort. We need Hugh's skills. One of his applications needs updating to help trace the Russian agents."

"I thought they were dead?" Carolyn asked. "There are more?"

"Three dead, but several got away, which is why security is in place. It's likely that there will be more dispatched. That means you are still targets, and so are we. Several people still are, not just the four of us in this room, but we may be able to pre-empt the attacks if we can trace them." Kathrine genuinely pleaded. "They killed Lady Paltry; they tried to kill the wife of an MI5 officer and him. They killed Justine and her husband. We do need Hugh and Michelle. Mel and 2B may have wanted sterner actions…"

"Others before them," Carolyn snapped.

"Yes, I know. We're going over old ground again. If the Russians get them, you'll not only lose them; the country will lose a very effective team. We'll lose the system that protects this country, all of us. Something Effi can personally attest to."

"That is true," Effi agreed.

"We can't call them." Stephie was trying to be unemotional. Carolyn held her sister's hand. "We can ask them for a call; they may respond; they haven't as much as they used to."

"I understand they've gone back to how they were when they first ran. Are they sailing?"

Neither Carolyn nor Stephie responded. Kathrine couldn't

read them. "Please email them. Can you do that now?"

"Why the rush?" Stephie hadn't moved to get her laptop. Her phone, like Carolyn's, was still in their flat, left behind to avoid detection. They only had laptops, so work for Carolyn and course work for Stephie could be processed or messages relayed.

"We have a window where the Russians may be regrouping, licking their own wounds, so to speak."

"Thought they had enough problems with Ukraine?" Carolyn added.

"It's all the same to Putin; don't they cover it at the university?" Kathrine knew Stephie was studying international relations as well as languages. Italian practical or colloquial too, thanks to the yacht's crew and Jules in particular. She knew they both had Greek due to the frequent visits. She'd had an update from an old contact at Nottingham University, where Carolyn had graduated and Stephie would graduate. Both, despite everything, with First's. Although Stephie didn't know that yet, Carolyn already had hers. She waited while Stephie booted her laptop and then did some complicated log-on.

Stephie typed a new message in the draft mail box.

```
Please call via FaceTime as soon as possible. We are still
in a safe house. Effi and Kathrine are here; we need to
talk, not message. Please call: C&S xxx.
```

"While we wait…"

"It could be hours; we don't know what time zone they are in or where they are, honestly," Carolyn insisted.

"We know, hon," Effi responded with a smile. "Tom and I have both told Kathrine and others that.

"I believe you. I wouldn't tell you either." Kathrine tried to smile. "Michelle wouldn't."

"Nor Hugh," Stephie added.

"No, I know. Why don't we order some takeaway while we wait? As long as it's not pizza, it's not good for my skin."

Carolyn and Stephie had gone off pizza since their kidnapping. They had ready-meals in the fridge, but a takeaway could be picked up.

***

While they waited, Kathrine broached the other subjects she wanted to raise. One concerned the immediate operation and four people's safety. That was reasonably discussed, even if it caused some surprise. Kathrine was impressed; they wanted to be involved, which put them in harm's way. The sisters both dismissed that caution, with Stephie pointing out the action in Turkey and the risks in Mykonos. Kathrine knew she didn't have the whole story from Mykonos or how close Carolyn and the other occupants had been to the raids by special forces from three countries. That ended with a firefight in the house before all three, the UK, the USA, and the Russians withdrew.

The second subject immediately raised questions. Kathrine started with, "Are you happy with your job, Carolyn?" She said it as a polite conversational query, but Carolyn saw through that.

"It's okay, why?"

"Get to use your languages much?"

"No, I'm doing corporate finance for this period."

"What about you, Stephie? What will you do after university?"

"I don't know yet. I thought about a law conversion, criminal law."

"Hear me out, but have you considered joining?"

"You must be joking," Carolyn laughed, but she had thought about it every time she met up with the spooks, as well as Michelle, Effi, and even Tom and Hugh. Being present for visitors like Kathrine, Mel, and 2B added to it. The element of excitement was there, she knew. It had ruined her relationship with Lizzie.

"You've considered it, then?" For once, Kathrine could read her. "Stephie?"

"Not a chance."

"Why not? Don't you admire Effi and Michelle? Didn't you enjoy the operation?"

"Not being shot at."

"You know that's not what I mean." It was the harshest she had spoken.

"Stephie," Carolyn calmed her sister. They had spoken to each other about it years before. Not so much recently.

The conversation was interrupted by a police constable carrying large amounts of take-away Chinese into the house. They didn't look impressed with the task or the weight. Stephie couldn't tell which.

Food was served, including to the security team. They were still eating when Stephie's email pinged. She checked.

`30 mins, we tried your phone so will be to this laptop, don't change wi-fi.`

***

There were no names used or greetings in the draft email. Stephie suspected Michelle had replied; she was always blunter. They cleared plates and repositioned on the sofa to wait. They had only drunk water, although Kathrine would have welcomed a stiff drink. She and Effi had a quick discussion with the security team. They were getting nervous about the amount of time they were on site.

"There are too many cars around us; I mean, we're attracting attention."

"Actual threats?" Kathrine asked

"Nothing more than before. We weren't followed here. But…"

"Okay, we'll try and be quick." They returned to the girls just as they could hear the laptop buzzing.

"Hello," Stephie answered.

"Hi, you two, and we see you have guests. Effi, Kathrine."

"They need to speak to you," Carolyn added. The video

picture joined the audio. It showed Hugh and Michelle sitting on a bed in what appeared to be a hotel room. The video wasn't very clear. The room was nearly dark. Just a bedside lamp throwing light. There was no indication of where in the world they were or what time it was there.

Kathrine spoke; she needed to get the meeting going. "Sorry, Michelle and Hugh. We needed to be in touch. Effi and Tom agree. Stephie and Carolyn mostly agree. The attacks here are very serious."

"We know; we're taking precautions." Michelle was sounding annoyed.

"They may not be enough." Kathrine insisted.

"We need your direct help, Hugh," Effi added.

"In what way?" Hugh, as usual, was more friendly and polite, even if his trust was very limited. Kathrine's play of calling with the sisters and Effi was trying to imply more trust.

"Your tracking app..."

"What about it?"

"We have some leads it could use, but it doesn't work."

"Mine does. I haven't sent an update since…"

"Old news," Kathrine wanted them thinking of now, not the past. "It's why we need your help now. It can help us trace the attackers and find links. You showed me years ago in Naples."

"I remember."

"Effi looks after the team you both met."

"Really?" Michelle looked at Effi. The light in the UK picture was better than their own disguising illumination. Deliberately murky to hide their location and current disguises. It was barely six in the morning in Kula Lumpur. Nearly ten in the evening in the UK. Not that the UK knew that. "Same team?"

"Yes, Greg, Troy, and Ali. They need your help. We all do." Effi was directly helping Kathrine; Michelle noticed. Effi was like a younger sister to Michelle, just like Stephie and Carolyn.

"Where's Lizzie?" Michelle asked.

"She wouldn't come; we're not great at the moment, not for a while."

"We're sorry, Carolyn, love." Hugh was sympathetic. "What about Jules? Have you warned them?"

"Do we need to?" Effi asked.

"He was with us in Enez," Stephie explained to Kathrine. Kathrine knew but just nodded.

"The Russians will know that too; the film is on the Internet for God's sake." Michelle sounded tired and stressed.

"I'll warn him, but I don't have my mobile; it's back in Nottingham." Stephie stated.

"That's okay," Michelle said, calmer. "We'll tell him, all of them. They've been helping Harry and Josephine, Hugh's old friends." Neither Stephie nor Carolyn confirmed they had been with the couple on the yacht.

Kathrine had another old connection confirmed: "Sorry to interrupt the catch-up and to be abrupt, but we need to know now. We need to get you safe. Russian activity is all over the place. They may have found you."

"We think we had one in Singapore," Michelle admitted. That meant they were not there now, Kathrine guessed, but that also meant more urgency. The next surveillance might not end as well. That was if they were clear now. She didn't ask. Michelle would have made as sure as she could.

"Putin is going all out for revenge. Our only hope to stop him is to capture assets," Effi said. Michelle knew capture was not on the cards. Captured could return to the field.

Kathrine had been briefed on most of what MI6 knew about Russia's revenge operation. Not directly, but from the tendrils that had extended out. Activity in foreign countries. Messages would be tracked if they were not deciphered by GCHQ or the NSA. The Americans were actively helping. She knew her defector, and every defector would help if they could. Names and faces were being analysed. The Americans were trying to mend bridges after the tracking of Hugh and Michelle. Kathrine still didn't trust the NSA or the CIA, but for the moment, any help stopping Russians was welcome.

Kathrine had passed on some of the information to Effi. They couldn't disclose the information to the freelance finance team or the sisters. Kathrine was already pushing what she could say or not. It had been part of the argument on the trip to the sisters.

"We can't hide forever, and we know you two have been running for years, sort of." Stephie continued the strained conversation.

"We didn't want this for you." Hugh sounded sad.

"We know that, but this can't go on." Carolyn was going to add that Kathrine wanted them to join MI6 but decided it was best not to.

"One sec," Michelle said as a brief close-up, allowed a glimpse of different coloured short hair. They could see the call was now on mute. All they could do was watch a discussion. It wasn't an argument, as far as they could tell.

***

Michelle eventually leaned in. "The yacht, I presume?"

"The Russians know about it; they may be watching it." Kathrine should never be surprised at Michelle's understanding of her operations. If Michelle had not run off with Hugh, she would have been a desk head, if not an operations lead, in MI6 by now. Kathrine realised that, with the financial control they had, Michelle and Hugh were effectively operations directors. MI6 and MI5 were dependent on them to organise and even plan funding, accounts, and logistics for hundreds of operations. She'd been told by the analyst team that much appeared to be pre-seeded, as they called it. In other words, Hugh, with Michelle's guidance, anticipated operational requirements by arranging accounts, credit cards, and even company names and facilities in multiple countries.

Kathrine wondered, not for the first time, what they had in place in the UK to protect them. She knew they had relationships with private air travel companies, hotels, and who knew what else.

The analysts only had glimpses of the network. All this had continued even though they were officially out of touch since Enez, Mykonos, and Naples.

"Like you are?" Hugh accused, snapping Kathrine back to the video call.

"We have, yes." Kathrine needed the pair. Now was not the time for withholding operations. "Mel and Baz ordered it, not me. They had good intentions too." Michelle and Hugh gave each other an obvious look. They probably didn't believe her. "I knew about it, but I wasn't in charge. As you probably know, I have been on extended leave."

Michelle nodded. "We can't believe they are dead, whatever they had planned for us. Is Sam back with you?"

"He is, yes, but he is with William Thatcher now. William is the effective head. Sir Rupert's replacement has been given another urgent task." Kathrine gave out more than she wanted, but she had to get Hugh and Michelle into the operation under some type of control and the Russians sorted. Michelle's mention of Sam also meant the couple did not trust him. Kathrine didn't fully either, but he could be effective.

"Are Harry and Josephine at risk?" Hugh pressed and refocused Kathrine on the task.

"We don't think so. They are looking for you, Tom and Effi, and the young ladies here."

"And Jules was in Enez with me. Andre and Natalie?"

"Yes, Stephie. They've also been in France crewing for the Rosenthals," Kathrine admitted, thus exposing more surveillance of the yacht.

"It's already a honey pot, then?" Hugh asked.

"Michelle, you know I can't say everything. We have indications. I can't say more, and you know that. But, yes, in some ways."

"The attraction will not be high enough without others." Hugh continued to surprise Kathrine.

Kathrine was not surprised Michelle was with him. He had a grasp of operations, in addition to his software and accounting skills. Michelle had probably spent a lot of time training her husband. Kathrine had seen him on the video shooting in Enez. She recalled his preparation for previous meetings and how, since she had first met them, he had progressed. The last time, handing over General Yegorov and his family in Naples, was in the same restaurant as the first time they'd met. The difference in approach and wariness was notable.

The couple had come under their own terms to the meeting she had arranged. A meeting to set up finance for a mission to Pakistan. A direct link she made because she didn't trust MI6's regular communications. She'd been impressed then. She had never been in control of the more recent Naples handover. A handover where certain others in MI5 and MI6 had hoped to also grab Hugh and Michelle. They'd never come close. They'd anticipated every move she had prepared with her own special forces and MI6 staff. The couple had been aided by her supposed agents, Effi and Tom.

Water under the bridge. Kathrine focused on the present. On the message application, there was another muted discussion, but not a long one.

"Okay, we'll make our way there. Yes, we know it will be a risk, and therefore we need to put in place financial protection should something happen."

"Hugh!" Stephie exclaimed. "You can't do that, the Russians; the others they'll…"

"Stephie and Carolyn" Michelle stepped in. "We've had this conversation before. We all know it can't go on. We have a mutual enemy who will track us down unless we prevent it or make it very costly. Even then, it will continue. We need to change things. For us, that means no longer running the finances, which is exactly what the service and Five want. We need to finish this. You'll also be at risk because we need to get you out of it too, and Tom and Effi."

"We're okay," Effi tried.

"Are you?"

"Michelle," Kathrine tried to regain control as emotions were running high. "Tom and Effi will be part of the protection in France. We'll extend that elsewhere. I need a proper planning session with you. Ideally, face-to-face, if possible, before you act as bait." She was explicit about what was being planned. "We tried that before using Tom and Effi, and we all know how that worked. If you, Stephie, Carolyn, and your Italian friends are on the yacht, then we know the Russians won't resist."

The line was quiet again. "We'll let you know when we are near. Effi arrange with the analysts if you can for a full handover of the funds." Hugh explained.

"It will take a while to get there, especially as we don't want to be seen. Port Grimaud won't be good for a pick-up, I mean in terms of protection and potential for civilian issues." Michelle added. "I'm sure you can prepare a warm welcome elsewhere. We'll send some suggestions. Tom, could plan that with Effi's help?"

"He can; they can," Kathrine replied. It was coming together.

"Please keep Harry and Josephine out of it. I'll contact them." Hugh was talking. "I'll send an update to the app; it will be a link to a download."

"We'll be travelling carefully, so we'll let you know. A few days at least."

Kathrine didn't know if that was to take precautions or because of the distance. She suspected both, but it was a reasonable outcome.

"We'd really like you in London?" Kathrine tried.

"Wouldn't you just?" Michelle was back. "You'll need to make the honey pot of the yacht attractive. If the Russians are probably watching it already, it puts Jules, Andre, and Natalie at risk too."

"In Naples as well?" Effi asked before Stephie did.

"Kathrine will know, won't you?"

"Possibly, yes, it's likely given the actions they have already taken." Kathrine was making no effort to sugar coat the risks.

"A couple of hours before I upload the app, Effi," Hugh added. "We need to go. Too long online; I don't want any tracking."

"They won't; they've offered help." They were both referring to the NSA and the Americans.

"And you trust them?" Michelle probed.

"Not entirely, but they are taking action." Kathrine could see the doubt in the expressions on the faces of Hugh and Michell. "They have already helped in some cases. Again, I can't say too much, but some of our assets worldwide have been protected."

Michelle and Hugh couldn't assess if that was true, but again, it was likely. "Stephie, Carolyn, you don't have to do this?" Hugh demonstrated his concern.

"You know we do, Hugh; you can't protect us from this." Stephie was becoming upset again.

"We'll be okay; we'll get to see you soon too." Carolyn held her sister's hand once more.

"It's anything but okay," Michelle paused. She sighed with a nod from Hugh, "but all right. We'll come. Kathrine, Effi." There was no time to acknowledge the simple names as goodbyes from Hugh and Michelle before they disconnected.

***

In Kula Lumpur, Hugh and Michelle were already preparing to leave. "I'll upload from elsewhere. We were online too long."

"I know, but any warnings?" Michelle was packing back packs.

"Not that I've seen. But…"

"You're being careful." She hugged her husband before looking into his eyes. "It has to end somehow," she whispered, her own concern.

"It does, but I'm scared. Not just for us, but…"

"I know, the girls."

"And Effi and Tom, plus Jules, Andre, and Natty, they

shouldn't be involved."

"But they are."

"That's our fault."

"I know," she said, holding his cheek briefly. "I know love, so let's see if we can resolve it." Michelle didn't add one way or another.

She didn't want to think about probabilities. They might not even get to France or wherever they picked up the yacht. The Russians could find them first. The Americans might try, and even MI6 couldn't be 100% trusted. "Different ID, we need a hair colour change and glasses. But you're right, not here." They left the hotel.

CHAPTER SEVENTEEN
Uliana Doubek

Uliana Doubek was as surprised as anyone to be standing in Vauxhall Cross reception waiting for her escort. She had already gone through security and been issued a pass. She was surprised because she had only agreed to move departments three days before. In her experience with the Civil Service Fast Track scheme, she thought it would be several weeks before it was arranged. She knew she was already on the Security Service's radar after the Treasury reports and incidents the previous year. She had become used to being obviously followed around by protection officers. She also now knew she had been followed before.

The only person she could talk about it with was her now-former boss, Paul Stubbs. Paul and she were both still not happy. Paul, in particular, with the death of a Russian outside his Darlington house. They had both spent several weeks in various safe houses with twitchy men and women watching windows and visitors.

The incidents followed Uliana researching and then sending a report tracing hidden Treasury funding for the Security Services. The report ended up in Russian hands and caused direct action by the Russians. People had died attacking or defending the connections. One man was in prison, awaiting trial for espionage. Uliana would have to testify about what she knew. Only about the report, not the rest, unless the defence lawyers decided to be difficult. She hoped Adrian Holloway would plead guilty and save all the risks.

Uliana tried to explain to her father what little she was allowed to say. That mostly covered her being away at no notice.

Several meetings were attended by a lady called Cindy Loughton, who seemed to know far more about her than she did herself.

After writing the report, she stayed with the Treasury longer than she had expected. She had carefully written other reports using her skills with AI analysis of spending patterns. The reports she wrote were all now carefully classified, with very limited distribution lists. She had uncovered more gaps and more potential savings. Not billions, as she had hoped, but several tens of millions across multiple departments. She'd had to hastily hand the programme over to a contract team of forensic accountants before she left to return to London. A new apartment was found for her within walking distance of her new office. Her original plan to look at NHS spending would be completed by others using her techniques.

She knew she couldn't afford the apartment, but Cindy explained that her new, unnamed boss would sort it out. She still had a rotating team of protection officers. Some of them were even friendly. Her dating and social life were non-existent.

***

"Hello, Uliana." The woman coming towards her was Asian in appearance, very attractive, and younger than she was expecting. Uliana was sure she had seen her before. She tried to place her. "I'm Effi; I look after the team of analysts you're joining this way." She led her through the plastic and armoured door, screening one person at a time, and into a corridor. She stopped at an electronic-controlled bank of lockers and pointed at an open one. "Mobiles, tablets, and so on are in there. You'll get a service mobile, and we'll port your number this week. You'll get all the briefings."

"I've seen you before." Uliana was rushing to keep up after just putting her small bag into the locker and locking it with her new pass.

"I thought I saw a glimpse of recognition. "Where was it?" Effi stopped and studied her. The gaze was intense, but not hostile.

"In Darlington, outside the office. You work with Cindy." She realised she had just been tested, but that meant this woman, Effi, was part of the surveillance team with Cindy or attached to it last year.

"Good. Keep an eye out for recognised faces. I don't mean your protection team or mine," Effi pointed out to the man trailing them. She suddenly realised that Effi was armed too. She took a deep breath. "Yes, and no with Cindy; she's Five, I'm here. Come on, we can talk in the office after you meet the team."

***

Uliana was lost in the maze of numbered, windowless rooms. Two flights of stairs and more corridors. Effi walked quickly. Throwing out occasional titbits of information like the canteen, which was pointed out vaguely as being, "Down there," and the on-site gymnasium, "it's down one floor from reception." She was just able to note the room number before they went in. It was a larger-than-expected room with a glassed-off separate conference room. Four desks faced each other, surrounded by clear plastic boards partially covered with photos and lines between them. Three faces, two male, one of whom was black, and a friendly-looking woman in her mid-thirties looked up.

"Hi, I'm Greg Birch." He was closest, and she shook his hand. Older than the woman, late thirties, she guessed.

"Greg will be your line manager and head of the team. Greg reports to me at the moment and up to Kathrine."

"Kathrine?"

"You'll meet her and her assistant, Sam, later, I'm sure." Just first names. She had noticed Effi wore a wedding ring. Greg didn't.

"Ali Watson," Ali shook hands. A very friendly smile from the attractive brunette.

"Troy, Troy Williams-Roberts," he said, appearing to be a bit shy and under thirty, and he immediately glanced at Ali. She guessed they were linked, although the way Ali was looking at her was a bit surprising.

"Okay, Greg will give you the in-brief. He'll also show you the systems. This afternoon, IT will be in to give you mainframe access for processing. We have received an upload of your systems from Treasury. Don't look surprised. This is the Secret Intelligence Service, and we have lots of secrets. This is another step up in classification for you. Everything in here, except the coffee," her quip got a smile from the team, "is highly classified, mostly Top Secret. Greg, Ali, and Troy can brief the rest and provide operation codenames, etcetera."

"I don't know what to say." Uliana had never seen a top-secret document. Until last year, she had never seen a secret one, let alone created one.

"Greg and the team have been appraised of your work. They've been asking for programming and other support for months, so here you are. Just to let you and the team know, we have received a new USB stick of reports by courier." Uliana was already confused. "IT is checking it at the moment. It should be with you soon. They know it's a high priority. We also have the new version of the app you wanted. IT will also forward the link to the standalone. Then, you can get cracking on that bit." Greg nodded. "Sorry Uliana. The team will let you know what we're talking about. We have several time-critical parts, so we can't spare too much time on normal inductions and training. You will get it, though. Your protection will be waiting for you when you leave. Now, I need to meet with Kathrine on other aspects."

"Hugh and Michelle are okay then?" Greg asked. Uliana reacted to the Hugh name.

"Yes. I've spoken to them. I'll tell you more in the next few days."

"Okay, thanks, Effi." Greg answered. Uliana looked shocked.

Effi Miani left them to it.

***

"Coffee? We have our own filter; we collect a couple of quid a week for beans and creamer. Rota on water."

"And it's not top secret? Sorry, Er yes, thanks, white no sugar, and that was?" She stumbled over the ordinariness of getting coffee. Her last one in a work setting had been with Paul Stubbs in Darlington. He knew she was coming to MI6. He was sorry to see her leave. Their mutual experience had made them close. Uliana enjoyed time with the family. Now she was back on her own in London, surrounded by spies, analysts, and security people.

"Effi, Effi Miani, or Larring, as she's married now. She's ex-field well, sort of ex." Greg partly explained.

"Kathrine and Sam?"

"Seniors, no second names. Kathrine works for or works directly for the Director, Sir Rupert, in the news. Now, she's… Doesn't matter. We don't know their surnames; we know them, of course."

"None of us do; they were all threatened, tied in with the attacks a few weeks ago." Ali added.

"I see." She wanted to say more. Perhaps once she knew her new colleagues better, she would. "And we're doing what?" She scrutinised the photos on the boards as she sipped her coffee. She hadn't even sat down at her desk. She could see a pack waiting neatly for her, together with two widescreen monitors. Both showed a swirling MI6 emblem. She needed to clear her head and hoped the caffeine would help.

"We're helping finance; they're our special team, and we're tracing the connections of the attackers." Greg stated.

"We're told you're a whiz on computers and financial analysis, so you can help us use Hugh's programme." Ali stated

"Is that Hugh Turnbill?"

"Yes, but how do you know that name?" Troy said it before anyone else could.

"It's a long story."

***

Effi had directed before she left that she could talk about last year with the team in the office but not outside. No work discussions outside the room unless as part of briefing senior officers elsewhere. The warning was directed at them all, not just the new employee. Uliana explained how she had found missing funds and written a report. A report that had caused several problems resulting in a Russian, she hesitated to state that part, being killed outside Paul's house the previous year. She also admitted that she had been followed and was now under protection following the more recent attacks.

"I saw that on the news; I mean, the shooting was linked to shootings in London. I don't mean linked; I mean it happened at the same time. Effi did mention it, but not specifics." Troy was keen to understand.

"They were linked; I know the press didn't say that or were told not to. We were told. I'm not sure what I can tell you. An HMRC lady was killed. I exchanged emails with her. A man is on remand, waiting for trial. He gave my report to the Russians."

"Allegedly," Greg added. He was a firm believer in innocent until proven guilty, and Adrian Holloway was yet to have his day in court.

"He did; I have to give evidence if and when it comes to trial."

"Oh," was all Greg could muster. He changed subjects; he knew from Effi and Kathrine that they needed Uliana's computing skills but also her analytical brain. "Why don't you take a look at the boards? It may be a long shot, but you might see faces you recognise."

"Do you have the ones from last year? MI5 would have them; they were watching me and the Russians."

The team glanced at each other. Ali was already typing into her system. "Greg, why don't we hold on to the photos until I get those up? You can take Uliana through what we get from Hugh. Don't forget induction admin, like how to get to and from the loos!"

***

By the time Uliana had joined her new colleagues for a brief lunch, she had already taken a look at Hugh's tracking application. To say she was impressed was an understatement. Now, they had to wait for a working version, cleared and delivered by the MI6 IT department.

It finally arrived along with the USB stick mid-afternoon. By then, Uliana had wondered around the boards but had not seen anyone she recognised.

"My former boss, Paul, might have seen them." She was watching Troy load the stick and hopefully access the working application.

"We can ask Effi," Greg responded.

"Ask me what?" Effi had returned. She was followed by Kathrine and Sam. The room suddenly felt crowded. They both shook hands with Uliana.

"Nothing on the boards," Greg reported. I mean, Uliana doesn't recognise any of them, but..."

"I was suggesting you show the photos to my former boss, Paul. He was also under surveillance."

"Good idea," Kathrine smiled at the nervous woman.

"I'll ask," Effi agreed. She would pass on the request to Cindy.

"The application?"

"We've only just got it," Troy was still uploading from the stick. They all watched the file transfer as the screen showed it creeping towards 100%. As soon as it showed complete, Troy clicked on the application. They then had to wait for another interminable period, as it just displayed *loading*. There was a lot of disc and network activity happening, indicated by flashing lights on the system's case but with nothing showing on the screen.

They had all just about given up when the opening screen loaded. It had two boxes as normal, but although Uliana had already seen the non-working screen and viewed some of the code, she could already see differences. The first box requested an account number; the second had space for a BIC, SWIFT, or bank sort code. A couple of menu buttons above the empty boxes held *previous* and *filters* as selections.

"Card numbers?" Troy requested. Ali handed over a slip of paper with two unidentified numbers on it. Troy typed the first in. A spinning wheel appeared with a message showing results with a changing number. It was going up from five minutes to ten.

"A crawler?" Uliana asked.

"Yes, it always takes a while, depending on how many connections there are and then their connections." The screen was now showing twenty minutes. Troy switched back to the operating system desktop and pulled up the financial reports section.

"Totals are wrong," Ali stated before Troy could. Uliana couldn't believe the large figure in front of her. Over a billion. She knew she had been hunting for that amount when she wrote the report. Back then, there were indications of more. Her analysis of other departments had only shown potential savings in the millions.

"In what way?" Kathrine couldn't read the numbers. She was putting off getting reading glasses.

"It's about half what was in their last report, back to near what was before…"

"We don't need to go into that." Sam tried to stop that discussion.

"I already know it was increased or replaced with funds directed from aircraft carriers overspend." Uliana stated this to some shocked looks. "It was around two billion I identified, and now…"

"One billion, one hundred and two million, is near enough. It was two point three-four last time." Ali was checking her own screens.

"They've…" Sam started, but Kathrine cut him off.

"We can trace the Treasury funds? With the application?"

"Possibly," Troy started, "with Uliana's help. There's another file on the stick. Another application."

"From Hugh?" Kathrine asked.

"It's on the stick, and IT has cleared it." Troy was asking permission.

"It's only on the standalone?" Sam was nervous about what the application might do, given what he had just heard.

"Yes, I can't copy the other apps except onto the separate partition on the PC."

"No sandbox?" Uliana asked.

"No," Greg was trying to keep up before Uliana and Troy

descended into tech speak, as he termed it.

"What would we lose?"

***

Before anyone could answer, the PC gave a bing, and Troy clicked back to the Hugh application they did know about.

"Jesus!" Ali expressed her shock. The system was showing a mass of interconnected accounts and additional links. The analyst team had seen this before, as had Effi and Kathrine, albeit with their own accounts. It was faster than before and had more detail. Sam and the newly appointed Uliana had not. She leaned in before Troy clicked another button, and the screen was duplicated by a projector at the end of the room. It made it easier to see, if not understand. Katherine thought the connections displayed looked like Contact Chain maps used by GCHQ and the NSA, only this time using financial transaction connections.

"That's going to take a while; can you click through Troy?" Effi asked. "See what's downstream." Troy clicked, and more webs of connections appeared. More account numbers Uliana was fascinated. Troy clicked again, and fewer connections appeared. Another click, and there was a single bank account and sort code. Troy typed that into a web browsing page.

"That's Moscow," was his only comment on seeing the NEWMRUMM pre-text. He quickly backed up the connections and applied a filter using the button and that code. Fifteen accounts appeared.

"Fifteen source accounts linked to Moscow." Greg announced.

"Proof of their involvement." Effi stated. Uliana didn't understand. "We got the account base card numbers from two dead Russians."

Uliana noticed the matter-of-fact tone from Effi. Kathrine and Sam were likewise unconcerned. Her fellow analysts were less comfortable with the casual mention of deaths.

Kathrine focused her attention. "Map and analyse, team. Greg relay your reports via Sam for a while. Effi is going to be away."

***

After Kathrine, Sam, and Effi had departed, Ali voiced what all bar Uliana had been thinking: "Operations again."

"It looks like it." Greg nodded.

"Effi is surveillance, or she was," Uliana stated. "She watched me in Darlington."

"She's done much more than that. Have you seen the Enez film?" Troy added.

"Don't think so." Uliana could see from their expressions that the other three had.

"You can take a look at home, not now." Ali didn't want them looking right then, although the standalone PC could access the Internet. "We didn't finish covering the third application."

Before they could do that, an IT technician arrived with another PC for Uliana to access the mainframe and run AI searches and code. It was connected to the standalone machine, not to the secure systems.

They had to wait till the IT man had departed, and again the attention turned to the third application. Uliana, this time with Troy watching, took a look at it. She went on her own system and began to download various applications that she needed for her own work and to help look at the application still sitting on the USB stick. Uliana installed a virtual machine manager. On one of these, she installed a Linux minimal operating system, which she then spent thirty minutes configuring, adding another virtual machine sandbox. The Hugh-supplied application was then copied to that controlled area. Troy explained to Ali and Greg what Uliana had done. Much faster than he could have done it.

"Now what?" Greg asked.

"Disconnect the other machine, just in case. You'll still have account reports and the tracking application."

"Which we should be working on," Ali reminded them.

"We can do both, but I know we all want to see what Hugh

has sent." Greg stayed in charge.

"Okay," Uliana went to act as Troy pulled the network cable from the first machine, which, of course, meant it couldn't trace accounts anymore. "It's a compressed executable with links looking at the source." She waited for approval from her new boss, Greg. He nodded. The application opened, and it started installing. It presented a web interface to a cloud system hidden by a tiny VPN. There were several buttons on the only page that Uliana could see. The first was labelled *Account Management*. The second was *Companies*. A third was *Travel*. Underneath that array were *Reports*. Off to one side was *Messaging*. Each button was a simple box with black writing on a grey background. Uliana didn't think Hugh Turnbill was worried about user interfaces.

***

"Messaging," Greg instructed as Uliana's mouse hovered between buttons. She clicked. There was a slight delay as Uliana noticed the web site change, although the VPN relays appeared to be similar. It would take more studying to see how they worked. It meant some server-side code was redirecting and hiding the connections. The screen now had a web-based email system. There were the usual Inbox, Sent, Draft, and Deleted folders. There was nothing in any boxes except the draft one. That contained one message simply called Hello. Uliana didn't wait.

Hello team. Hope that's still Greg, Ali, and Troy. Hugh here with Michelle. At some stage, we might come and talk to you direct again. Need other issues resolved first. You have three files/apps. My usual reports, the tracking app, which I'm sorry I stopped updating but should work now. Slight interface change. You also have an app you won't have seen, which includes your access to this messaging system. Your use is flagged to me. I will also be able to see what you do with it. I can't provide detailed guidance yet, but should something happen to me, it will give you a start.
For messages, please only use the draft mail box. **Don't send**, and there's no receive working. I monitor it through a different system. Effi, Kathrine, and others know how it works and have the same access to their own mail. If you have questions, I will try to answer them, but it may take a while. I'm not always online.
This app creates the reports (using button) you regularly

receive and has the latest one separately on the stick. It can be run at any time and adjusted. You will notice the total number has decreased. We have returned funding to what it was when Michelle left.
The accounts section is the most complex. Please don't adjust settings until you fully understand. Emails from Five and Six come in with requests; they get parsed into this app, and then the accounts background app adjusts requirements or provides access. Other sub-routines can create or amend settings for those accounts, e.g. create a credit/charge card with credit or place funds in a new bank account.
Companies section allows creation and dissolution of trading companies globally. Lots of background code here. Again, you should not need to adjust.
Travel section allows manual bookings or adjustments to other bookings again, coming from email requests. It's also how we have manually supported operations for Effi and others. We have also called booking companies direct by phone for urgent needs. Effi and Kathrine know about those too. High risk of exposure that way but sometimes necessary.
For Kathrine, William Thatcher, and Sam.
This application gives you the control you wanted over the Treasury funds and sub-bank accounts. It also once had the *Deadman-Switch* settings, but we have withdrawn that threat and code. You have your money. We will continue to support until the outcome planned is successful or…
Team - good luck! If you watch the accounts section, you can see the system running as soon as you connect it. It will work in the background, whether you are connected or not. Try not to break it.
Regards, H&M

They had to show the message to Kathrine and Sam after they were called down by Greg. Effi was already elsewhere, and her whereabouts were not discussed. Greg could see the relief on Kathrine's face. She used one of their landlines to relay the information to William Thatcher. She came back to the group to watch an endless stream of numbers, locations, and accounts running in the accounts section.

Kathrine would send a note to Effi and Tom, who were both on their way to Hereford, to brief Tom's former colleagues. They would be supporting another part of the operation. That also meant Greg needed to relay information on the connections to

Sam to get to MI5 and Special Branch. Effi, who had been initially tasked with that component, was now away.

Uliana had to keep shaking her head at what she was seeing and now knew. She was already caught up in the intrigue. She was planning how to access and manage the system on the AI. How the web interface could be improved. First, she needed to understand the code. She had access to that by looking at the web source code, even if she couldn't see the server code behind calling other scripts. Kathrine and Sam left them to it. They were happy to have the Russian account connections, let alone control of the money. Kathrine thought that calling it half the money might stir up old issues. Operational funding would continue. That was the important thing, and Effi's recommendation of Uliana was already proving successful.

Kathrine had other issues to resolve and hopefully keep others alive. Sam would no doubt complain to William Thatcher that it was only half the money. Hugh and Michelle still had access and, no doubt, some control, so they still needed to act. Sam would try to spin it to his own advantage. Without Mel, Kathrine had no access to internal security to check up on Sam, and even Mel had not pursued Kathrine's concerns. Mel and 2B had both wanted control of Hugh and Michelle, as well as the funds. They were gone, but they had the money and its oversight, if not direct control of Hugh and Michelle.

CHAPTER EIGHTEEN
Tom and Effi

Tom and Effi travelled independently to Hereford. They had on-base accommodation, and someone had at least found them two adjacent rooms in the Officers' Mess. Tom was slightly annoyed to have missed the departure party from the Joint Staff College. Farewells had been limited, including a frosty one with the commanding officer, despite the praise the unit had received for preventing an attack.

Tom was pleased to be back in Hereford. It had been his base before he had been injured in Afghanistan. That had led to meeting and being recruited by Kathrine for the mission to Pakistan to kill Bravo-One-One. His future wife had acted as his fake wife on that journey. Effi had a different name as he had. It was also where he first had contact with Hugh and Michelle, albeit message and email contact.

Now his wife's presence added to the positive feelings of being there, even if he would rather she not be involved in the planned actions. He'd barely been on site for thirty minutes when he was invited on a run. After that, Effi joined him on the shooting range. They were both out of practice, and Tom was out of breath from the run.

"Stop protecting me," she told him over a drink before dinner.

"I'm not."

"Yes you are Tom. I love you, you know that. I know you love me, but let me do my job." Outside of the bedroom, it was unlike Effi to be sentimental or express her feelings so clearly.

"I just want…"

"No, Tom. I'm part of this. They came after me as well. I was at Enez too." Tom knew that. He'd watched his wife kill someone just as he had. "I'm trained to do this. You're just trained to run and shoot," she added a laugh to soften the comment.

"You sound like Michelle. Advising, teaching, poor Hugh."

"And you sound like Hugh who is anything but poor. That's also why we've ended up in this mess. I don't mean this Officer's one."

Tom managed a smile. "Kathrine's mess."

"We were complicit. We agreed." Effi was finishing her drink.

"You and I both followed orders."

"Did we, are we?"

"Sort of."

"After this?"

"What dinner?"

"Funny! Be serious."

"Too much seriousness, not enough yachts and fun, diving, snorkelling…" He was thinking. "This will not be easy, physically or mentally?"

"What's next, after?"

"I don't know. Army life, get promoted, become a CO. You as Mrs. CO."

"I'd end up shooting people. So would you."

"I could leave, while you climb the ranks at…"

"Too much politics. I don't want to be Kathrine in ten years. There's the others to think about too. Carolyn, Stephie."

"They'll be fine."

"I hope so. Kathrine's plotting." Tom waited for more but Effi decided she wouldn't tell him, or not tell him yet, what she meant. "Let's eat." They went through to the dining room where there were several old acquaintances and colleagues Tom knew. It was nice to be back in the military fold. The college was too full of ambition in Tom's opinion. The regiment was more like home.

***

Their first evening had been spent in a briefing room with two Senior Non-Commissioned Officers. The SNCOs were team leaders and were joined by the current commander of the 22nd SAS. They were starting preliminary work on locations. They would cover other participants and the layout of a yacht in the following days. Tom knew he had to get back to special forces fitness quickly. He needed the team to have full confidence in him. His rank didn't matter here. The SAS and the Royal Navy equivalent, the Special Boat Service, were similar to many military special forces. It was a meritocracy based on ability. Yes, they were under military command and carried out military orders, but day-to-day details dispensed with ranks. Most teams were led by an experienced SNCO, normally on their second or third SAS tours. Groups of teams were led by officers. Sometimes teams had an officer embedded who was not the leader, their rank would normally designate. Tom Larring had already been in combat with individual teams and then led several teams during his second tour in Afghanistan. His reputation was enhanced by his rumoured participation for the spooks in Pakistan, and the YouTube video allegedly of him in a firefight in Turkey. His visit for a formal briefing had been to a limited audience, but the CO had been there.

He had to recount the Enez operation in more detail for the briefing group. It was the only way to explain the plan and expected participants. Many were civilians, even if they were associated with the security services. Effi took some of the barbed comments with good humour, but she also knew she would have to demonstrate her capabilities. Her own film was also available to any sceptics. Tom took some pleasure in naming the various people shown, even if he hated to watch and be reminded of how Liam Green and Lila Cotton died. His summation of the shootout was a sobering reminder to all present that losses could be expected and not always avoided. They all had their own experiences on the battlefield to reflect on.

Tom was permitted to casually mention, without too many details, that they had together destroyed a target in Pakistan. That got Effi more respectful looks. She also provided some guidance on surveillance and counter-surveillance. Tom had benefitted years ago on the streets of Manchester. Effi took two teams out, one to hide and one to search, on the streets of Hereford. She then backed it up, with both teams looking for her and Tom individually and together. The SAS men were surprised at how hard it was to follow her and Tom, and how she always seemed to spot them.

Effi then criticised the all-male make-up of the proposed team. She called back to Vauxhall, and the next day Cindy Loughton appeared with another member of a surveillance team. Effi vaguely recognised her from previous actions. Dagger-Three-Seven, Holly Kirkwood, was once again amazed to be included in such a mission. Her previous role in arresting Adrian Holloway had been stressful, but she had also been praised for her actions then and in the immediate aftermath. The two new women were more current in shooting, but both started to be put through physical fitness training in return for surveillance training. The team was working hard and fast. It would not be perfect. It never was Tom knew, but it should be enough. SAS-level fitness would not be required, and they would be ready without risking training injuries.

Hereford and the surrounding area were also on the lookout for any unusual activity. That was nothing new for the town or the camp. Strangers asking questions or appearing in the wrong place quickly attracted attention. The fact that Tom and Effi, as well as Cindy, may still be under direct threat was known to base security, even if MI6 and MI5 security weren't needed on the base.

Two intensive weeks to train were all the time that could be risked. Failure to prepare meant preparing to fail, as many of Tom's initial trainers had repeated. Tom knew it himself but also knew that no plan survived first contact with the enemy another old saying. Every day that passed meant that another attack was likely or that the Russians would learn of MI6's own plan. Yet Tom and Effi, when not exhausted from the training effort, did not understand how the Russians would stop. Not when Putin remained in charge. In the Salisbury and other attacks, his organisations had demonstrated patience over years to take revenge. The recent attacks were faster and more overt, but they could continue for decades.

***

Kathrine visited only once to relay the latest intelligence on France. She had managed to get a small team from the UK to start watching the area. Tom and Effi had wanted a team from Dubai, but they had not yet been allocated. Baz Butler's absence was felt in that way too. His deputy was not as friendly. The resource constraints were the same in MI6, who were already stretched to cover threats worldwide. Effi told Tom that she had also asked Jermaine Harris for support from Dagger, in addition to Cindy and Holly. Not to watch the yacht, but for anyone interested in the yacht. She also told Tom and Effi that she thought Hugh and Michelle were now in France. Tom and Effi didn't confirm that they knew that.

"How do we get the Russians to bite?" Tom did ask, neatly changing the subject from Hugh and Michelle. He didn't ask how the planned activity would stop the longer-term threat.

Kathrine let him get away with it. His change indicated and confirmed what she had suspected. She suspected that the sisters had been in more contact, with the couple although they were still in a safe house. Laptop screens couldn't be read by the CCTV, but the sisters weren't as skilled as they needed to be in hiding activity they were trying to keep confidential. That was why they needed training in the Service.

Kathrine answered Tom, noting that Effi was watching her like a hawk. Kathrine realised that Effi knew what she knew. The problem with clever spies, she thought, is that they are clever. Sam didn't understand that. She was having to keep him out of some aspects, like today, because he would tell William Thatcher what the Head of Operations didn't need to know. William needed to have deniability and not have to issue orders. If he was to be the new Director when this current crisis settled down, he needed distance. If he issued actual orders, or was briefed on too many details, he couldn't brief the FCO, or the politicians, without potentially lying. The alternative was having to endlessly spout operational security restrictions. Politicians didn't like that, especially if they had to face the media.

Sam would never understand the sensitivities involved. She still hadn't ruled out that he had provided information to others in MI6. Disclosures that had risked her operations as information went to the Americans who almost took disastrous action. Sam's lack of empathy had been apparent before Liam Green was sent to Pakistan, twice, and then Turkey. She missed having someone like Liam. Utterly dependable. Effi could be like that with more trust. Michelle would have been like that if she hadn't runaway. Kathrine could only sigh at past mistakes despite her successes. She had pushed her luck. Previous heads of the service had given her a lot of leeway. Especially Sir Rupert. She took a moment to wish his recovery well. He was improving very slowly.

Tom and Effi were again demonstrating what a good team they were. Kathrine continued, "We need to lead the Russians down this garden path. I've put some things in place. Some inadvertent chat will take place near the yacht about preparations for owners and long trips."

"Who?"

"The couple of messages that I did get…" She waited for a reaction and was pleased that she didn't even get a facial expression change. "No matter. What about Italian cooperation. I'm assuming Jules and Andre will do it. Carefully, I hope. I've warned them via draft mail about potential Russian watchers and their own risks. Natalie too."

"They can take care of themselves." Effi claimed, but she saw Kathrine's unhidden expression. "Okay, we can warn them via Stephie. She's in regular contact with Jules. Oh! No phone. They are together sometimes. She'll relay via Hugh," Effi explained, "like the rest of us."

"Good." It was confirmation of more contacts with Hugh and Michelle, "They'll also tell the current users, that the owners will be taking a long trip or losing the boat. We can't go all in telling them. It needs to look real, otherwise, the Russians will know."

"I see." Tom was thinking of what to tell Kathrine about his side of the operation. He had no reason to suspect Kathrine or Thatcher would leak anything, but he didn't trust Sam or others that Sam might talk to. Was his absence an indicator of that lack of trust from Kathrine? Power plays had taken place in MI6 regarding the defection and associated incidents. Effi had told him that Jamie McKenzie had been promoted to Head of Russia Desk, but now that seat was vacant. As was Mel Kennedy's role. Deputies would be interim heads, but they wouldn't have the background. Formal appointments at that level would have to wait for the current director's, future to be resolved. Elliot Parnell was notably absent from any discussion of the operation or Vauxhall. William Thatcher was in charge if only unofficially.

"I'm sure you'll keep some details to yourself, Tom, or selves, I should say, Effi." Tom didn't hide his surprise this time. She still seemed able to read his mind, or at least read his actions. "Keep it that way." Now the couple both looked surprised. "There will be many moving parts in and out of the services, and here. We can't be certain that we don't get a leak, accidental or otherwise, in which case our attackers could resurface, which would not be good," they all knew, "or they may back out and wait."

"They've waited years." Effi was referring to previous attacks.

"True, which is why we need to entice them. Do you need me on-site? I told Hugh and Michelle that I'd brief them face-to-face."

Tom was surprised at the implied offer. Kathrine was indicating her willingness to be in the firing line. Effi asked, "Do the Russians know you are involved or were involved?"

Kathrine admitted her own and MI6's lack of knowledge, but only after a small implied criticism: "I'm not on film or in their records. Some long distance stuff in Naples when we left. We did confirm they tried to intercept. We have the debrief from our asset."

"You mean Oleg?"

"Yes, Oleg," Kathrine said, briefly contemplating how he and his family were. "He said, as far as he was aware, no one in FSB or SVR has my identity, but they did know a senior woman at director level is operating in MI6. They could have meant Mel, not me." Kathrine didn't know. "They did know her from previous interactions. She coordinated body returns." That got a raised eyebrow from Tom but no comment. "We don't know what else they do know. There was no attacker outside my home, as far as Special Branch has been able to detect. As I said, they may have photos from Naples."

"Good on your ID, but we were all in Naples." Effi added.

"Yes, we already know who they've tried to get to." Effi was going to bristle, but Kathrine continued with a raised hand, "I'm not underplaying it. Not for any of you. I don't like this approach, but I can't see any other way to draw them out."

"I don't think I'll need you as bait then." Tom considered what Kathrine had and had not said. As usual, he needed to read between lines and expressions. Effi may tell him later. Then, he might realise he had missed some implication or message. Sometimes being under fire in Afghanistan was better than all the spy wheeling and dealing.

A knock on the door dragged him and Effi back to more exercises and more range training with Cindy, Holly, and the rest of the assigned team. Kathrine returned to London.

***

Tom and Effi's team was formed of two split troops from the 22nd SAS. The Sabre B Squadron had been assigned. Tom had worked with several before on his tour in Afghanistan. He knew the others by reputation. They knew him. There were six men from a boat troop, two with sniper skills, and four from the mobility troop, with two communications specialists adding to the planned team.

The next task was to bring in the rest of the bait, as Kathrine had put it. That meant Stephie and Carolyn. Ideally, Jules and Andre too, if he could persuade them to come with Natalie. He would rather they knew something. They could also give more information on the yacht to the boat troop members. They were busy researching Sunreef 70s and similar motor yachts, but Tom and Effi both knew that Hugh and Michelle's yacht was customised during its construction in Poland and then further modified in Italy. When Tom was onboard, he was always finding odd storage areas, and the engines, navigation, and other systems often baffled him. He suspected only Hugh, or maybe the Italians, knew what everything did or hid. His colleagues in the Boat Troop were already fascinated.

CHAPTER NINETEEN

Sidorova

Ula Sidorova was shaking after the man's approach. An American from his English accent. His Russian made him sound like a Muscovite. Her mind had thought FSB or SVR, but they would not have approached it like that. She was not arrested, or, she should say, grabbed, by a team. The man had watched her; she knew. She told herself off for not realising he wasn't just interested in her. He was obviously interested in who she was. Her counter-surveillance skills were out of practice despite the recent escape.

Her time in Moscow had dulled that operational edge before she fell from grace and recovered. Now her fall was further, with no hope of recovery. Her only hope was to escape and hide. At least she now had money and whatever was in the still-unopened briefcase.

The man at breakfast had indicated another surveillance. He had given her a room number. How did he know her name and that she was in the hotel? She checked her room. She had placed a do not disturb sign on the door and placed a tell-tale. It was all undisturbed. The briefcase and suitcase remained where they were. She didn't have a screwdriver to try and pick the lock of the briefcase. Its fastening was more secure than normal briefcases.

She checked the two mobile phones. They both had more missed calls. She was concerned they would be tracked, but she was balancing that risk against access to the Internet. She had looked at further routes out. She would need to drive the BMW again or try and fly out, but for that, she needed a passport. Driving to Astana, the capital, was over twenty hours away. Crossing south into Uzbekistan or Kyrgystan would again require a passport, and both were also long drives.

Her ethnicity and lack of local languages would be noticed the further away from Russia she fled. She could return and plead for forgiveness. She would not be believed, especially if the man from the restaurant was right and others were looking for her here. They had already tried to grab her at the library back in Russia.

If she went to this unknown man, then what? Who was he? Who did he represent? She could guess the CIA, the local secret service, or even the British. Perhaps he was a reporter, but how would he know who she was?

She reviewed the brief encounter. What was his accent? He had spoken Russian and then English with an American accent. CIA, then, or what? How could he help her? If he was masquerading as an American but was really SVR, FSB, or even GRU, she would have been grabbed already. He had to be a western agent. She checked the one gun she was carrying. The other two were in the briefcase. She headed for his room.

***

The door opened after a brief pause from her knock. The man opened the door wide.

"Come in, Ula." He stepped back, holding on to the door. He ignored the gun pointing at him.

She waved him inside; he left the door and moved back into the room. He didn't raise his hands. She shut the door, but not fully closed, in case she needed to make a rapid exit.

"Sit," she ordered in English. He perched on the unmade bed.

"No need for the gun; I mean you no harm."

"Who are you?" The gun stayed pointed.

"Gavin." He decided to tell her his real name. He didn't think she would shoot him, but then again, who knew what a former colonel in the SVR might do?

"How do you know who I am?"

"FSB sent an alert out; we picked it up." She didn't look

surprised by that announcement. Gavin considered that she knew she was being hunted. "I was surprised when you walked into breakfast."

"It's a coincidence you are here?"

"A little. A man was looking for you last night. I was watching him."

"Who?"

"A smuggler."

"How did he know I was here?"

"Your car, I'm guessing."

"Not my car."

"No, but you drove it. Is that how you got through the border?"

"No." She didn't add an explanation. "You were following the smuggler?"

"No, one of his clients. A Russian we are interested in."

"Who is we?"

"You know." He watched her consider his answer. "The bigger question is: why is he trying to watch you? He can get his car back."

"The men who drove it are dead." From her statement, he didn't believe she had done the killing. "And another man, he carried me, I mean, drove me across the border."

"Smuggled you."

"Yes. They shot each other. I took the car." He appreciated that there was more there that she wasn't telling yet.

"What do you want to do now?" The important question. She could shoot him, but he thought that was very unlikely. It would attract attention, and she was already on the run. Why she had not continued to her destination, he didn't know. Did she have a plan?

"I need to travel. Get away."

"Where to?"

She was suddenly unsure. He could see the strain on her face. His briefing had very little. He had no idea why a former Colonel was running. Then again, there were many people crossing out of Russia for various reasons.

"I don't know. I have no passport." He realised she was on the verge of collapsing from the stress or strain. "They will kill me if I go back. They wanted revenge and tried to take it. They arrested the generals and…"

Gavin didn't know what she was specifically talking about, but it was already a snippet of new information. He was aware that Russia had taken aggressive action against the British. There had been alerts and warnings. He needed support. He needed to get her somewhere safe, away from the smuggler or anyone else who may come calling. That meant abandoning his current plans for the smuggler's client. "I can help you, if you'll let me."

"Money, I have money."

"Money always helps, cash?"

"Yes."

"I am not a defector, not like…" She stopped herself.

He waited to see if she would continue. The gun was now pointing at the floor. "We just need to get you safe. I can take you away from here, then we can think and plan." Gavin had his own emergency extraction plan, which involved getting to the southwest coast of the country near the city of Atyrau. It was over eight hours away. That was before a planned long-range helicopter pickup with assets flying from Baku. If they turned up? The fear of a spy in a foreign country, that they will be abandoned. Further escape would be from the base there. If he could get the CIA to agree, and if he could get the frightened colonel to agree?

He took the time to explain his idea. Using his own phone to show her the route.

"What after?" She asked.

"You can come with me to the USA. We can protect you

there."

"Not defector."

He understood that she didn't want to think of herself in that way. "Then where will you go?" He had to push now.

"I have money."

"No passport."

"I'll get a passport." She was becoming angry. The gun was now re-directed.

"More smugglers. Police, SVR?"

She went quiet. Her words of agreement to accept his help were almost whispered. "Yes, okay." The gun was lowered. She seemed surprised that she was still holding it.

"Go back to your room, collect your bags, and come back here. I'll then get my car. Not the BMW. I have to make the arrangements. I can check you out of the hotel without being seen, and then we can get going again without the smuggler and his friends following."

"I keep money." She was trying her English.

"Your money. You keep it." Gavin wasn't worried about that or where it had come from.

"I have a briefcase too."

"Your bags?"

"No, a briefcase from Russia was in the truck."

Interesting… Was that the reason why his target was waiting? It would have to be a very large sum of money in cash to provoke personal interest. The man had plenty of money. "Bring everything back here. I'll be waiting."

***

It was less than thirty minutes before she returned. In that time, he had used the application and told his superiors some of what had happened. *Extract via Exfil*, were his instructions in the message back. He'd said he'd have to abandon the watch of the suspicious oligarch. His supervisors didn't seem to mind. He sent that message as a *fait accompli*. They normally didn't like those messages.

He'd only just finished typing and reading when his door was knocked. She had an overnight bag, a suitcase, and a briefcase with her. The gun was no longer in sight. He quickly sorted out his own room.

They left the hotel through the rear entrance. Gavin had gone down to reception and checked them out. A different man was sitting uncomfortably in reception, but he took no notice of Gavin and couldn't hear him clearing accounts for two rooms. Gavin declined help with his bags or the offer for a taxi from the man operating reception. He paid the extra charges without complaint.

Down the rear stairs and out the back. He helped Ula with her bags. They casually walked past the BMW and retrieved Gavin's own SUV around the next corner. Gavin had persuaded Ula to leave the phones she had obtained in her room. He wanted to tell her to leave her gun as well, but he knew she wouldn't. She was still living on her nerves. Gavin had left his weapon untouched in his bag. He didn't want to scare her. He hadn't seen anyone loitering by the BMW. No one was looking for him, but Russians or others could be looking for the colonel.

After loading the bags, he drove out of the city. He constantly checked his mirrors to see if they had been spotted. He saw no tail. That didn't mean a more professional one wasn't there or other methods like drones weren't in use. Still, he could see no reason why they would be followed. After two hours, Ula took over the driving at a gas station. It gave him a chance, with her permission, to look at the still-locked briefcase. He recognised the type. There was a chance he could open it. He had some equipment in another part of his bag. He asked Ula to stop and reassured her while he retrieved the kit. They were back underway in under a minute.

The conversation was stilted, with the main discussion on the route and traffic. He noticed her checking for tails too. He had to keep telling her to stick to the speed limits and not to worry. After fifteen minutes, he popped one lock. He was out of practice and distracted by the road. The concentration needed was making him car sick. He had to keep stopping and taking some breaths. Another ten minutes, and the second lock popped. He noticed the tracker as soon as he opened the top. He quickly removed it and launched the device out of the window.

"Problem?" Ula asked.

"Maybe. A tracker, I don't know if it was active. We have to presume it was."

"They will follow."

"Probably, yes, but not anymore." He rummaged around the case's contents, looking for any other trackers. He didn't find one. "I think it activated when I opened the case."

"They will find us."

"No, they will find the tracker. We'll be long gone. They don't know this car, that I'm with you or anything else."

"They know a lot."

"Not this."

"I hope so. They'll kill me, torture me. Other things."

"That's not going to happen, we'll be gone soon." Gavin hoped he wasn't misleading her.

They drove on. He needed to examine the contents of the case. There were Russian and Arabic documents with security markings. A USB stick was also present. He wouldn't even try to read its data. That would need special handling to avoid the loss of the information. He could see Syria mentioned in one document, along with what looked like bank account details. This could be a major treasure trove.

He moved the contents into his own bag while looking for another tracker. He asked the woman to slow down while he threw the briefcase away. "Just in case," he told her. He wanted time to photograph the papers and send them in.

"They are important?" Ula Sidorova was watching the road with only occasional glances at Gavin and the papers on Gavin's lap.

"I think so. There's a lot here, some in Arabic; do you speak it?"

"No, just English and Russian."

"Your English is good too." He offered her a smile.

"Not in practice speaking it," she tried to say in the language.

"You're doing great. We get this to my bosses, and you'll be looked after very well."

Gavin could not believe his luck. He now needed his good fortune to get the information and his new friend out of the country.

CHAPTER TWENTY

Oligarchs

Russian oligarchs were not renowned for their pleasant demeanours or their willingness to accept failure. Sanzhar Kaliev was personally experiencing some of the more hidden aspects of how he had amassed wealth and power following the Soviet Union's dissolution. This man did not belong to the older generation; he was too young. Instead, he'd risen to power and influence through his connections to Putin. He was replacing a deceased, less amenable man who had not paid sufficient tribute in terms of subservience and money to the Russian leader.

He'd had his own publicised fall from grace and apparently left Russia under a cloud, creating a false narrative to conceal his true actions. He'd been waiting for the cash and, more importantly, a briefcase to arrive. He'd received neither. An upset customer. A very upset customer with connections to armed help had waited for Sanzhar Kaliev, standing by a BMW car parked near a hotel in Aktobe.

The discussion hadn't started pleasantly, despite Sanzhar's attempts at friendliness.

"Again." The Russian was smartly dressed in a business suit without a neck tie. He looked immaculate. Sanzhar couldn't see what he looked like. Both eyes were almost closed from his injuries. He could vaguely make out the two men closest to him. They had insisted he knew more, when he didn't.

"Sir, my men…"

"Your idiots."

"My," he stopped attempting to correct their description.

They were idiots. "Sir, they went to collect the goods as planned from the truck."

"The driver?"

"Adylet Tsoy, he has been dependable for you and me."

"Not this time."

"I don't know," he said as he waited for another assault, cringing into the chair he was tied to. "He was killed, according to my sources." The watching man laughed. "My police contacts say they killed each other at Martuk, the handover gas station."

"Someone else was there?"

"Yes, evidence of a woman, hair in the driver's cab."

"The woman at the hotel?"

"Probably, yes. She claimed to be the husband of one of my men. But I didn't know that then. The hotel wouldn't tell me." They'd already discussed how Kaliev should have forced that conversation.

"You didn't see her."

"No, just the car. I wanted to get your goods. They might have still been in the car or the truck. I needed to check that too." He wanted to wipe the blood from his eyes, but he could barely move. "They were not there. Some police or medics could have taken them." He was trying to shift blame.

"They didn't." Some information Sanzhar didn't know. "The woman? She checked out with this other man. An Iranian?"

"That's what they said. I did insist then."

"Too late."

Sanzhar knew it was all too late. They wanted to know what the man looked like. He had a fleeting memory of the man at reception. The man and the woman had checked out together, but they were in different rooms. Sanzhar couldn't search. His belligerent approach had meant that the receptionist had called the police. He and the failed watcher had left. The failed watcher was already dead. His body was lying in a drying pool of blood on the floor. Sanzhar knew he would soon be there. He didn't know why this failure was so important. He'd had other failed deliveries when the bribery used had not prevented a search. Not that he'd failed this man before.

"You've put us all at risk. My own masters are very unhappy with the loss. I will have to compensate."

"I can repay the money." A last desperate plea.

"It's not about the money." It was the last thing Sanzhar heard.

***

The oligarch did not like Kazakhstan. What should have been a brief visit to collect his goods at the airport had turned into a disaster. He was a conduit in that chain of communication. He knew he had failed. Previous success wouldn't matter. He needed to leave while appearing to have discovered what went wrong. He would call his contact. Not direct. Not now. He was supposed to be exiled. He could use his hidden wealth. Avoiding sanctions and the Americans. Asia was a good place to go. Lots of women, cheap people, and far enough away not to be seen as a threat. Yes, Thailand or Vietnam. Wait for this failure to blow over. Others would attract the president's ire.

He didn't know about everything in the case. A USB stick was due to go to North Korea via South Korea. A place he flew regularly to. He didn't know what was on it, although he could guess. Probably a Bitcoin wallet paying for arms sales, alongside arms orders. Before that, he was due in Syria to hand over more regular paperwork. Another place he'd rather not go to. Now he had nothing to send or courier. For him, the cash was trivial, merely money that had been hidden in one of his homes. If it had only been money, the smuggler would not have paid such a high price.

He would report what he knew, fly to Thailand, and wait. He carried out his own searches for the mysterious woman and the case. He knew it would be fruitless. He had a few contacts in Kazakhstan. One had just gone. He had money, a lot of money, but his main areas of influence were in the Middle East and Far East, not the former Soviet 'Stans. His conduits to Syria, Lebanon, and Iraq were built on selling arms. He'd helped arrange initial contacts with the Iranians. Suddenly required weapons in the battles against Ukraine needed to be sourced. North Korea was another conduit. It also allowed Chinese indirect elements. He saw what had happened to others who had failed the president. He would need to be on his guard.

He was well aware of what happened to those that displeased the president. He'd known Yevgeny Prigozhin the dead head of the Wagner group. He helped supply arms to the mercenary organisation in Africa. He hadn't known Prigozhin would be so stupid as to plan a coup or whatever he was doing. More concerns for his head of security to consider. A few days in Bangkok, he thought, would reduce stress in several ways. Plan other locations out of reach of any possible punishment.

CHAPTER TWENTY-ONE
CHAIN 3865 Tarot CC 00643

"Strange request?"

"Connections. Don't worry about it."

"The normal team…"

"Given other tasks."

"Not got a lot."

"Early days but?"

"Previous files had comms with Syria. Radio tied into flight details into Damascus."

"From?"

"Bangkok or Phuket. At least two from Aktobe, in Kazakhstan."

"Any details?"

"Normal flight radio traffic plus some coded requests. Calls to Syrian regime folks. Still plotting them. Then we have the little pearls."

"Which are?"

"Co-located calls to Iran. All burners. Just meta at the moment, but if they call again we may get something. That's all historical."

"The new stuff?"

"Aktobe call to Moscow. 3 minutes plus. In the details. Geo was Kremlin area, nothing definitive. Call to Syria immediately after. Then a flight to Bangkok. Don't have the same number in Thailand and the burner has not been used again."

"Keep watching. Flights, calls radio. Gonna share another file with you. Your eyes only. Nothing the team can see."

"On?"

"Read it. Langley ops. Background on Tehran links and proposed action. With all the other crap happening some people are proposing stronger action."

"That doesn't always go well. Remember the Navy chase."

"Exactly, but mood has changed especially against Russia."

"Okay I'll read it and let you know about Thailand." He knew the additional information was not coincidental.

CHAPTER TWENTY-TWO

Meetings

Port Grimaud was not showing itself off as it normally did. The weather was dull and grey, with a persistent drizzle. Michelle didn't mind. It provided good cover on their brief walk past the yacht's dock. Hugh was desperate to take the boat and sail off over the horizon, never to be seen or heard of again. Certainly never to cross paths with various security services. Instead, bearded and carrying a walking stick, he and Michelle, in her own disguise, appeared as a much older couple.

Although Hugh and Michelle knew that Andre and Natalie were on board, they didn't approach. Jules was in the area too, although they had not seen him. They both knew that MI5, MI6, or Russians would also be nearby. They needed the Russians to be watching and to catch glimpses of anyone involved. Those observations needed to be controlled. Their cover as an elderly couple was enhanced by their wish to see an adjacent dock that was for sale. That was what they had told the agent before heading to view. The agent was happy to let them go on their own, given the miserable weather. A large golf umbrella only reminded Hugh of the ones in store on his yacht. It had once been his home and refuge. For months he'd been away. Before that it had been docked when not in use by their now sold home in Mykonos.

Watchers for the couple would have to be further back in adjacent road houses if they could obtain access. Michelle didn't mention if she had seen anything. Hugh knew he wouldn't be able to tell. The weather didn't favour an extended conversation. Michelle was plotting. Hugh was reminiscing both with their own thoughts. The rain hammered onto the umbrella. They wanted to be glimpsed. They were baiting the trap. It was a risk to be seen, but one that would require action to turn watching into a capture or kill. Hugh's heart rate was remarkably calm. Perhaps it was some limited acceptance of the outcome he expected.

Hugh and Michelle returned to the Agent's office. It was a chance to get dry, but they claimed another appointment and didn't stay for the offered coffee. They would let the agent know about the dock. They wouldn't need it.

The false elderly couple walked steadily to their next planned location. The rain wasn't easing.

"Hello, Harry, how are you?" Hugh was standing taller, but it still took Harry Rosenthal a few moments of surprise before he recognised Hugh Turnbill. It had been years since he'd seen him.

"Hugh, my God, please come in, come in." The rain was continuing in earnest.

"This is Michelle, my wife." Hugh introduced Michelle, who only shook hands once the door was closed and they were away from any watchers of the house. Hugh and Michelle knew they were putting them at risk.

"Josephine!" Harry called his wife to the entrance hall.

***

"Visiting the Rosenthal couple," Jermaine remembered the names from the original investigation. Jacqui and Dave had reported to Kathrine, and she was telling the small joint team.

"They stayed for under an hour. No chance to follow them after." Sam was unsurprised at that report.

"You have contact, though?" Joe Carpenter asked.

"Yes, to the team in Vauxhall, primarily email discussions between Uliana and Hugh, so Uliana says." Sam responded. Effi, who had been running the team, was away with Tom somewhere. They weren't in Hereford any longer, and Kathrine claimed not to know and that they shouldn't find out. Sam suspected they were also in France.

"Other targets?" Joe asked.

"You're here." Kathrine smiled.

"I didn't mean me." Joe smiled back, "or you and Sam." He included Sam because he had been in Naples. Therefore, he was probably in Russian pictures connected with the defection that Joe and Jermaine had eventually been briefed about. Despite the tension in the room and the seriousness of what was being planned, the practical aspects were progressing. Morale had improved. Joe didn't know why he had been personally targeted, but he blamed it on his one parliamentary public appearance. "Timeline on when they'll be ready?" Joe asked.

"A few days in the area, according to Tom's last note. They need to pre-position and get settled." Kathrine replied.

"You think the Russians will take the bait?" Joe was sceptical.

"An unknown, they can be patient as they were for Salisbury, but the recent attacks didn't demonstrate that."

They had a short break while they waited for DCI Sam Fox to be shown in. He was alone this time. A friendly nod to Jermaine before he sat down and joined in the latest discussions.

"Tom and Effi are deployed." Kathrine didn't say anymore or add that they were included with two of Jermaine and Joe's teams.

"Know that. We have irregular contact with Cindy. Another one of those blasted email set-ups." Jermaine was trying to exert some control with Joe.

"I wondered why they weren't here." Sam Fox didn't know about strange email set-ups. "My two are back with investigating forces. With the perpetrators probably overseas, the investigation is stepping down."

"We need to stay alert, though." Kathrine made it clear.

"Of course. You are obviously planning something you won't tell me about."

"Overseas," Joe stated before Kathrine could.

The DCI decided he didn't want to know. He suspected they

were baiting a trap. He needed to concentrate on targets in the UK. Several of them were believed to be out of the country. "Sir Rupert's protection is still in place. No change there." Sam offered.

"Harper sisters?" Kathrine knew, but let the policeman brief the details he did know about.

"They've left protective custody as planned after they were escorted to a small airfield. A private jet went to Turin according to the flight plan."

No one mentioned that they were probably in France with Tom, Effi, Cindy, and Holly. Kathrine knew a special forces team was there too, travelling via a different route.

"As I said, we don't know. That aspect of the operation lies with Tom and Effi."

Sam Fox managed not to say what he thought of that. He didn't believe they didn't know. He also recalled other actions when he was first investigating Hugh Turnbill. There had been a special forces operation at sea and another one on the Turkish border with Iran. He decided to concentrate on UK protection and operations. "Any specific threats coming my way?"

"Nothing we've detected. GCHQ, NSA, and our colleagues around the world are all on alert." Joe tried to reassure. His own safety was part of the watching. His family had returned home with an additional team of house guests watching and protecting.

Kathrine or William Thatcher's assistant, Sam, had raised multiple questions with the acting Director, but had not been taken into confidence or encouraged. Sam knew Thatcher was distancing himself from any fallout. He needed to have that distance. Sam understood, even if it devalued his own role and prospects in MI6. Sam was keeping quiet as much as possible.

The other Sam, DCI Fox continued, "One piece of better news, relayed from Interpol. There have been several sightings of our female target, Lina Smirnov, or whatever her real name is. She crossed into Spain. Madrid police are hoping to apprehend her soon. They may have already gone in." Understandably, the Spanish police weren't updating the British authorities on a live operation.

"You've advised them of the danger." Joe asked.

"Yes, they also want her for a killing there. Your photo recognition helped tie her in. That's why they are telling us what little they have."

Sam Fox updated them on other details. Where weapons had been identified. They gave him more information on electronic surveillance. Joe had the possible identity of a Russian Embassy official who may have received the text messages. CCTV had been traced, and with GCHQ, they had combined locations. The woman had not ventured out of the embassy. That information had not been shared with MI6 or Special Branch. Joe wanted a word with her first without others entangling. She was not on the diplomatic protection list.

The meeting broke up. It was unclear if there was a need for another. Sam Fox did promise to update them if Spain was successful.

***

The Russian special group was meeting at the same time. Once more, the three men were in a Kremlin side room. They had just spent an uncomfortable fifteen minutes with their President. He was again distracted by other news and only wanted progress, not excuses. Volkov and Egorov were relieved not to be the focus of the displeasure. Instead, Kovalenko had to answer.

They were repeating the review of the list of targets. The successes had been quickly dismissed by their leader. Instead, he focused on the outstanding targets and failures. He wanted results quickly.

Kovalenko was angry that he had been the focal point of Putin's ire. Mostly, it had nothing to do with the operation. As with all three participants, there were many other issues to be dealt with. Political prisoners smuggling messages out of prison had been the complaint voiced today.

"Yegorov?"

"Utah, from SIGINT, but no actual location. He's not with his family. Australia or New Zealand, we think for them." Volkov told them. "We've deployed assets there. Do we take the family without him or wait for him to join them?"

"He's being debriefed by the Americans?"

"Undoubtably."

Egorov joined in. "He will have given them everything he knows. Part of the deal."

"If he'd been stopped in Turkey…" Kovalenko didn't continue. They couldn't rewrite history, and no one in the room was responsible for that. "Wait for Yegorov. We'll get them together." It might be the only opportunity they would get.

"We'll send the woman. She made contact with her control."

"She is safe?"

"So far. In Spain. We need to get her out of Europe or back here. The police have her picture everywhere." Volkov added. "We only have surveillance assets in Australia; we'll split them for New Zealand."

"They can't act directly?" Kovalenko asked, wanting to pressurise the SVR.

"Not trained. They would likely fail against a protection team."

"Needs must." Egorov wasn't helping.

"We have to find them first, then act. Do you want more failure?" The other men backed down. Volkov knew how to run an operation. He also knew the limitations of the information they had. They all knew that finding their targets was difficult, especially alert targets. Taking revenge, there was no other word for it, against heavily protected targets, was very different from the recent attacks in the UK and around the world. None of them wanted more failure. They also knew that an attack in Utah or finding an actual location was unlikely and very high-risk. The Americans were fully alerted after the UK attacks. It wouldn't stop political manoeuvring against any of the participants inside the group or outside.

"Sidorova?" Kovalenko let Yegorov drop for now. He returned to the list.

"No sign, but we had an alert of a possible helicopter

extraction from Atyrau." Egorov briefed even though it was overseas. It was his organisation's assets hunting the missing ex-colonel. "The local authorities," he meant Kazakhstan's limited air force, "complained about airspace violations. We received electronic intelligence."

"How is not important. Where is that?"

"Kazakhstan, south-west coast. There is no sign of her at the other border crossings." They all knew that. Egorov didn't want to admit the next part, but he had to, as it impacted other operations. "We had an issue in Aktobe, also Kazakhstan," he added. He was receiving hawk-like stares in response. "We thought it was unconnected. Another operation, but now connected with ours."

"Go on."

"Information and finance for Syria." His two comrades were staring straight at him. He was very glad they weren't still with the President. "The information is missing with associated accompanying funds. It is possible that Sidorova was involved. How, or why, we don't know. The receiver of the information has interrogated the courier organiser. Something went wrong just over the border from Russia. The driver was killed alongside the two men sent to pick up the information. It was a regular route. A woman was involved, according to the smuggler. One of the other two men killed was associated with my organisation." He wasn't a serving officer he had established.

"Who was the contact?" Egorov told them. They both whistled. "Thought he had run away?" Kovalenko's admission demonstrated he wasn't completely in Putin's confidence. None of them were.

"Dubai?" Volkov understood the implications.

"Not directly, but confirmation and payment were in the goods. There are other opportunities, too. Requests for help in the UK and USA. Other matters are not connected with our joint operation."

"They will have the IDs for the new assets?"

"No, just logistics." Egorov hoped that was true. He didn't

know everything that was in the briefcase. "We tracked the briefcase holding the information." His comrades looked more hopeful. "It was on a road to Atyrau, but the tracker was by the side of the road. It was only when we were given the intelligence on the helicopter, that we investigated further."

"The helicopter?"

"US military."

"The Americans have her and the information?"

"Yes. We must presume so." Damage from the lost information was still being assessed. Putin had been told the real reason why he was angry. Egorov couldn't complain that the transmission method was stupid, not when the former KGB man was the president.

"We need to accelerate Dubai, or they will be warned."

"It may already be too late. We don't have complete control." Egorov revealed his concern.

The use of the Syrian team had been debated before. Volkov had exposed his disagreement. He had been against the policy. The exact timing of their plan was not known. Communications were limited. The Syrian group of four had been given photos and locations. How they would deal with their targets was unknown. Volkov allegedly had operational control. "I will send an urgent message." Volkov added. They took a break while Volkov contacted his team to send messages to Dubai.

***

After the calls, they spent a few minutes discussing the finance team.

"Activity around the yacht?"

"They think it's being prepared for a longer trip. We have glimpses of the targets that were the crew. Large heavy bags being loaded. Possible sightings of targets. They are clearly preparing something" The crew were of lower priority. "I haven't requested a response yet."

"Hoping to ensnare others?"

"Exactly."

"We had the messages of these sisters no longer in protective custody."

"Yes. It's very risky to dig further; unless I get higher authority, I'm not going to risk that asset." The others knew very little about what the SVR man was saying and couldn't pressure him. They had to have assets after this revenge mission, or the Russian intelligence effort would be damaged for decades. They'd lost a lot of UK resources in the last 12 months.

"But you had flight tracking."

"Public flight trackers, a plane with two young women and others flew to Turin. We had no assets to watch where they went next."

"The yacht?" Kovalenko asked?

"A good guess, but they could be anywhere. We can't put bulletins out in other locations without risking further exposure." Volkov was again concerned about the longer-term impact.

"We can send more assets to France, just in case?" Egorov encouraged and asked.

"We need support."

"I shall ask GRU." Volkov didn't voice his concern at Kovalenko's suggestion. The last larger GRU deployment in Mykonos had failed.

CHAPTER TWENTY-THREE
Dubai and Spain

Doug Masters was on his way back to his apartment. He and Calvin had a dinner reservation planned. The operations they were assigned to continued, even with the absence of 2B calling the shots. They were back in a limited routine, both missing Lila and wondering too often about the future. They had received some messages with alerts and warnings on potential Russian actions after the attacks. The assaults attracted little news attention in Dubai. The Embassy was warned, and via their local contacts, they too were warned.

Doug, having been at Enez, was more obviously at risk of Russian retaliation. Not that the Embassy or local Five and Six operatives knew he had been there. The video on the Internet was not that clear. No one had asked or implied. Calvin did, but he wasn't telling others either. They both knew he had been lucky to get away from Mykonos.

Doug was taking extra precautions. He varied his route to and from their apartment. It was not always easy, given fixed transport links. He'd used the bus to return from his regular contact meeting with his local control. He'd walked and used the metro to get there. At this time of day, the bus was relatively quiet. He was going to take the lift, but decided to give his body a workout. He headed for the stairs entrance.

"You'll need this." The man was American. It took Doug a few seconds to realise where he had seen the man before. He had been dressed in a t-shirt and grabbing a target that Doug and others were watching. It was connected to an anti-terror operation in Pakistan. The man had been based in Dubai, and they were following him when the Americans grabbed him. The American was dressed just as casually, except for the thin gloves on his hands. He passed over a set of gloves to Doug and the Sig Sauer pistol, barrel first. "Twelve in the mag. You've got two in your apartment, one in the corridor. We've got two friendlies on the floor below, plus us."

Doug was quickly reorienting. "My associate?"

"Don't know," Doug was not reassured. "We only just got the heads up. Drove here. We saw them go in. Russian coordinated but Syrian or some other idiot connections, according to Langley. We got some SIGINT on it kicking off. We were told you were their target. Had the alerts before." His delivery was rapid while he scanned the foyer.

A young black or mixed-race woman came into the area. "Car watcher we've got. No fight." Pure Texan accent. "Van's ready."

"You were on the bus." She looked annoyed at having been spotted. "I didn't figure it out. Good craft."

"Thanks, are we going up?" She took out and donned some gloves, before pulling another Sig Sauer out.

"What about locals?" Doug asked.

"They don't know; they are not going to know. I'm going to need you both to come with us afterwards, sorry."

"That's okay; I'm done with Dubai anyway. My fingerprints will be everywhere."

"For the new weapons and elsewhere."

"Okay."

Doug didn't think it would be an option on him. Would the USA implement such an outcome ending badly? No, he didn't think so. If they wanted that he'd already be dead. Instead, he wondered how he would tell Thames House or Vauxhall what was happening. He had the email account Hugh had given him. Not that he had used it. He briefly wondered if the man and his wife were okay. He hadn't heard from Tom or Effi either. He guessed they would all have been targeted, as would the sisters. There was also that almost crazy woman, Justine. They'd gone to the airport together after they sailed back to Greece. Despite the immediate concern, he welcomed the chance to play a part. He hadn't forgotten Lila, and his own need for revenge.

"Good, let's grab ourselves some targets."

***

The three of them moved towards the stairwell. Doug could now see the earpieces.

"Roger that," the man said.

They stopped two floors below his apartment and one below the other assets. Doug knew there was another fire stairwell at the other end of the building. "We have them bracketed on the floor above. The other stairwell, there's another friendly there. He's dressed like me. We'll lead you follow, okay?" Doug knew he couldn't get in the way of their tactical formation. He would hang back, even if he wanted to be in the thick of it.

They moved very quietly up another flight. There, they met another member of the team. Doug didn't recognise him. "Elevator in relation to your front door?" The first man asked.

"Closer to the other stairwell." Doug and Calvin had rehearsed emergency egress. They knew how to get out via the three routes available. They were covering two of those. "I could go up the lift, the elevator." The three Americans had a quick whispered discussion.

"Sorry, I need to keep you back, just in case they start shooting. Marietta will go." The woman had a name. She nodded, exited the stairwell, and they saw her jog towards the lift. "Yeah," the leader responded to a voice comm. "Keep them in the foyer, or preferably outside. Sure, let them call the police. We're going in. On my call." They moved up the stairs. The man who had been waiting lay down before he pulled the stairwell door open. Doug couldn't see. He did hear the ping of the lift.

The shots were loud in the echo of the bare-walled stairs. The lead man jumped over his partner and sprinted down the corridor. Doug saw a man exit from the opposite doorway to the other stairwell. He sprinted past the prone Marietta, who had pulled a gun from her victim. Doug carefully followed the man, who had been lying down along the corridor. Shots could be heard from inside his apartment. The other three were already inside. A man was dead or dying, half-sitting by his door.

"Clear!" He heard the shouts, and he entered his apartment. Blood was smeared on the corridor wall just inside the door. More blood spatter decorated the wall opposite. Marietta appeared from one of the bedrooms to the left of the front door. The other three were in the lounge. Two injured or dead men, both of middle-eastern appearance, were face-down on the floor.

She shook her head and said, "Your friend. Sorry." Marietta indicated the bedroom she had come out of. It was Doug's room, the one he had once shared with Lila.

Doug didn't want to look. He was suddenly very tired. He went over to the two men lying prone, both covered by the others. The lead man was now speaking on a mobile phone. Standing by the window.

"Photos, fingerprints, two minutes to Exfil." He reported.

"I just need my passport and laptop. The other laptop is…" Doug told them.

"I got that one already. I'll get the others." Marietta returned to the bedroom where Calvin was lying.

"Passport's bottom drawer, right-hand bedside table." He didn't say there were still some of Lila's things in the other drawer on the other side of the bed. Her side. He watched as they turned the first man over. His face was severely injured. They took his photo anyway before pressing his fingers onto a phone screen. The man was dying, judging by the blood gently leaking from his chest. The other man was in better condition, wounded, and silently watching them. He appeared to be praying.

Doug kicked him as soon as the identification details were done. He pointed his gun at him.

"Not him," the leader said. "Not yet; we take him. The other is yours." The three men pulled the lightly injured man to his feet. He said some words in fast Arabic, that Doug didn't manage to translate. He nodded at Doug. Doug took aim and pulled the trigger. The Sauer wasn't as loud as he thought it would be. He wasn't satisfied.

"Sorry, I have to see." He went to his bedroom. The woman, Marietta, was coming out. He didn't want to see but knew he had to. Doug wasn't squeamish. He'd killed before including removing a team member when he over stepped with the Harper sisters. That was with Lila, dead in Enez, and Calvin now dead in Dubai.

Doug walked around the bed, avoiding stepping on Calvin's inert body, and found the picture of the three of them in Lila's drawer. He took it. Some of Lila's underwear and a book were still in there. He'd never completely cleared Lila's things away. He left them where they were, shutting the drawer. He stopped briefly placing his hand on Calvin's shoulder. His eyes were already closed. He had a flashback to the dead Lila. She was lying on the deck of the yacht as they sped away from Enez. Nothing could be done despite the efforts to save her. Lila's body had several bullet wounds. Doug blamed himself for allowing her to be in such an exposed position. He knew Tom blamed himself too. He briefly wondered how the man was and where he was.

"We need to go," the woman called from the bedroom's doorway.

"Yeah, sorry." Doug could see that Calvin's throat had been slit. He would blame himself for Calvin too. If he had been home? He hadn't been and therefore hadn't been killed either. Doug noticed the other wounds to Calvin's arms and one leg. They had tortured him before killing him.

Marietta handed over his passport but kept the laptop. She had found or had always been wearing a backpack. Doug wasn't sure. The last few minutes were a blur that his brain was struggling to keep up with. He saw the other laptop, Calvin's laptop, already inside. They prepared to leave the building. The passport was his proper one. He had his fake one in his pocket.

They dragged the weeping attacker with them into the lift. Doug wanted to kill him. They left the door open. One of the men was completing the ID checks on the dying man by the door. He casually completed a headshot. It echoed in the corridor. The lift was open. Doug saw a fire extinguisher preventing the door from closing.

Two of the men were holding their prisoner by the upper arms. He was dripping blood on the floor.

"Guns away." The lead said this as the lift reached the ground floor. There were a few residents waiting, annoyed by another man blocking access to the lift. They walked swiftly past and out of the main doors. A black van with dark-tinted windows was idling at the kerb, waiting. They all climbed in. Another prisoner was already on the floor. The wounded man joined him, also tied with a plastic cable, a gag in his mouth, headphones, and finally a bag over his head.

"Sorry, Doug, just the bag, okay?"

"Yes." Doug momentarily feared for his life, but if they wanted him dead, he would still be upstairs. He could hear approaching sirens. Not too close. The view went dark. He felt Marietta lean across him and click his seat belt shut.

"Don't worry you're fine." Marietta stated.

"You're good, Doug. Just some stuff you don't need to see."

"Okay." Dog tried to relax.

***

A ten-minute steady drive through traffic, then a faster drive before the van again slowed. He heard some discussions from the driver with someone outside. The vehicle accelerated again. It slowed and came to a stop.

"Wait here," Doug heard the lead American state. He heard raised voices before the man returned. "We wait." The vehicle was getting hot. Doug could smell aviation fuel.

After about twenty minutes, he heard a shout of "Okay." The only words in the van were from one of the men, telling the prisoner to keep still. There was a grunt. Doug had accidentally pressed down on the man's leg. He couldn't see if it was the injured one or not. He didn't care.

They disembarked the van. Doug felt Marietta guide him. Briefly, he felt the heat of the sun was on his head's covering and shoulders before he walked up a slope and into a cooler space.

"Sit," she told him. He recognised a bucket seat used in military transport. "Don't speak for now." He didn't. He heard the engines start up. The plane taxied and took off. Marietta sat next to him. He couldn't see her, but she handed over a water bottle. He managed to take a drink. He still had the gun. He was still alive.

It was a short flight before the boarding process was reversed. It was getting darker and cooler. Marietta sat him down in a chair. She whispered to him. "Al Dhafra Airbase, we flew in from Al Minhad. The Australians gave us a lift. They aren't happy. We'll be moving soon. Have some food on the plane. Do you want more water?"

"I'm good."

"Okay, sorry again about your friend."

"So am I."

***

"Joe."

"William, sorry about the lateness of the call. We've had a Dubai attack."

"Damn." William Thatcher waited for the bad news. It hadn't come from his operations desk; therefore, as far as he knew, it wasn't an MI6 asset. It still could be because they might not know yet.

"One friendly dead. Waiting on ID. Two presumed attackers were killed at the scene. The Emirates' authorities are not very happy. We also have one friendly going with some Americans out of Al Minhad Air Base with Australian cooperation. Sort of Australian cooperation I should say, don't think the Americans gave them any choice. They had two unknown prisoners, with them, described as Arabic. I need your folks in Dubai to dig more."

"I'll get them moving. The friendlies?"

"Connected to all the mess. Baz Butler ran them which is why we got the alert. Calvin D'Jabe and the former Doug Masters. They shared an apartment. Doug was in Enez. Calvin in Mykonos.

I don't know who made it and who is apparently with the Yanks."

"I'll speak with Dubai. Have you told Kathrine?"

"Not yet. It's very hot off the press, and we'll have journalists, politicians, and diplomats all stirring the pot. I need to brief my DG. We had an Op that they were doing there too. You need to warn others once more if it's coordinated."

"Thanks Joe. I'll tell Kathrine and see what Langley will tell me. She can alert the others. If she has contact."

***

The Spanish police took no chances in apprehending the woman, who was identified in London as Lina Smirnov. A full counter-terror team surrounded the hotel they had discovered she was staying in. They waited to assault the building at 3:00 a.m. Previous entries by counter-terror operatives had covered CCTV access and gained a presence in the spare room next to the target. There, the surveillance specialists had drilled a minute hole through the wall to insert a specialist fibre optic camera. The attacking group of six black-clad officers entered the corridor silently. Other officers would follow to cover other hotel room doors on the floor. They knew from the feed that the room was locked and latched. They knew where the latch was.

The first two officers placed small plastic explosive charges on the main electronic lock and the position of the latch while keeping to the side of the spy hole in the room's door. They were careful not to allow their shadows to pass across the viewpoint. The corridor lights were dim but not dark enough for night vision goggles to be required.

One man lay awkwardly across the corridor, his weapon pointing at the door. He was very exposed, but his low position would not be expected, and he would be lower than the door blasts. The two on the right side of the door retook positions. A man on the left had a battering tool ready, but he was behind the remaining two officers. The team leader raised his fist. They leaned back from the door. As he dropped his hand, the explosives were detonated. The sound was no more than a small knock. They were through the door and surrounding the bed. Guns pointed at the still-sleeping woman. They took no chances. One officer each took a limb. The legs were pinned under the sheets. The woman was waking but was quickly gagged and hooded. She was cuffed and her legs shackled before two officers carried her onto the floor. She was heavier than they expected but still light compared to their regular weight-training exercises.

They held her there as they unceremoniously searched her body. No weapons were found under her t-shirt and panties. A knife was under her pillow, as one of the other officers discovered. A gun was in a bag below her sleeping position, along with a variety of travel documents. There was relief all around. She was taken out by the attack team and roughly thrown into an unmarked van. Four officers sat in the van, which departed even as more police and forensic teams arrived. Congratulations would wait; at the moment, there was just relief that the operation had gone smoothly.

***

It was nearly twenty-four hours after Doug had left his Dubai apartment. Most of it he'd spent on planes or on short waits for them. For the transatlantic section, he was at least unhooded. At a refuelling stop somewhere, he was back with his head covered for the descent, landing and take-off. His gun was taken back, not that he resisted. He was left with his passports and the photo of the three of them. He didn't attempt to remove the hood. The team he had travelled with left with their prisoners at that point. Others joined.

"See you around, Doug." The team leader grabbed his hand and shook it. They'd told him he would be going further. They didn't say where.

Marietta said, "Goodbye." She placed her hand on his shoulder. "Sorry again about your friend," she repeated. He could only mumble his thanks. They hadn't spoken on the flight.

There were "See ya's" from the other three. Nothing from the prisoners, although one had received some limited medical attention on the journey. Back under his hood, he had to wait until they were level at altitude before two suited men let him take it off. They had a bag of clean clothes for him, including a puffed jacket. They didn't introduce themselves, but they did hand over another sandwich and a coffee. Black, but he didn't care.

He was hooded again, for the landing, and he could feel the cold despite wearing his coat. He still couldn't see but there was enough light to know it was daylight again. He'd dozed off on this shorter trip. Another van journey. They slowed for multiple security checks before they drove into a garage.

An obviously armed man pulled his hood off. "This way," he said, opening a door to the garage, revealing a short corridor. A WC was off to one side. A utility room was opposite. American appliances, he noted. They walked a few steps through another corridor. A small grey-haired woman was waiting at the entrance to a large lounge overlooking a snow-covered garden.

"Hi Doug, I'm Aileen; you know, Oleg, I believe." Doug watched in disbelief as Oleg Yegorov stood up from a large armchair.

Aileen knew it had been proposed to bring another defector or escapee, a woman, to the house. Thankfully, when Aileen found out her name, more sensible plans had been enacted. She wasn't entirely happy that the new man had been transported to her, but he wasn't a threat to the defector. There was a possibility that the men's interaction might reveal more details, not that Oleg was reticent. They would have audio and video recordings, sometimes obvious, sometimes not.

Oleg gave Doug a bear hug. After a suitable period of hellos and expressions of disbelief, Doug asked to contact his employers. He was surprised his request was permitted. He was escorted through several guarded doors before he was shown to a secure landline phone. The call had already been put through.

***

The former FSB Colonel, Ula Sidorova, luxuriated in a hot shower. Her journey to the room was long and tiring, but uneventful. That was if you ignored the car, the helicopter with a short refuelling stop at sea, more helicopter time, and then the transfer to a small jet. Another refuelling stop. She was asleep for that one and only woke on landing. Another take-off, landing, and then a car journey to a large house. She wasn't blindfolded. Gavin stayed with her until he left the house. The briefcase contents were gone, but her other bags, including the cash-filled suitcase, were in her room. She guessed she was in the USA but had no idea where.

There were several guards in the house. Ula no longer had any guns or phones.

Before going to her room, Gavin said his farewell. "I'm heading off, Ula. You'll have others take care of you."

"Will you be back?"

"I'll try." Gavin's own future was unclear. Returning to Ula was possible if she spoke to him, but she was reluctant with her assigned interrogators. He may not be blown in Kazakhstan, but it would be risky to return. Gavin didn't want to go back. He wanted to spend some time in the consumer paradise of the USA. He wanted some time away from checking his back and having every contact meeting a possible trap. He had his own debriefing to attend. He couldn't stay with the colonel, even if he wanted to.

She was attractive, but he could see the coldness in her. He watched her switch her demeanour on and off when she met men. She hadn't tried with him. He knew it was fake and a reluctant fake too, but he could also see how that would have worked when she was less tired and better dressed. He knew she would face a long debrief and that her former employers would try to get her. He noticed the security at the house and their journey. He'd had the alerts. People were concerned.

He'd warned Langley from the helicopter. An imminent threat in Dubai from a four-person Syrian team going after a target named on papers as Doug Masters with a pseudonym and his associate Calvin D'Jaste. Gavin didn't know them; he would have been very surprised if he had. He didn't have the group's ID in the papers, as far as he could tell. There was a lot of information there, but not all of it in Russian, and his limited Arabic wasn't sufficient. It could be fake. There was always that risk, but the documents looked real. He'd handed the contents in his own bag over at the refuelling stop. It was on its way for a full analysis, along with the USB stick. That could contain copies or even more information.

He insisted he stay with Ula in case she gave more information on the journey. He was her friend and ally now. She had shared morsels about herself and why she was running. He knew she was ready to talk. He told Langley that he was getting more information. He also wanted to make sure the suitcase of money didn't disappear. Langley agreed to let him go to the safe house to safely deliver her to the rapidly assembled second debriefing team. Gavin didn't miss the second terminology. Ula had hinted she had lost her job due to a defector. Her mood swung from glad to have escaped to angry that she had been forced to run, with varying emotions in between. They were both tired. Gavin slept on his flight to Washington. Ula slept in a warm bed. She felt safe for the first time in months.

CHAPTER TWENTY-FOUR
Surveillance

Holly and Cindy were enjoying strolling around Port Grimaud. The weather had improved which made the exercise warmer and drier. They appeared to any passing watcher as tourists, especially when accompanied by two of the SAS team. They seemed quite happy with the arrangement. The non-tourist appearance had to extend to clothing where weapons could be concealed. The suddenly better weather meant concealment was harder. Not that the team were expecting a firefight. Their task was to check for Russian watchers of the boat or the crew.

They used obvious mobile phones for communication rather than hidden radios. Effie was receiving their calls and texts. Tom was still preparing action including picking a launch site for the SAS vessel, if that was needed.

Stephie and Carolyn Harper had insisted on appearing in the town. Public walks past shops and out to the marina area without actually going to the yacht. The MI5 and SAS watchers spent most of their time seeing who was watching the sisters. Carolyn and Stephie knew they might be targeted before the yacht. A risk they knew they had to take. Their only comfort was that various large men were nearby as were Holly and Cindy. They'd been introduced to the support team not long after they arrived in France. Faces they needed to track so that no one took unnecessary risks.

"The woman with the yellow dress." Holly announced. She was holding hands with one of the SAS men, who was very happy with the situation.

"Likely," Cindy confirmed.

"Any threat?" The other SAS man asked. He wanted a better position than the exposed street, if there was a risk.

"Just watching," Cindy reassured him. They were all browsing a tourist shop. Carolyn and Stephie were sitting drinking coffee at an external table of a nearby restaurant, *La Coupole*. The woman they suspected changed position. She had a phone call in operation.

"Trouble?" The first SAS man added. A fit looking man had joined the woman. The man wasn't as skilled as the woman. He glanced at the sisters.

"Selfie," Holly announced ensuring the woman in the yellow dress and the new man were the subjects of the photo. Cindy and the other SAS man repositioned between the sisters and their watchers, just in case there was an imminent threat. They were now standing by a clothes shop called *Sud Fashion* where Cindy checked a bikini but looked at Carolyn and then at the two watchers. They were on the opposite side of the road allegedly browsing postcards at a shop called *Gourmandises*. Stephie followed her sister's glance and smiled at Cindy, acknowledging the hidden warning too. Cindy with her escort moved to another shop's display.

"Good sightline here," the SAS man whispered in her ear. Cindy could sense his readiness.

"Easy, they're just watching."

"Sorry," the man tried to relax. She rewarded him with a kiss on the cheek while holding up a string bikini. The SAS man had to laugh, he could imagine the woman wearing what little cloth she held up. He refocused his attention on the task at hand. The two pairs now had the watchers bracketed.

The man and the woman moved away. Breaking the surveillance contact. Two pairs, Cindy and Holly with their respective SAS men moved to follow. They changed plans, Holly and her man returning to the cafe, taking a table near the sisters. Phones were against heads. From all external appearances they were making and taking calls. Carolyn and Stephie went to move, but Holly just raised her hand briefly. The sisters called a waiter and ordered another coffee.

***

Tom was watching from Harry and Josephine Rosenthal's house. Hugh had introduced him. Harry and Josephine were initially amused and then concerned about the turn of events. Now they were watching an obviously armed man as he in turn scanned the dockside using a pair of military binoculars.

"You knew Hugh back then, worked with him?

"No, we met after a job we were both involved in."

"He was finance, a banker we thought."

"He is. Very specialist finance."

"For the government?"

"Yes."

"So why were they looking for him. They told us they thought he'd been killed. Josephine was accused of having an affair with him," Tom managed not to comment.

"You don't need to be coy, Tom. We met some of his girlfriends."

"He's married now."

"The sisters said. We met Michelle. They didn't say more. Like you they don't say much."

"They can't my dear," Harry said tapping his nose. "Let's leave Tom to it." Harry took his wife to the rear of the property.

***

The focus of Tom's observation was not currently the Richtung Süden III, but two men who appeared to be watching the boat. Tom did have a radio.

"Samba 2, no change." Tom heard.

"Roger, Samba 2," Tom replied. Samba 2 was one of his SAS colleagues. He was sitting fishing on the wall. Tom had a flashback to Lila Cotton sitting on the wall in Enez. He didn't think the same outcome was about to happen but he knew his team were in vulnerable positions. He moved the view of his binoculars back to the motor yacht. He could clearly see Andre and Jules working on the vessel. They were loading the heavy closed bags and more obvious provisions on trays from a small van. Natalie appeared and claimed a tray of food from Jules. They all knew they were being watched.

"Samba 2, approaching Hotel 1 and 2."

"What were they doing." Tom thought. He quickly moved the glasses to look at the docks approach. Sure enough he could just see Carolyn and Stephie. Thankfully, they walked past the end of the dock and did not approach the vessel. Tom's mobile went.

"I've told them." Effie said. "You know what they are like."

"Samba 2, Samba 5 and 6 also following, Hotels."

"Roger," Tom managed. On the phone he told his wife, "Tell them again. More hostiles in the area."

"I will," Effie hung up.

Tom was cross at the sisters deliberately putting themselves in danger. He understood that the Russians needed to be baited into the trap, but he didn't like who was acting as the cheese. The Russians were much more dangerous than mice. He had to stop thinking like that. They were all in danger unless the Kremlin could be persuaded to call off its actions. He refocused on the two watching the boat. They had also seen the sisters and were on their own mobile phone. They did not follow them. Tom's phone rang again. Not Effie this time.

"Kathrine," Tom answered.

"Tom, progress?"

"Some, watchers on the sisters and the boat. Have one woman and three men spotted so far. The woman was initially on her own. Using phones, you might get SIGINT. You should have photos soon."

"Good. I'll check with Cheltenham. Michelle and Hugh?"

"Hoping to see them soon."

"Your hosts."

"Doing a great service." Tom smiled at Josephine who was

delivering another cup of coffee.

"When?" Kathrine wasn't prevaricating.

"Two days, maybe faster."

"Okay, be careful." A rare comment.

***

The Russian team reported their findings back to their masters in Moscow. Positive identification of the sisters. A lot of activity near the yacht including the sisters going near but not on the boat. There were many tourists around and the team were not certain they had not seen either of the two couples. They had their own photos, but identification was not aided by the poor quality photographs they had been sent. They did confirm that the yacht's crew were on and off the vessel. One possible sighting of one of the main targets, the man. He'd briefly been on the deck. They were almost certain of that.

The older couple that lived in Port Grimaud had been seen, but not on the yacht. They seemed unaware of the crew's activities. The team, were stretched and inexperienced. They also had to brief a GRU team who themselves had to stay out of sight. Six military looking men who had entered Europe illegally, would be obvious if they strolled around town.

CHAPTER TWENTY-FIVE
CHAIN 3865 Tarot CC 00643

"I'm guessing things are not going well."

"Good guess. Your report went down well."

"After your edits."

"Things have moved on. Russian activity and Brit response."

"Getting hot."

"Looks like it. What have you found so far?"

"Honey pots on the systems. As instructed I didn't go further. More access from UK, you know who, to those systems."

"No need for more. Leave that be. The Brits are promising more info. Don't want that upset."

"Okay."

"So, the yacht?"

"Yes. I was surprised you wanted us back looking."

"I was surprised to be asked."

"There's lots of activity nearby. Limited direct. We have encrypted radio, no decryption. Phone calls all over. Not getting transcripts just metadata. Had UK, France, Italy, Russia connections."

"Messy chain map."

"Yes. I have the new AI plotting which makes it quicker, but we have multiple groups converging and operating. There's some UK and Russian military stuff too. Brits don't know who, they have a formal request in for support."

"We're going to give it."

"Oh, okay, well, the Russian is GRU, as well as SVR signatures."

"That's not good."

"Hence my alert. Christ knows what they are capable of."

"Brits?"

"I can assume it's SAS or SBS from the signature. They planning on a war?"

"We all hope not. If the GRU does chemical, all hell will break loose. They need to heed the warnings after Salisbury."

"If he'll listen." He meant Putin. "That would drag in the French as well as everyone else. They don't know as far as I can tell."

"Keep watching. Brits are out for revenge. Russians the same or reprisals. Global activity there. They're losing assets, Russians I mean, looks like a big mistake. More chatter from Moscow. Main locations?"

"It's still seems to be mostly near Port Grimaud. Neat St. Tropez. A lot of cell traffic, mostly burners, they're geolocated near the radio transmissions."

"Any systems use?"

"You said not to look."

"Impossible not to, I understand."

"Well…"

"Coincidental? Accidental? These things happen."

"Got it." Reluctantly he added, "Some, not all in that location and off the yacht, but nearby. Just saw VPN encryption packets heading on the network. Same design as before. No decryption and the targets are global cloud servers. Could be any or all of them."

"Okay. Come to ops when I call. Might need your input

when it goes down."

"Okay."

"The Kazakhstan stuff?"

"Interesting, not my usual area. Langley involvement and Navy. Lots of chatter, most is encrypted, but some going to that…"

"Don't fret. Langley had an op. Went well. More damage to the Kremlin."

"Tied in with Dubai."

"Yes. More chains, but not for you, we need you focused on the big stuff."

CHAPTER TWENTY-SIX
Michelle and Hugh

Michelle and Hugh were in an Air B&B on the outskirts of Cannes. They both knew that two other rentals were in operation, hosting a variety of people. Not that the couple had told all the others where they were. Hugh, in particular, was in a contemplative mood after his reunion with Harry and Josephine.

"Having regrets?" Michelle was reading his mind again.

"Not about you," he said, giving her a loving look. "I wouldn't have lasted long on my own."

"No, and who knows what would have happened?" It was not the first time they had discussed what had happened. How they had ended up in the position of setting themselves and their friends up to be attacked by Russians. Hugh thought they had a lot of deaths on their conscience.

There was a knock on the door. Effi and Tom were greeted with hugs. They sat in the rental house lounge, discussing the operation. Tom took them through what had been planned. Michelle and Hugh listened closely. Effi watched her friends to see if they agreed or not.

"Too much risk for you, Stephie and Carolyn." Michelle eventually commented.

"I can't see a way of avoiding it. We have to draw the Russians out and give them a big enough hit; they will not try again."

"A bloody nose won't stop Putin."

"It might not, not in the long term, but he's acting now. Not just us, but any target he can find." Tom tried.

"I agree, it's optimistic…"

"We don't plan to fail," Tom quipped with a shrug and a small smile.

"We get an end result; we're out of the picture, and removing their assets will be a major setback." Effi sounded very professional. "The UK team had some success. The Spanish police have captured the woman who probably killed Baz and Mel and that poor delivery driver. Others have been identified and are being looked for. The police want extradition, but the Spanish want her for another murder."

"Some good news," Hugh replied.

"Better if she were dead," Michelle could always be blunt." The room lapsed momentarily into silence.

"Are you going to tell them?" Tom was looking at his wife.

"Tell us what?" Hugh asked. He was suspicious of missing information once more.

"An attack in Dubai. They got to Calvin." The reports had been clarified and passed on by Kathrine. "Doug got away. Other stuff is happening. The Americans saved Doug. Kathrine passed some info on."

"Half the story as usual," Michelle expressed her opinion. "Is Calvin dead?" Michelle asked.

"Yes, sorry to say that."

"He was with Doug and Lila when they kidnapped Stephie and Carolyn." Michelle was almost absent-minded in her statement.

Effi still didn't know all of that story. She returned to the Dubai information. "The attack team was captured or killed. There is lots of diplomatic activity with the Emirates. We only have a bit of the story."

"Bloody typical Kathrine." Hugh was scathing.

"I know Hugh, I know, but it's not all Kathrine. She needs information from the Americans and others." Tom attempted to placate his friend.

"It doesn't matter. You can get everyone away?" Hugh asked pointedly.

"That's the plan. I have a full team in support."

"Some of the ones outside?" Michelle, as usual, missed little.

Effi had to laugh. Tom continued, "No plan is perfect. It could all be pointless if the Russians don't take the bait."

"Then we'll all be looking over our shoulders for years," Effi commented.

"No change there," Hugh grimly stated.

"You have your bits ready?" Effi asked Michelle and Hugh.

"Couple of days," Hugh answered.

"Just need a location?" Michelle had pulled a sea chart from the desk.

"You're the sailors; where do you suggest?" Tom looked to his friends.

"Just there, deeper water, just in international waters, but still in view of the coast, provided the weather is good."

"Better than the last day or two."

"We need calm seas."

***

"Will this do?" Michelle was looking sceptical.

"Limited choice with the time available." Hugh wanted more. "It has space, and it's only for a limited time. Still a few hours, probably eight. Cruise speed."

"And that exit?"

"It's good. Trains, planes, and automobiles." He tried a joke. Michelle appreciated it.

"The gear for the yacht?"

"We have ours in store, as do the sisters. Andre and Jules

have the rest. Natalie hasn't used it. Andre said he'd make sure she could. We can all help."

"We need spares for debris."

"They know."

"Sorry."

"Don't be."

***

"We have an alert." Egorov of the FSB had called Volkov of the SVR

"From where?"

"France."

"You have the team ready?" Volkov knew but wanted confirmation.

"Already alerted. The GRU team Kovalenko organised. Two hours to be in position. They have the new inflatable high-speed assault boat with them. They got one from the Special Military Operation. The higher-speed engine. It will need to be; the target may be capable of over 70 kmh."

"That is quick."

"The boat, even when loaded, will be quicker and lighter. Six-person team onboard. Radio and logistics on land."

"The team as ordered."

"Yes."

"Have you informed the President?"

"Not yet, nor Kovalenko. I wanted to be sure we were ready, and we agreed to act."

"You are taking a risk." Volkov understood that he would be implicated too. Nevertheless, they needed to be sure.

"I know, but..."

"I understand. This could go badly wrong. Publicly wrong."

"We will carry out the mission, but the president should

fully understand the risks. Mykonos and the losses in Europe and Dubai."

"I had to brief him. And Kovalenko won't tell him; he just agrees with everything."

"Perhaps not." A lot was being inferred. They were both taking risks with the conversation. Neither had disobeyed. Reluctance could only go so far.

"The president will still insist."

"I know, unless we can persuade otherwise." He gave the appearance of agreeing, which did match his own unvoiced thoughts.

Egorov knew he had pushed as far as he dared. "I don't have a target count, but several appear to be on the motor yacht. Ones we missed before. The finance man, the team claim is onboard. They are preparing to sail soon. Fast loading of provisions and bags. The surveillance team is exposed watching."

"A trap?"

"There is nothing to indicate it. All normal activity in preparation for a trip. They are complacent."

"We cannot be."

"I know."

"We request presidential go-ahead after a quick brief."

"If he will see us."

"We must insist, but keep preparations going."

"I will."

***

"Who on the list?"

"Mr. President, we have the sisters, the couple, possibly both couples. A lot of goods. It looks like a long trip. If we had a submarine?" He didn't bother to finish that thought. The Russian Navy was not performing well. Losses in the Black Sea meant few resources could sneak into the Mediterranean. Operating in that area was fraught with difficulties. The British, French, and US navies would all be watching and tracking. A torpedo could destroy the yacht at sea. If there was a submarine available. He hadn't asked.

The president didn't offer. Instead he focused on the targets. "The finance team?"

"Definite on the woman. That's recent, the man from a couple of days ago but they didn't see him leave."

"The MI6 bitch?"

"Yes, Sir." Kovalenko wasn't sure which MI6 woman was being discussed. Two were probably on the boat but disguises made that hard to distinguish them. He didn't tell the president that. The man didn't want to know about problems. The report from Spain had not been received well, although the president had at least listened to the explanation. No one explained that it put a delay on any operation in New Zealand. They were short of assets. The losses not just in the UK were denting operations all over the world. There had been arrests in several countries. Others were running, or trying to return home, under emergency procedures. Putin didn't want to know that either.

Kovalenko kept to the main operation, "We also have the crew from the incident at Enez, plus one who wasn't there." The finance man, Hugh Turnbill, had been seen. Briefly on the deck before disappearing into the cabin. Another bad photo. If the surveillance team got too close, they would tip their hand. They'd warned them only that day, after they got very close to the sisters. They were told to back off. The plan would grab them, or kill them, on the yacht at sea. Well away from prying French eyes ashore. That was if, and when, the yacht left with the targets. Their presumption was that the finance man would be on board too. Other possible sightings always had the pair together.

"The team is ready?"

"They are, but it's…" Volkov tried to speak.

"Risky?"

"Yes, Mr. President."

"We are at war, enemies everywhere." Privately, the

president did not call Ukraine a Special Military Operation. Putin was emboldened by his success against the Wagner Group and the continuing disunity in the West. The politicians there were focused on elections and their own domestic issues. "It is time to strike." He declared.

"Yes, Mr. President." Kovalenko answered on their behalf. "My team will do it." Volkov and Egorov had to leave. Their own futures were now very uncertain. If the mission failed, Kovalenko would also be exposed. He stayed behind, probably to ensure he wasn't blamed. He'd already deflected any responsibility for the previous actions.

***

"All set?"

"Yes." The man from the Russian surveillance responded to his equally watched wife.

"Keep your eyes peeled. I could still come with you."

"No. You need to collect the others; organise them, not me."

"You still need organising," Michelle stroked his cheek.

"By you," Hugh hugged his wife, then stepped on board his new acquisition. He didn't want to look back. He had a brief recollection to when she had walked away on a beach to return to London. He'd dropped her off. Just a few weeks before he met Stephie and Carolyn. That was after he had first run. Michelle had been in charge of the hunt for him. At that time he thought he might never see her again. There had been other occasions since. He knew this was another occasion. It didn't make it easier. Just like before, he watched his wife switch personalities to the operational MI6 field officer she had once been. She was now. He was just an accountant with an interest in sailing with time running out. A feeling that had been building since before Enez.

He'd already had an emotional reunion and departure. Effi and Tom but in particular Stephie and Carolyn. He'd not had a chance to speak to the crew he had come to know and like. They were already on the yacht. There had been another argument about who would sail the yacht he'd just boarded, and who would helm the Richtung III. Stephie, Carolyn, and Hugh could all manage the yacht. Adding Michelle and the crew to the ability to helm the motor yacht. Even Tom and Effi could do that as well as several of Tom's colleagues from Hereford. They also needed to consider who could swim best. Hugh's slight cold tipped the balance. He'd already done one dive. Part of the bait but leaving the trap.

Using scuba with a cold was not advised. He'd even tested for COVID just in case. He was clear. Hugh was annoyed, although not directly witnessing the fate of his former home might be less upsetting. The time away had been different, but he missed the life of moving between Greek islands. Not without a care in the world. They had never had that. There was a very small chance they might escape again. He thought back to Enez. Liam dead. Lila who he'd never known dead. The four Russian attackers lying by their vehicles, watching Tom and Effi finish them off as Doug ran to catch up.

He needed to think of happier thoughts. Right back to Michelle visiting at his home in Surbiton. He could picture her flicking through a yacht magazine, playing mind games with him. He thought she'd come to arrest him. Instead she took him to bed and expanded his ridiculous plan to take some money to taking it all. Protecting him and keeping him safe. He knew he wouldn't have survived this long without her. Now he had sent her to board a yacht they all hoped would be attacked by the Russians seen in Port Grimaud, perhaps others too.

He couldn't change it even if he wanted to. For the most part he didn't. He didn't want it to end either. He knew he had accepted his fate on some occasions. Resigned to the possibility he and others may die. It made a strange thought process to review the past and future. It also focused his mind on what he could alter. To be successful; however unlikely meant he needed to do his part. Sail this yacht to collect whoever survived. Make sure his absence from the main vessel wouldn't be noticed. Hope that no one hunting them spotted this yacht.

The boat was a third-hand 2011 model. The Lagoon 400 came with a small tender. It needed refitting, which was why it was going relatively cheap at just under €300,000. Acting as a broker, Hugh had purchased it for that purpose, he told the selling agent.

The hulls and engines were sound. Speed would have been nice, but stealth was more important. The sails were in adequate condition. It had space on the deck for everyone, even if staying for a longer period would be cramped. Hugh took a few moments to lament what would happen to his pride and joy. The recent months away from the boat now docked in Port Grimaud did not lessen his sadness. Focusing on the new yacht, stopped him from dwelling on his friends and wife.

On board, after loading cash-purchased supplies, he spent nearly an hour ensuring he knew the working components properly. Getting out of the Sanremo Marina was straightforward on the engine. Hoisting the sails alone was a little harder, but the bay was quiet. Three to four hours, he thought, depending on the wind. Four hours before the people he loved could be dead. He might join them. He put that morbid thought aside. No boat was following, according to the yacht's limited radar. Not the slick system on his own proper boat. Not the speed either. He managed to get the mainsail correctly rigged. A stiff halyard winch, caused a brief delay. The jib had been easier. The vessel accelerated with the breeze. He tacked to regain his planned course of 220 degrees. He had a portable GPS to check his position, route and track. He adjusted the helm. The weather was better. Nineteen kilometres in the breeze. Under four hours. He tried to enjoy the trip. He had the laptop and a satellite data connection via a handset. There were still electronic actions to do. He had to do those too, not even Michelle could. No one else either, although the new woman back in Vauxhall Cross seemed capable. He re-checked the radar. He used the laptop.

CHAPTER TWENTY-SEVEN
Not The Yacht

Hugh had navigated to the agreed-upon position. This far from the coast, a deeper part of the seabed lay beneath the keel. A deeper ridge and fin than the motor yacht, which should be on its way to the rendezvous. There was little to no swell to disturb the very pleasant evening. His mind was drifting to other anchorages. Greek waters off sheltered coves. Private swimming and sun bathing. Snorkelling and diving were mostly done by him and Michelle. Sometimes the crew joined in. What would happen to Jules, André, and Natalie? She put up with his poor Italian and attempts to help cook. They saw more of the crew than Stephie or Carolyn. Not that they had seen any of them properly since Turkish ports and shootouts.

He looked at the radar, which showed regular sea-lane traffic, but they were clear of those coastal routes. Nothing appeared to be coming near him yet. A fishing pole with no bait hung out from the deck. If someone did approach, it would appear his presence was innocent, although it wasn't a fishing area. No current was moving the hull. The vessel wasn't completely still, but it would only drift a few meters. He could use the engines to nudge it back. Hugh fiddled with ropes and made sure the vessel was ready. He threw additional lines into the water and made sure the platform boarding ladder was clear. It looked a little rusty. He attached another spare line over the transform at the stern. The small tender was also ready. For the fifth time, he checked the little engine on that vessel. The fuel tank was full.

Hugh walked around the deck as darkness began to fall. He was about to switch off his exterior lights, a breach of sea regulations, when he saw the lights of an approaching motor boat. It was moving quickly. Hugh tensed. He had a pistol but no other protection. He couldn't outrun the boat.

It slowed. "Are you okay?" It was in French. A glamorous-looking woman in shorts and a polo shirt shouted, with a handsome man at the helm watching.

"Night fishing." Hugh shouted back, indicating the rod.

"Too deep here." The man said Hugh was still tense. Were they innocent sailors or there to get him?

"We're going to Saint-Raphaël."

"Very nice." Hugh had never been. "A couple of hours here, hopefully catch something, then I'll sail back to St. Tropez."

"There tomorrow. Perhaps we'll see you then."

"Perhaps."

"Au revoir."

"Au revoir." Hugh breathed. The motor yacht was a very new-looking Sunseeker 76 model. The woman walked back to the man at the helm and placed her arm around his waist. Hugh had so many memories of being in the same position as Michelle on the bridge of their own boat. He gulped air. He had to focus. He casually noted the French name of the motor boat as it sped away. *L'Espérance Éternelle*, hope eternal. A promise of a good outcome. He waited till the vessel was well away.

He made sure nothing was on the radar; he'd missed the Sunseeker on the screen. It made him doubt the radar's performance. He was doubting everything. He recalled the time when he'd first run. Buying the Sunreef yacht and preparing had been okay. Leaving with just him on board had not been easy. He enjoyed the sailing, not the hiding. It was much better after Michelle joined him. Even when Stephie and Carolyn had been on board, he'd been sacred. Afraid of a misstep or failing to hide his real identity, now everyone seemed to know.

He switched the exterior lights off. The radar still showed nothing approaching. He was fretting. He had an infra-red beacon ready. It wasn't time to switch that on. He rechecked that the sails were ready to hoist. The breeze was minimal. They might have to use the main engine.

Below deck, Hugh Turnbill made sure that the first aid kits were ready, hoping they would not be needed. The last time he used one was in Enez. This had to be the last time.

The others had just over 115 kilometres to navigate. He switched to nautical miles for the calculations. It was 62, which meant two hours on a fast cruise. Less at high speed. They should be half way to his position by now.

***

Stephanie and Carolyn were both on the flybridge. Stephie was at the helm, with Carolyn switching her attention from instrument displays to her sister. Together, they edged the Richtung Süden III out of the marina before accelerating away. A brief burst of nearly forty knots. Like her, Stephie knew her sister was recalling other fast rides on the yacht. There had already been tears when they realised Hugh wasn't on board. They might never see him again. The fast departure was to make it look like the yacht was being stolen. High speed and late in the evening. They wore dark clothing.

"What next?" Carolyn asked. She had been quiet for several days, Stephie thought especially, since they'd left England.

"I don't know; we've got to survive this first."

"We'll be okay."

Stephie adjusted the course to avoid another boat. She needed to watch. She could recall previous times she'd helmed the yacht. It included the first time with a man they then thought was called Olaf. They knew he wasn't, but it was a while before they found out it was Hugh. The last time Stephie had sped away was from a dock in Enez, Turkey. That was after shooting on the dock. Thankfully, there were no shots this time, but there were shots to expect in the future.

"You and Lizzie?" It was a strange time to have the conversation, but Stephie didn't want to talk about what would happen in the next hour or so.

"Over, she texted me."

"Harsh."

"Confirmation." Carolyn didn't add details. "She hates all this."

"Luxury boats, holidays, private jets?"

"You know what I mean. What about you and Jules?"

"Don't know. We have fun."

"When you're not arguing."

"There is that."

"What are we going to do? We can't go back."

"You have an alternative career." She didn't add her dark thoughts about whether they would survive.

The rest of the crew, including Michelle, were below deck. She had been the last onboard. The sisters had barely recognised their friend and sometimes mentor. A not unusual occurrence that also went back to their first meeting. More recently, there had been a disguised meeting at the sailing centre in Nottingham. Another emotional reunion that had been cut short by the need to move and hide.

Before Stephie had opened the throttles, Andre helped Michelle on board, even as he lifted the rear gangway and finished untying. Jules was at the bow, port side hull, also untying. They stayed in their respective positions, each equipped with military-grade binoculars. Natalie was in her galley.

They had cover from two members of Tom's team ashore and strict instructions to avoid a firefight on the pontoon in the marina, if at all possible. No one wanted anything like the battle on the dock at Enez. It still amazed Tom that no Turks watching the shooting had been hit. Plenty of others had been. Bad luck for the dead and good fortune for those slightly injured. In Justine McKenzie's case, luck had not held.

Somewhere ahead of the yacht, Tom's best friend, Hugh, was waiting. He hoped the wait would not be in vain. Hugh had wanted to be onboard, but someone needed to helm the yacht.

Not The Yacht

Hugh's sneezing had clinched it. There was a presumption that Hugh was not being followed. A big presumption.

Tom and two more of his men had sneaked onboard the Richtung III the previous night. The large, heavy bags had been deposited near the engines in the sterns of the catamaran's hulls during the previous day. Even though the smell leaked through the vessel. Effi had arranged it after talking to Michelle.

Tom and his assistants had rigged the boat, not with ropes for a sailing vessel. It was a difficult and upsetting process for Tom and the crew. They all liked the boat. They all had happy memories of being on board. Yes, there had been bad times, notably Enez, but many happy days and trips. The two assistants deployed from Hereford were now in position on their own boat. They were waiting for the hoped-for and planned response.

It was crowded in the main lounge. Not helped by those on board being unwilling to go in other rooms. Wires and blocks were distributed around. No one wanted to look at them. Small antennas were also visible, and if anyone looked closely, there were pulsing red LEDs.

Tom, already in a wet suit, walked back in from the stern. He joined the rest of the passengers and crew. Weapons were obvious. The wetsuits and armaments for everyone else were scattered around the room. They checked that the guns were ready, just in case. Tom was listening to a radio channel. He checked the screen of the interior radar display. There were too many contacts to break out who might be following. He felt the boat slow to a normal cruise. If the bait wasn't taken, they would return and go again. They'd sail back, motor back, Tom corrected. Hugh would sail.

Effi looked at her husband. She had returned from the master suite, which was the women's changing room.

"Stinks down there."

"Hardly surprising."

"Rest of you need to change; the side cabin, port side, and master suite are clear." Tom instructed. "I know we should have time, but let's not waste any."

"I'll go, then spell the girls." Michelle pulled off her wig. She seemed to change her posture too, becoming younger and taller. Her eyes and expression still showed the strain. Her only comment on Hugh's well-being was, "He'll be fine." It was hope, not knowledge.

They rotated through changing. They also rotated more gruesome tasks. Knife cuts that would sting in salt water. Blood was needed. DNA evidence. Michelle had once pulled a similar trick with Hugh in England. Faking his own disappearance as a possible murder victim to buy time. It felt like a lifetime ago.

***

The radio spluttered, "On you." They were only 20 miles out. It was the message Tom and Michelle had been waiting for.

"Roger," Tom replied, looking at the radar. "You half a mile behind them?"

"Yes, had to delay due to other traffic. Catching now."

"How many?"

"Six estimated."

"Samba execute." Tom ordered.

"Roger." Cindy's voice added no more details.

The remains of the team on land would now move in. They had the Russian surveillance team to deal with. Tom had not been explicit as to what that meant. He didn't know how Holly or Cindy would act. He knew what the SAS members might do. The ones on their boat, chasing what they believed was a Russian boat, would be very aggressive.

There was silence on the radio. The rest of the motor yacht was watching. Weapons were readied. Michelle was looking back into the darkening sky. Danger was rapidly closing. She was managing her own fear as best she could. She knew Hugh's moods. She hoped he was okay alone on the yacht. He was waiting for them all and hoping they would all make it. She hoped for that too.

Stephie was still helming, with Carolyn standing next to her. Jules and Andre were at the rear, staring sternward, their guns ready. Natalie stood next to Michelle. She was unarmed and dressed in her wet suit, but she looked nervous. Ellie paced near her partner. She and Tom had argued. He wanted her to sneak back ashore and join Cindy and Holly with their SAS support. Ellie had sworn at him after he half-heartedly suggested it. She stopped him before he started with one word. "Pakistan." He shut up and concentrated on the radio and radar. Time dragged, and the boats chasing were closing, despite Stephie's initial increase in speed.

"Anything?" Carolyn was looking for the stationary yacht.

"Maybe." Stephie pointed at a blip.

Carolyn waited, checking the charts, before she shouted, "Two minutes!" It had to be the yacht; if it wasn't, they had less than five minutes alive. Stephie began to slow the Richtung Süden III's progress. She was letting the pursuers close faster, although that action might delay the pursuers while they tried to figure out what she was doing. They'd be more concerned when she began a wide 180-degree turn. She was using that manoeuvre to slow their yacht to a standstill. Tom and Effi now moved to the bow to face the attackers. Others joined.

The engines were just a background hum, with the waves lapping against the slowing vessel. It was almost peaceful until, at Tom's signal, they all opened fire. They knew they were well out of range. The boat's position would allow the superstructure of the yacht to act as a barrier to the fast-approaching speedboats, but not where they were standing.

As soon as the first few shots fired, flashes could be seen, and the sounds of a response echoed across the water. They were still out of range, but not for long. That meant the Russians were going to come in hot and angry. That was what was required, but it brought its own risks. The Russian RIB was very quick.

Tom immediately started to usher everyone rearward, before anyone received an unlucky hit. This was going to be close. The boat's engine's ceased. Stephie and Carolyn came down from the flybridge, ducking as they went to the stern. Tom returned to the bow. One of the forward-facing windows took a hit. They could now hear the approaching RIB and the bullets hitting the infrastructure. That included the now-empty flybridge.

At the stern, Andre and Natalie were first in the water.

Andre used a wrist compass to get his bearing. They could see the flashing beacon through their goggles. Natalie was the least experienced diver, despite recent training experience. In the distance, they could just make out a yacht's mast. It was gently bobbing a few hundred meters away. A long swim in daylight in a pool. It was almost dark at sea, although there was little swell to block the view. Tom wondered if they were shooting high to get a capture, not a kill. The Richtung Süden III was now just drifting.

Stephie and Carolyn joined Michelle, going overboard. Michelle and the sisters were pausing to glance back at the yacht they had so many happy memories of. Jules was right behind them, bringing the second tank for the four of them to share. He checked the bearings and found that he could see the infrared strobe. He only delayed to fire his weapon inaccurately towards the rapidly approaching Russian RIB. The four briefly paused as they heard shots above the noise of the scuba nozzles before ducking under the water.

Tom redirected his fire at the approaching small boat. He was not expecting to hit it; he just wanted to gain some critical time. Effi also opened fire. The RIB lit up once more with return fire flashes. Tom flicked the switch without thinking about it. A complete commitment with no way back. Now they had to rush. He pushed Effi lower down as they crawled around the bridge to the protected rear deck. Sixty seconds left, he estimated, not taking the time to check his watch. They jumped in together and swam as hard as they could. He had a bearing but no time to check the strobe. There had been no time for flippers, and like the others, they were also sharing a tank.

The explosion knocked them deeper. He almost lost the tank. His ears hurt with the overpressure. He fought blackness. He felt Effi's hand on his, pulling him back to the surface. She'd been just in front of him. He'd protected her after all. He thought his ears might be bleeding. He wondered if the tank was working. He couldn't seem to get any air. Water filled his lungs. He surfaced, gasping for breath. A head was in front of him underwater; he pulled Effi up. Other hands grabbed him. He wanted to escape their grip. Effi wasn't moving.

***

The flash of the explosion momentarily blinded Hugh before he heard the rumble and even felt the breeze of the shock wave. He'd already heard the distant shots. He scanned the water. He had to wait and hope. He looked around. He could still hear a motor. It was moving fast. He couldn't tell where it was coming from or going to. Was that the Russians? If it was they were doomed.

***

The SAS team saw the flashes before they heard the gunfire. That was earlier than planned. This was not right, the leader thought. They'd been radio silent after the Execute call. Their own weapons were ready. They quickly closed the distance, then opened fire on the Russian boat, which was now within fifty meters of the yacht. They were a further 250 meters back, with their own helmsman slowing their approach. The Russians started to turn to return fire from their rear.

The explosion almost knocked them out of the water. By the time the helmsman had steadied the craft, all they could see was wreckage. The Russian boat was gone. Bits of wood and fibreglass were bobbing. They had to use their night-vision goggles to get a better view. The explosion was earlier than planned, too. The briefing had stated they would pincer the Russians between the motor yacht and themselves, dispose of the Russians, reorganise, and then blow up the yacht. Something had gone wrong. There were a couple of bodies in the water, but no one was moving. They didn't start to search for survivors. They could not stay to check. The local radio crackled with reports of the explosion. They didn't reply. The helmsman turned for the coast and their pre-agreed pick-up.

CHAPTER TWENTY-EIGHT
Sail or Not

Volkov and Egorov stood, waiting to be called in to see their president. They both looked out the window, wondering if they would ever see sunlight again. Kovalenko was already inside, weaving his version of events.

"The surveillance team too?" Egorov had already heard it but wanted to hear it again.

"Everyone. The two from before who were trying to get across Germany." He received a nod in response before saying, "Police, shoot out. They didn't make it." That was new, equally disappointing news.

They already knew that the GRU team from France had not reported in. The last satellite message from the fast motor boat had been sent, confirming they were intercepting. Since then, all they had were garbled reports of a large explosion at sea. Coast Guard reports were just alerts to shipping to head for the site to see if there were survivors. There weren't any. Not that there was a huge response. The media always claimed there were too many other small boats in difficulty, overloaded with illegal immigrants desperate to get to a European shore.

The surveillance team's status was officially unknown, but they were either dead or captured. They had not checked in or called for an emergency extraction. If the British or Americans had them, who knew what would happen?

There had been follow-up reports on partial body remains that included complaints from the French about potential Russian nationals. The Russian Ambassador to France had publicly declared it was none of France's business, given the explosion was in international waters. He then thanked the French for returning the remains. An about face that only a seasoned diplomat could pull off.

There had also been ramifications for the actions in Dubai. The Emirates did not appreciate the Syrians being used in their territory. Something the Americans supported by the British had been only too willing to confirm.

It had also been confirmed via discrete sources to the SVR that the former Colonel Sidorova was also in American hands. Other risks were exposed. More assets had to make swift exits to prevent being captured or killed. Neither of the waiting men knew what had been in the lost briefcase.

The oligarch who had been waiting for it had also disappeared. He'd allegedly been on a private flight. He'd gone from Kazakhstan to Bangkok. A few days later, his plane crashed on its way to Laos. What he was doing in Thailand or why he was going to Laos was unclear. It was another private plane crash carrying someone Putin no longer needed. Egorov knew all about such crashes. He'd been involved in arranging one the previous year. This time, the Americans were suspected, or so the Russians wanted the world to know. He wasn't the first oligarch to have an *accidental death*. Egorov hadn't arranged anything. He didn't know whether Volkov had. He couldn't and wouldn't ask.

It was also clear that Sidorova's information was lost. Her knowledge would be combined with Yegorov's. Were they working together? Neither man considered that element. They were not responsible for her interrogation or release. They didn't know. Two generals in prison awaiting a presidential decision had been asked. Neither could explain it. Not knowing sealed their fate. An announcement would be made public later that day.

"A lot of assets were lost."

"Some successes."

"The deaths, you mean?"

"Yes."

"Are they really?"

"I know what you mean. Now we will have to find out who the replacements are."

"Not just that. We will have more losses to come. Those being questioned." He trailed off. Any captured might be tortured, or at least interrogated, and might deal just to save themselves.

"Do we have anything positive to report?"

"Paltry is reported as dead. We have the other enemies dead, and the initial reports from the Mediterranean had multiple bodies. Men and women. A blow to our enemies."

"That's a small success without identities. Our operations world-wide are degraded. The boat was a trap."

"It is destroyed, and there are several deaths on it."

"We don't know who."

"Correct, but we did try to warn." He stopped as the door to the president's office opened. Before they were shown into the room, Kovalenko was escorted out. He was between two guards from Putin's personal staff.

Putin came to the door. "Gentlemen, tell me how you plan to retrieve this badly planned operation?" He was looking at the back of Kovalenko. Volkov managed not to smile in relief that the security man had been blamed. He glanced at Egorov. He could also see the relief there. They both entered the lion's den.

***

"Katherine, you are looking well."

"Thank you, Sir. For a dead man, you're looking pretty good yourself." Kathrine smiled at the former head of MI6.

"Recovering. I could have done without the move. Coffin," he laughed, "hard to believe. Wasn't that in some spy thriller? East Germany?"

"Possibly, Sir," William Thatcher agreed. "We are all sorry for your loss."

"My fault; I should have anticipated some ridiculous

revenge. I'll miss her." A rare personal statement. Kathrine and William gave him a moment to contemplate what had happened. "The other losses are…"

"Upsetting. We took action."

"So, I've heard. Joe Carpenter and some Special Branch detectives were here. They didn't have details of your plan, Katherine? Successful?"

"Mostly, we await a full report."

"And I'm part of that."

"All the suspected targets are, except Joe and myself. Not that they have my name, according to debriefs." Kathrine explained.

"The other targets, the detective, Sam Fox, said there are multiple ones."

"We don't know. There are deaths reported. Not just the attackers."

"A honey pot."

"Yes." Katherine would admit that.

"But a good beekeeper will have removed the honey?"

"A good beekeeper would. Yes, Sir," Katherine followed the thinking, "but bears were nearby."

The dead Sir Rupert Paltry looked at one of his former best agents and his chief of operations, his acting successor. He decided not to press for now. "The future?"

"A careful retirement for you, Sir. We're sorting out a house and protection. South Coast unless you wish to go overseas." William Thatcher knew that an analyst team in his own service was preparing the cover without knowing who it was for.

"No matter, William. Out of the limelight, the coast will be nice. I might try some sailing." His eyes demonstrated his recovery. "I'll assist, of course, if I can?"

"Your advice would be welcome, Sir." William Thatcher would need a sounding board. Not an unusual situation with former heads of the intelligence services.

"Thank you. I want to be useful, but I can't complain about this." He was staying in a very private suite at a small health farm that sometimes had other uses for the security services. He was still recovering, as evidenced by the drip and hospital bed. "Will Putin restrain himself?"

"The Americans had a hotline call. We sent our ambassador, not that he met her personally. He appears to be focused on his recent successes in Ukraine. There are a few live assets to send back as and when. He has a journalist and others to switch with. We will still be on our guard. Best of all, we have control over the finances. They are back in-house." William Thatcher didn't explain that it was half the money. Much of the rest appeared to have been donated to various charities; how much was unclear. Greek lawyers had not returned calls.

"A long-term objective, I seem to recall."

"Yes, Sir Rupert."

"The sailors?" He asked explicitly. Kathrine knew he knew. He hadn't mentioned sailing for any other reason.

"We don't know. One was definitely on board. Michelle."

"That would be sad news." Sir Rupert remembered her.

"Yes," Kathrine decided to provide more despite the beekeeping discussion. Our Bravo-One-One team is also missing."

"That is upsetting."

"A great loss to the service and the Army." Thatcher added. Kathrine nodded in agreement.

"The man, the sailor, what was his name? The one we chased way back when?" Katherine knew that Paltry knew the man's name.

"Turnbill, Hugh Turnbill, Michelle's husband."

"Yes, I recall. His fate?"

"We don't know if he was sailing or not. No reports from the yacht. The SAS team arrived as the boat exploded. They found

Sail or Not

no survivors. We have two captures from the Port Grimaud operation. There were no casualties on our side there, but two more Russians died. A Special Forces team was involved. Not directly part of my plan." Katherine could guess what Tom and Effi had ordered or advised. She hadn't asked. They hadn't said.

A nurse interrupted their discussion. They weren't to tire out the dead man.

***

Outside the room, William Thatcher looked at Kathrine and asked, "Do I need to know?"

"Not unless you want to?"

"Arrangements for funerals and so on?"

"With Sam."

"Something he can do."

"Yes, Sir." By failing to say anything else, she was condemning Sam to suspicion in front of his boss.

"No sir, Kathrine, not alone." He decided to add something. "I'm keeping an eye on Sam." Kathrine just nodded. "Our incoming security head will be told. I'm thinking of asking that detective, Sam Fox, to take a look at several things. Of course, I may not get confirmed."

"William, I think you have a billion reasons why you should."

"The money is no good without loyal assets to use it. You'll carry on as Ad Hoc Operations?"

"If you wish."

"Kathrine, I need good people I can trust. The service needs good people. We have lost a lot. Not just Mel, but we'd only just sorted the Russia Desk out."

"Jamie will be missed."

"Yes, the whole team is in shock. We still need something back in Moscow, but that is going to be hard." He stopped to look at her. "Anyone else hiding there that I need to know about?"

There was a lot hidden in the question, especially with the caveat.

"Not in Moscow." A suitably ambiguous answer. "Sam doesn't know." She was implicitly saying that there were other assets in play. "We do have the analyst team and the software. That has great potential for tracking opposition assets. We used it to help in France. An operational test, if you will. They got us their rentals, cars, and plane tickets. We had them all before they started, including the one who was first watching the yacht."

"Yes, I need to understand that more; we need to see how we can protect the capability but use the output. The HMRC woman has settled in well?"

"Yes, Uliana is very promising. I'll have to replace the team leader.

"Effi?"

"Yes, but two of the members are overdue for promotion; the third should also be rewarded. They were caught up in the previous business but had done nothing wrong."

"I recall. I'll support your recommendation."

"The two from Five in Port Grimaud did very well. I'm pretty certain we can poach them. That's if Joe Carpenter and Jermaine Harris can be persuaded. They liked being overseas."

"What do they know?"

"Not everything; even I didn't have all of that." A rare admission from Kathrine. Thatcher knew she did know more, but she'd already told him that the team had not shared all their plans. "They know the SAS team returned to shore. They assisted with their exit. The rest of the news is still very limited. You and me, the individuals concerned."

"Let's try and keep it that way. What about the others?"

"Very deep." She didn't add anything about the sea. Her answer also confirmed that some from the yacht were alive, despite reports to the contrary.

Thatcher had seen the SAS report. He asked, "Will you tell me?"

"When you want to know." Katherine looked to see if that question was coming. Thatcher decided he didn't want to.

***

William Thatcher, now acting head of MI6, understood what Sir Rupert Paltry meant when he'd briefed him about Kathrine months before. Before the Treasury report and defectors.

"She has more secrets than the services combined. She'll tell you what she thinks she needs you to know. Nothing more. She trusts no one."

"Not even you?"

"Not even me."

"Why do you put up with it?"

"There are plenty here who don't want me to. Mel's an exception and similar in some ways." Mel Kennedy was still alive at the time. "In the end," Sir Rupert had continued, "she has never let her country down, or me personally. Some exceptional operations, Bravo-One-One among them."

"I've only read the précis."

"The whole file is fascinating. The planning, the forethought. It was how she became involved with the finance pair. Read it when you're in this seat."

"If, Sir."

"When William. Then, you'll discover how rare her talents are. We've let others get away or caused them to leave. Perhaps she'll tell you about some of those." William Thatcher now knew Sir Rupert was referring to the former and now possibly dead Michelle Turnbull, née Houston.

Partial remains of two bodies out of six total had been pulled from the waters of the Mediterranean, according to French reports. Most appeared to be Russian nationals. The two female ones were very partial and remained unidentified. DNA on blood stains on the wreckage added confusion.

They left to head back to London. There were other missions to plan and information to turn into intelligence. The

Americans had another defector to share. A former general would soon be on his way to New Zealand. An ex-Dubai-based agent also needed resettling. He couldn't come back to the UK. He was another one who was officially dead.

Kathrine looked at the rain-drenched trees and noticed a glimmer of sunshine trying to escape the clouds. She wondered if her complicity in the plans had been fully understood. William Thatcher was looking at her. Yes, he understood and either guessed or knew. She doubted if anyone else did.

***

Nine people gathered in a large farmhouse in the Tuscan hills. Two sisters, three married couples, and the semi-boyfriend of one sister. There were a couple of bottles of wine, partly empty, on the terrace. In the distance, the sea could just be glimpsed. There had not been a lot of talk. There had been many wet hugs and anxious waits. The house was new as a possession, even if it was old, and rambling as a structure. The main house had been refurbished before the previous owners ran out of money or willpower to complete the full refurbishment. It now belonged to a group of companies equally new and with a suitably indecipherable ownership chain. Most of the plans for the people enjoying the facility had already been made. Replacement lives needed to be implemented. Software applications were adjusted with updates and different versions sent to London buildings.

"We're done." A phrase repeated in Greek and then in Italian. "Low profile; no airports, train stations, or anywhere else with cameras."

"We are going back to my father." An Italian statement. "Outside Naples. We have a new restaurant for our chef." There were smiles from the crowd.

"We have another two weeks. Sight-seeing, we think. Ears are still recovering." A pat of a partner's knee.

"We'll join you." A nod of agreement.

"Then what?"

The sisters looked at each other. "As we said." More arguments and discussions would follow.

The *Sailing Clear* series has been a long gestation of multiple interlinked ideas and plot lines. It feels like the right time to lower the sails, drop anchor and say goodbye.

Of course, the characters may have a say in that. Each book has had the main protagonists sail off into the distance for an unknown future. Perhaps they are waiting to fire up an engine and motor away. Because of course, the yacht is not a sail yacht. They motor around the Med' and only rarely is a jib raised or a tack required.

The Sailing Clear Series:

Sailing Clear

Sail Chains

Sails

Sail(or) (K)Not

Acknowledgements

Research is never easy so my thanks to DARPA, MIT and Sir Tim Berners-Lee for the invention of the Internet and the World Wide Web.

Once again, I wish to express my general thanks to the content providers of the Internet, without their generosity it would be impossible to research many subjects. The cast of thousands if not millions who contribute to the content, official and unofficial. As a lone author the Internet provides me with access to much of the World's knowledge at the click of a button.

Thanks again to my family for their encouragement and help.

A special vote of thanks to the creators of Scrivener - Keith at Literature & Latte which is my primary authoring tool.

Any mistakes remaining are mine.

Phenweb Publishing

Phenweb.co.uk
Twitter/X *@philip_g_henley* Facebook *PhilipGHenley*

The Sailing Clear Series

- Sailing Clear
- Sail Chains
- Sails
- Sailor Knot (This book)

Sailing Clear

The first part of the Sailing Clear series

Missing girls, missing money, missing man, luxury motor yachts and the people chasing them.

An old MI6 undercover mission to prevent terrorists entering the UK via sex trafficking routes went wrong. The undercover agent is assigned to a new role.

A man lost in the shadows manages the hidden finances of the security services but dreams of a better life sailing the Mediterranean. When he runs off he is hunted, but he may have been killed by an organised crime leader. The police are assigned to find him.

Two sisters run away to Greece from the sexual abuse of their father.

The characters intersect as the hunt commences. Then, the security services need to find options to deal with the fallout.

The undercover agent now in her new planning role

is assigned to trace the missing financier, but a corrupt cop may give them all away.

Sail Chains

The second part of the Sailing Clear series

Captain Tom Larring barely escaped alive from a mission in Afghanistan. He now has another task. Effi Miani has been undercover in the Middle east but is needed for the same operation. Together they must find Bravo-One-One who is the highest priority target for MI6. He is believed to be building a chemical weapon in Northwest Pakistan. A previous MI6 operation has already failed. A leak or a traitor inside MI6 may have destroyed that mission, so extra precautions must be taken otherwise, this team will also fail.

Tom and Effi need a faultless back story before embarking on their mission. The operation needs financing and a cover story. The help of a former disgraced MI6 officer, Michelle Houston, and her lover, Hugh Turnbill, is sought. They successfully control the laundering of black funds for the security services whilst sailing clear of the security services. Some of the MI6 leadership wants to gain direct control of the money and the couple, despite previous agreements. They want that control regardless of the risks to the operations in Pakistan. They think they may get leverage using two former teenage runaways connected to the couple.

The hunt for whoever leaked the information continues. Suspicions are raised. The internal security team needs to prevent the traitor putting the financiers and the operation at risk. An MI5 team is on the trail of a suspicious Saudi diplomat. He may be connected to Bravo-One-One.

Closed missions should not be re-opened. The NSA and GCHQ are monitoring and tracing communications using secret programs and techniques, but some secrets should not be shared with allies.

Sails

The third part of the Sailing Clear Series

Despite the declared end of the pandemic, there are still threats to the UK, particularly from Russia. Friends from across the Atlantic who like to meddle continue to track and follow the shadowy financing team supporting the UK's security services. They assured the UK they would not, but disparate agencies in the USA have different agendas.

Michelle and Hugh Turnbill are now married. They still manage MI5 and MI6's clandestine funds. They occasionally sail around the Greek Islands with the Harper sisters or stay at their new house in Mykonos. They desire a normal life but are aware that caution must still be exercised, and complacency avoided. A Treasury probe investigating missing funds puts their way of life and lives in danger.

An unhappy assistant in the Treasury has been leaking information to someone who appears to be a journalist but he is actually sending the reports to Russia. The Russian security services launch an urgent investigation and may well take more direct action. They discover names and some photos. Information previously covered up by a Russian general.

MI6 needs to protect the system, but some elements still want more control. Kathrine commences an operation to protect them. One of her old assets needs to escape Russia.

Russian forces are closing in and are keeping an eye on the Treasury. MI5 is keeping an eye on them in an effort to identify the source of the Russian information. The finance team needs to dodge all the other teams trying to take control of them and the money.

Sailor Knot

This book and the fourth part of the Sailing clear series

To The Survivors

An apocalypse threatens human kind. A lethal virus is detected that attacks mankind and mammals. The Government must act, and whilst the authorities struggle to find a cure, they have to plan for the worst. As the disease spreads it is not clear how many will, or will not, survive, nor what the survivors will have to do to live. They will have to cope with their grief and loneliness before they can attempt to rebuild society. They will need to find water, food, shelter, and power and then face the other threats to their survival. If they survive, there may be hope for human kind. If they survive…

Semblance of Storms

A novel of writing, lust, storms, secrets and relationships…

All that is required, by his publishers is to write a fourth book, not like the flop that was his third. His successful first two books bought him fame, some fortune and disputes with his terminally ill father. He wants his son to help with his half-sister. If only her mom, wouldn't give confusing messages on what she wants; possibly him. A family friend and lawyer will help, as he always has done but there are secrets in his past too.

His new book will be a tale of boy meets girl in his usual elaborate and descriptive style. His agent, wants him to produce it soon but he has his own pressures from his new investors. There might be a movie deal to be negotiated. The new investor is represented by an attractive woman who is infamous for other reasons.

His editor, wants him to finish the book so she can stop his publisher asking for the advance back. She hopes he has written something as good as his first published book. He does too. He needs to concentrate on writing this book not drafting anything else. Old lost, and possible new loves and lusts, keep distracting him. The idle beach lifestyle diverts him as do post pandemic visitors.

Just when he begins to make progress on the last chapters a hurricane approaches his home in North Carolina. If he goes to visit his father, another storm may await in Houston. His neighbour and that family add further complications and secrets that need to be hidden or avoided, especially from the FBI.

Re-Semblance

The sequel to Semblance of Storms

The lies and actions have caught up with him. He's banished from the beds of his lovers. They tell their own stories now.

The ramifications of his actions continue, even while he remains caught up in the activities of the authorities. He faces his legal and personal punishments with self-guilt.

He has a new home waiting for him on Emerald Isle. There are new babies and there is a continuing need to hide the parentage of one of them. He is trying to resolve the issues until tragedy strikes once more.

Now, he's fighting for his life and trying to recall his past.

His lovers and friends rally around to help him recover. Perhaps he can reclaim the life he wanted.

The Demise Trilogy

The Complete Demise Trilogy in one Volume

- *An Agent's Demise*
- *An Agent's Rise*
- *An Agent's Prize*

An Agents Demise

A complex thriller based on the lead up to and aftermath of the second Iraq war and the lead in to the events in this book.

Intelligence analysts and agents have gone missing, some may have been killed. The press and the police suspect there is a serial killer on the loose. John Slater was near the latest victim, he is evasive, appears to have no history, and he might be the killer. The second Iraq war and the intelligence network may link the victims and so The Metropolitan Police's Special Branch investigates, with the help or hindrance of the Intelligence Agencies. The mistakes made in creating the dossiers used to support going to war are supposed to stay buried on both sides of the Atlantic, but still a killer strikes and is everybody telling the truth?

An Agent's Rise

The sequel to An Agent's Demise.

The Demise operation was shut down the killer allowed to disappear, but the conspirators have not all been caught and the efforts of MI6 and the CIA to cover up the dirty deeds of the security services only results in more deaths and destructions. Slater returns to tidy up, but how can he reconcile his new life with what he is asked to do.

The newly promoted Detective Chief Inspector Hooper has not forgotten who his target is but there appears to be another assassin on the loose.

An Agent's Prize

The conclusion to The Demise Trilogy.

The conspiracy is over the mistakes and cover up are hidden and buried for good. Both sides of the Atlantic can concentrate on the threats from Islamic Terrorism. That is what they all hope. They want to enlist a hidden black asset in the chase, but there are risks to that approach. Meanwhile the FBI is still investigating what really happened. Is the conspiracy really over?

Al Qaeda plan new atrocities and MI6 with Homeland Security will try to stop them. The newlywed Michael Johnson can help but his wife is still recovering from her injuries and she is suspicious of her husband and the authorities. From the streets of San Francisco to the suburban towns of England the terrorists are plotting an outrage.

The Observer Series

Part One - The World of Fives

Read how the story started. In, The World of Fives, we find Cathy an Observer in The Interplanetary Geographic Service observing the planet Fivur as an exceptionally rare convergence of moons and orbits creates massive tidal shifts on the planet's surface. Carlo, a Fivurian, must overcome the impact of the tides on the planet's power system, whilst keeping his love Sello safe. Meanwhile, Cathy tries to persuade her superiors to intervene and save the lives of the planet's humanoid population. If she can save them they will need a new home but Earth factions have different ideas. Meanwhile another intelligent species on the planet, the Sharok, wait to feast on any human or Fivurian who ends up in the water.

Part Two - Intervention

The continuing story of Cathy Rodriguez, a Senior Observer, in The Interplanetary Geographic Service. Cathy is recalled from her Observer duties as she is asked to establish first contact with a new life form. Meanwhile the Conspiracy to prevent humans changing their non-Intervention policy continues to try and kill her. Together with Marta De Jaste, a Senior Investigator, and Tony Briggs her former jailer and security officer, they travel to the chosen planet. On the planet Tullymeade, Karloon Niesta, a disgraced scientific observer, detects a strange anomaly.

A discovery that will change his planet forever. In deep space two groups of survivors try and recover from their battle in orbit above the planet Freevur.

The Persuasive Man

A tale of greed, insider trading love and misfortune, spanning the globe as a terminally ill businessman realises his luxurious existence will not help him. He tries to account for his past actions, his life, and loves. Ranging from London to Shanghai via New York, Hong Kong, and Dubai, his greed and behaviour alters his business and personal relationships. His persuasive ability brings him success, but at what cost?

Whether he is in his New York apartment, his French Château, or his St Kitts home, he does not know which relationships are real and which are false due to his past behaviour. Now he has to decide what to do with his money and how to say goodbye.

Landscape

She is a PA who dreams of running her own art gallery. He is an IT technician gambling away everything he wants. They meet and fall in love. Their relationship is threatened by endless bets even whilst they share their love of paintings. Years later some dreams are fulfilled others are dashed. Will the former lovers meet again?

Not Too Much

Alex has everything. He's one of the most eligible bachelors in the world. He's chased by the Paparazzi and once went out with a communist. Now he hides from publicity whilst trying to find a soul mate.

Victoria is a struggling waitress in a London restaurant. She shares a flat with Sophie an aspiring actress whilst trying not to give up a dream of making a success.

They meet and try to make it work in this contemporary romance

Take Four

A short story covering four people's points of view.

Mark King is a songwriter who secretly wrote a huge hit for the artist Louise Kline. She is a successful singer who claims to write her own material. Her half-brother Joel Kline helps to run a record company. He allowed the falsehood to continue. Joel chases wannabe pop stars and takes out escorts. One escort, Tamsin, meets Mark and there is a mutual attraction.

Inspiration for songs for Mark comes from the events around him and the people he meets. He likes Tamsin. He longs for Louise.

Following an attack by her current boyfriend, Louise is thrust further into the media spotlight.

Each protagonist tells their part of the story in this contemporary romance set in the music industry.

Counter

Ben Walker, The Count, is off the grid hiding because of what he took. A life in the shadows with covert military operations was terminated. He sought revenge. He tracked down the chain of command. LC is the man who tried to have him killed but he made an offer to be a different type of hunter.

Now Walker has taken information and money and

gone into hiding. LC wants Walker and what he took. He will take extreme measures to get it. LC has also disappeared. He is wanted too.

The hunters are now hunted.

Helen Lawrence is part of a team cobbled together from the maze of Government agencies. They set out to try to find Walker so that he can help find LC who has also vanished. The team members are not all they seem and if they do find him then the real hunt needs to start. She has her own problems and desires without an entanglement with Walker.

The missing data is valuable.

The motives of the agencies are unknown.

The bullets are real.

Printed in Great Britain
by Amazon